WHAT FANS ARE SAYING ABOUT THE *GREAT AND TERRIBLE* SERIES

VOL. 1: PROLOGUE: THE BROTHERS

"An amazing book. . . . The whole story was great, but the ending gave me goose bumps and the best feeling inside. Can't wait for the next volume."

—Hila Hopkins

"Thought-provoking and compelling. . . . I love the way it has caused me to think differently about my mission on earth and to look at my husband and children in a different light."

—Hillary Johnson

VOL. 2: WHERE ANGELS FALL

"This book is incredible! It broadens the spectrum from just our mortal scope and makes readers contemplate our place on the eternal battlefield. The plot is suspenseful, the characters are believable, and the setting is one of the most changing and oftentimes contentious areas of our world: the Middle East."

—Kaleb Valdez

"An edge-of-your-seat thriller. . . . I can't wait for volume 3 to be published. . . . I have read the *Left Behind* series and this series is shaping up to be far better."

—Mike Heiner

VOL. 3: THE SECOND SON

"It's a rare author who can spin a heart-gripping, page-turning story while at the same time filling it with truths about the things that really matter from an eternal perspective. Chris Stewart has done a masterful job. . . . I stayed up all night to finish it and then was mad that it was over!"

—Emily Watts

"Stewart weaves a stunning tapestry of storyline from start to finish with these characters to whom we are drawn, and come to love as our own . . . and with other players who defy all humanistic virtues and become objects of our righteous hatred. This book cannot be ignored!"

—James Parks, Vietnam era military pilot

"A stark reminder of the serious security issues that we face in a free and open society, *Fury and Light* also underscores the powerful and undeniable influence of good people who are motivated to help. With this book, Chris Stewart continues with another hit in his long line of winners."

—Brian Tarbet, Major General, Army National Guard

"It isn't often that a book—let alone a series—comes along that has the power to move, inspire, and thrill in a page-turning adventure that leaves the reader wishing the story wouldn't end. Yet, this is precisely what Chris Stewart achieves in *Fury and Light*."

—Dan Jensen, Homeland Security Expert

REVIEWS OF CHRIS STEWART'S NATIONAL-MARKET TITLES

"Stewart writes with . . . Clancy's knack for spinning a thrilling global techno yarn."

—*CNN Sunday Morning,* Off the Shelf

"Fast and furious. The author writes in a crisp style and tells the story with a certain authentic touch."

—*Stars and Stripes*

"His mix of fact and fiction explodes off the page with the immediacy of a live CNN war-zone video feed."

—*Publishers Weekly*

FURY & LIGHT

THE GREAT AND TERRIBLE SERIES

by
Chris Stewart

VOLUME 1
Prologue: The Brothers

VOLUME 2
Where Angels Fall

VOLUME 3
The Second Sun

VOLUME 4
Fury and Light

VOLUME 5
From the End of Heaven

VOLUME 6
Clear as the Moon

THE GREAT AND TERRIBLE

VOLUME 4

FURY & LIGHT

CHRIS STEWART

DESERET
BOOK

SALT LAKE CITY, UTAH

Library of Congress Cataloging-in-Publication Data

Stewart, Chris, 1960–
   Fury and light / Chris Stewart.
      p. cm. — (The great and terrible ; v. 4)
   ISBN-13: 978-1-59038-629-3 (hardbound: alk. paper)
   ISBN-13: 978-1-60641-685-3 (paperbound)
   1. Terrorism—Fiction. I. Title.
   PS3569.T4593F87 2007
   813'.54—dc22
                                           2007008319

Printed in the United States of America
Publishers Printing, Salt Lake City, UT

10 9 8 7 6 5 4 3 2 1

author's note

The technologies depicted in this book and their potential effects upon society are real and accurately portrayed. While the possibility of an EMP attack and the widespread devastation it would cause are well-known among the military and intelligence community, they are much less known among other government offices and the general population. Why this is the case I have often wondered, but have no explanation.

There is a great deal of information available regarding the subject. I encourage interested readers to pursue their own research and would suggest the Senate reports referred to in the narrative as a good starting place.

the story so far

In the premortal world, Lucifer and his followers reject the plan of the Father and wage war on the faithful, trying to win souls to their side. Jehovah and Michael lead the cause of the valiant, and Ammon, Luke, Elizabeth, and Sam are among the warriors who help to save many who otherwise would have been lost. Lucifer, enraged, vows to remember these great ones and to continue the fight for their souls in the mortal world.

And so the battle continues in the next estate. Lucifer and his minions, including the master teacher Balaam, whose pride was his downfall in the premortal conflict, wreak havoc on the inhabitants of the earth, snaring leaders of nations and stirring up hatred and bloodshed. Chief among their conquests is Prince Abdullah al-Rahman, second son of the king of Saudi Arabia. When it becomes evident that his father and older brother favor allying themselves with the democratic government of the United States, Prince Abdullah makes a pact with a mysterious stranger in return for knowledge of how to bring them down.

Meanwhile, in the Agha Jari Deh Valley of Iran, Elizabeth

is born Azadeh Ishbel Pahlavi, only child of Rassa Ali Pahlavi, grandson of the last Shah of Persia. Her mother, Sashajan, dies within twenty-four hours of her birth, but she lives a happy childhood, raised by a loving father. Everyone who knows her recognizes a special quality that she possesses, a sort of radiance or spiritual maturity that sets her apart. Lucifer's followers find her, and the adversary sends one of his mortal servants to murder her, but she is protected by Teancum, a heavenly messenger sent by the Father to preserve her life so she can fulfill her mission on earth.

Crown Prince Saud, heir to the throne of Saudi Arabia, also finds the Pahlavi family. Recognizing how precarious his own situation has become, he forms a desperate plan to seek help from them if the need should arise. He also contacts his friend in the United States, Major General Neil S. Brighton, asking to meet him during his upcoming trip to Saudi Arabia.

General Brighton, newly appointed as military liaison to the National Security Advisor, feels the weight of his assignment and the price it exacts from his wife, Sara, and their twin sons, Ammon and Luke. The boys are doing all right, basically on course with mission preparations despite a lively lifestyle. Neil wishes he could say the same for Sam, the foster son he and Sara have adopted as their own. Sam's abusive birth parents have made his road difficult, and even the love of the Brightons is not sufficient to give him a testimony of God's love for him. Instead of going on a mission, he chose to join the army, and now he serves in an elite Delta unit specializing in covert missions in the most dangerous regions of the world.

Neil Brighton travels to Saudi Arabia, and during his meeting with Prince Saud, a servant comes running to raise an alarm. A "Firefall" has been called—code for an assault on the royal family. Too late to help, Prince Saud learns that his wife and children have been assassinated, the first step in Prince

Abdullah's plan to take over the leadership of his country. Prince Saud flees with his second wife and his only remaining son, a boy of four, taking them by helicopter to Iran and consigning them secretly to the care of his distant cousin Rassa Ali Pahlavi, Azadeh's father. On the way back, his helicopter is fired upon, and he barely has time to get a Mayday message out, pleading for Neil Brighton to rescue his son, before missiles destroy the chopper. Abdullah's spies intercept the message, and the race is on to find the last son of Prince Saud. What no one knows is that Rassa has persuaded his powerful friend, Omar, to smuggle the princess and her child out of the region.

Soon the mercenaries of Prince Abdullah flood into the valley of Agha Jari Deh, seeking the young prince and the man Rassa. When Rassa refuses to surrender the boy, they burn him to death before Azadeh's eyes and begin the grim task of killing all the young boys in the village, as well as any of the villagers who oppose them. Their work is interrupted by the sudden arrival of American soldiers—Sam's unit—dispatched to help Prince Saud's son. The Deltas frighten off the remaining enemy soldiers, but they are too late to do much good. Destruction and carnage are everywhere, and they hold out no real hope of finding the royal child they have come to rescue. After a quick assessment of the situation, the captain orders them back to the choppers, but on his way, Sam feels an impression that someone needs his help. He turns back to see Azadeh and feels instantly that he knows her somehow. As his platoon leader pulls him away, he calls to her to find her way to Khorramshahr, a U.N. refugee camp on the Iran/Iraq border, where he promises to have someone find her.

Azadeh, shunned by the people of her village, journeys to Khorramshahr. Conditions in the camp are bleak, but when Azadeh reaches out in prayer she is led to a new friend,

Pari al- Faruqi. Pari, an old woman who has been at Khor-ramshahr for years, has chosen to brighten her surroundings with murals on the walls and flowers outside the door of her plywood shack. She shows Azadeh how to find the beauty even in a hard life, and the silver cross on her wall symbolizes her relationship with a deity very different from the one Azadeh has been raised with.

Sam and his good friend and fellow soldier, Bono, orches-trate Azadeh's escape from the camp and make arrangements for her to be taken to the United States. Soon afterward, they are invited to join the Cherokees, a super-elite classified unit of the army.

Prince Abdullah, spurred on by Lucifer himself, continues his plan for the destruction of all his enemies, beginning with his father and expanding to include the United States. The nuclear warheads he acquires from Dr. Abu Nidal Atta, deputy director of the Pakistan Special Weapons Section, are soon put to use.

The carefully planned sequence of events begins with the assassination of Israel's prime minister. When the *Knesset,* the Israeli parliament, meets in emergency session to determine a course of action, a powerful explosion rips through the room, killing most of the government leaders. Such an outrage can-not go unanswered, and Israel's military commanders give the order to "light the Pinball," sending bombers out to a stan-dard list of hostile targets.

Inside one of those targets, a Saudi crouches with his hand on the trigger of one of Prince Abdullah's nuclear weapons. When the bomb is dropped from the Israeli aircraft, he ignites an explosion from within the building, thus making it appear as if Israel has dropped a nuclear bomb. The world is stunned, but only the United States stands behind the Israelis, who plead their innocence. King Abdullah al-Rahman of the House of Saud addresses the U.N. General Assembly, denouncing the United States, and the ambassadors agree nearly unanimously to kick the U.S. off the United Nations Security Council.

The next piece of the puzzle slips into place as King Abdullah offers five million dollars to a Chinese general in exchange for allowing a single crate to pass uninspected through the port facilities at Shanghai.

Sara Brighton, unable to reach her husband, Neil, at his emergency post in the White House, is prompted by the Spirit to pack up the car and leave the city with Ammon and Luke. Soon afterward, General Brighton receives a phone call that he must take: King Abdullah is on the line. Abdullah tells him to warn his president that he has only seven minutes to live. Neil immediately sends out the code FLASHDANCE, signaling an imminent attack, but he is too late to do anything but run for shelter as the aircraft with the smuggled crate descends into Reagan International Airport. In a few milliseconds, Washington, D.C., is annihilated in a nuclear fireball . . .

"In this the beginning of the rising up and the coming forth of my church out of the wilderness— clear as the moon, and fair as the sun, and terrible as an army with banners."

—Doctrine and Covenants 5:14

chapter one

The president of the United States was almost dead.

His helicopter had not survived the shock wave that blew outward at the speed of sound from the core of the nuclear explosion. The burst of super-heated air literally tore the rotor blades from *Marine One,* sending the chopper tumbling toward the ground a few miles up the Potomac, the shattered fuselage crashing against the rocky shore. Advanced engineering saved the president from instant death, the crash-resistant steel frame around the presidential cabin absorbing most of the shock. Baffles braced the occupants against the impact, while foam-filled fuel tanks negated the post-impact fire.

Still, it wasn't enough. Twenty-five g's of impact tore the cabin apart, ripping the president from his seat belt and sending him through the air to crash against the cabin wall.

Another Secret Service helicopter, half a mile ahead of *Marine One* and so protected behind a rocky bluff along the river, had circled back to the crash site. The agents had pulled the president from the wreckage and evacuated him to Raven Rock.

But they were too late. Too much damage had been done. By the time the president's stretcher rolled into the compound, he was just a few moments from death.

His heart was in the process of rupturing, the left aorta beginning to tear away from the chamber, his chest filling with blood and body fluids, the pressure compressing against his lungs. One by one, his other organs were beginning to shut down, his blood pressure cascading downward with each beat of his tearing heart. His breath grew shallow in his chest. His lips were turning blue now, and his face was graying.

Yet he fought the falling darkness, concentrating all of the power and emotion that had carried him to become the most powerful man on the earth on simply taking another breath.

Still, the heavy blanket kept on falling.

He cursed the fading light.

No! Not now! Not *this* way!

The darkness grew more heavy.

Still, he forced himself to breathe.

He forced himself to think.

He forced himself to *live*.

But with each breath, he felt more shallow, more peaceful, more filled with light . . .

Inside his mind, he started walking, his feet stumbling over sharp and jagged rocks. Just a few paces ahead, he saw the soft moss and wet grass. Then a cliff, with a bright blue sky stretched beyond it. He kept on walking. The ground grew marshy, his steps soft and light. The rocky edge. He stepped toward it. No more pain. No more anguish. No more disappointment or regret.

Relief was right there before him, at the edge of the cliff.

He took another step and then stopped. Hesitating, he turned around.

It can not end like this! he screamed inside himself.

He *would not* pass away, stepping over the cliff. Not with his nation wounded, bent and bloodied and brought to her knees. He had sworn a sacred duty. And his work was not yet done.

So he took another breath, then turned away and forced himself to walk back.

* * *

The president choked and the military doctor leaned toward him. Turning him on his side, the physician cleared the airway, then gently laid him back down. The president reached up and took the doctor's hand, the doctor returning his desperate grasp.

The physician watched the president very closely. He had been in combat. He had watched others die. He had seen the look before: the desperate face, the moving lips, the fluttering eyelids fighting to keep the light. And he knew what was going on inside the blood-stained head.

He watched the dying president, his heart racing in his chest.

The physician had heard unspeakable things pass through dying men's lips. So he braced himself as the president tried to talk.

Could they trust a dying man to make the most important decisions a president had ever made? Could they trust a dying man to do the right thing against the greatest crisis the nation had ever faced?

A new fear grew inside him as the president began to whisper through clenched teeth.

* * *

"Tell me what you've learned," the president gasped to the army general who was kneeling at his side. The four-star told him what he could. "There was a nuclear detonation over D.C.," he started. "It's very early, sir. We don't really know what's going on."

"Who did it!" the president demanded.

"We don't know, sir. We know the warhead wasn't delivered by a missile, but that's about all we have. It could have been a ground package, a small watercraft coming up the Chesapeake Bay, inside a private aircraft . . ."

"Who did it!"

The general shook his head. "Sir, we don't know—"

"Find out. You understand that!" The president's fist tightened up.

"We will, sir. We think we have enough information in our database to track the fingerprint of the uranium explosion to its source, but it might take a couple of days . . ."

"Where is Caddy Johnston?" the president demanded, looking for the vice president.

"Again, sir, we don't know." The four-star's voice fell into a whisper. Far too many *don't knows*. "There has been no contact with him or anyone from his office. We are thinking—"

"Who is left? Who will be in charge here?"

"Sir, we are trying to establish communications with your offices in D.C."

"Will *you* be in command, then!" the president hissed, using every ounce of breath.

The protocol for the chain of command inside Raven Rock was very well established. And yes, besides the president, with no other civilian authorities in the mountain, the four-star was in charge.

The general finally answered. "Sir, if you should become incapacitated, I would be in command of Raven Rock." It was clear from the pain on his face that the general wished that wasn't true.

The president lifted his head, forcing himself toward the general while pulling desperately on his hand. "Don't you let them get away with this!" he breathed. "You understand me, General Hewitt. Don't let this go unanswered. I'm dying, that is obvious, but I am of sound will and mind, and I'm ordering you, as your president, to retaliate. I'm initiating a *White Wolf.* Do you understand?"

The general nodded slowly. "I understand," he said.

"Say it to me, General Hewitt. I want to hear you say the words."

The general hesitated, glancing anxiously over his shoulder to the other officers and civilian officials standing nearby. "You are initiating war plan *White Wolf,*" he repeated after turning back to the president.

The president almost pulled himself into a sitting position, a trickle of red drool, half spit and half blood, forming at the corner of his mouth. He glanced past the commanding general to the other nearest officer, a female captain who was the army general's aide. "You copy that," he demanded. "I said *White Wolf.* Understand!"

The captain nodded slowly. "*White Wolf,*" she repeated.

The president fell back, his lungs deflating as he rested on the pillow once again. Then he slowly closed his eyes, his face relaxing with relief.

The doctor watched him, almost crying with desperation and despair.

The dying man had spoken. He was still the president, and they had their orders. Now there wasn't any choice.

chapter two

Minutes after the president took his last breath, the four-star general moved into the Command Center, followed by half a dozen military aides. The Command Center was high-ceilinged and semidark, damp, almost moldy, cavelike, and chilly, partly because of the cold rock, partly because of the cooling systems designed to protect the multi-million-dollar computer systems that had been jammed into every foot of available space.

Built in 1956, rebuilt in '74, the underground emergency command post known as Raven Rock had fallen into neglect as the Cold War had wound down, then been seriously upgraded after the 9/11 attacks.

With a full-time staff of 350 people, including representatives from all major military commands, enough room for 2,600 more (most of them bunked up four to a room), 700,000 square feet of underground office space, a secret tunnel that connected the underground command post to Camp David (which was only a few miles away), a thirty-ton blast door, air vents hidden deep in the woods, a gym, a television and media studio, 500,000 gallons of purified water, a small hospital and pharmacy (prestocked with every known prescription currently being taken by all of the senior senators, representatives, military advisors, and presidential aides), Raven Rock was capable of administering an entire shadow government without coming up for air.

Adequate, but all business, the amenities inside the underground command post were sparse. Fake windows with landscapes had been painted on a few of the cement walls, and the lighting in the hallways was adjusted on a twenty-four-hour cycle to simulate the rising and setting of the sun. Small, cramped, and bleak, the quarters had perpetually damp floors, and the constant hum of equipment and computers permeated the air.

A private conference room had been built at the back of the Command Center. The darkened glass was soundproof as well as bulletproof, though no one understood exactly why. The four-star army general stalked into the room, where he found most of the senior staff. "Anything from the Pentagon?" he demanded as he walked through the door.

"We've established com with the Command Center underneath the Pentagon," the director of communications answered quickly. "Colonel Jackson is the Duty Officer today, but he's the most senior member that we have so far."

"You're kidding," the general shot back.

"No, sir. The Pentagon command post had less than three minutes' warning. The evacuation plan was under way but there was some confusion regarding whether it was a *Blackjack*, which would have ordered the senior Pentagon staff into the command post, or a *Swordfish*, which would have ordered the evacuation of the premises. At any rate, it wouldn't have mattered; most of the members of the Chiefs of Staff were already at the White House for the weekly briefing."

The general lifted his hand. "And the vice president?" he

questioned. His voice was low and absurdly calm. Devoid of emotion, he was rolling through the checklist, stone-cold and expressionless, not really feeling or thinking anymore.

He knew the procedures. He had drilled this a dozen times in his career. Then suddenly, despite his low voice and stony expression, something deep inside him started screaming, *This can't be real!*

The Communications Officer, a marine captain who had to be in his mid-twenties but looked like he was getting ready for his junior prom, shook his head. "Nothing from the vice president's office, sir, but every indication is that he is dead. Like the president, he was in a motorcade on the streets in D.C. when we received the warning. We got the president out on the choppers, but the vice headed back to the Situation Room at the White House. It looks like he might have been above surface when it happened." The officer nodded to the aerial footage of downtown D.C. that was being flashed into the Command Center from the military satellite, allowing the blackness and carnage to finish the thought for him.

"Anyone from the Congress? The White House Situation Room?"

"The White House Situation Room is just coming on line, sir. The NSA is not there. Colonel Brighton didn't make it either, sir. Last report, he was still at his desk. He's the one who called the president and the Pentagon. He saved an unknown number of lives by his actions, at the apparent sacrifice of his own. As far as civilian leadership, we've confirmed that Congressman O'Brien and a couple dozen others have been evacuated to Mount Weather—"

"Who in the world is O'Brien!"

The marine officer glanced down to his cluttered console and his notes. "He's the third-ranking member of the House Military Appropriations subcommittee."

The general's face turned pale. "The third-ranking member . . ."

"Actually, sir, he's the third-ranking *minority* member. He was en route to Philadelphia—"

The general cut him off. He didn't care. Some second-term congressman from Topeka wasn't going to help him right now. "Who else? There must be someone!"

"The line of succession has been cut way, way down the chain. The vice president, the Speaker of the House, the president pro tempore of the Senate, who would be third in line . . . all of them are missing. We can't presume until we know, but all of them were . . . you know, in the city at the time."

"There has to be someone else, some civilian authority that we can turn to?"

"No one at this time, sir."

The general flinched as if he had taken a punch. Again, his mind was screaming: *I must be dreaming! This can't be real!*

He quickly looked around, taking in his staff. The Continuity of Operations Command Center inside Raven Rock had been designed for one purpose, to administer the COOP, or *Continuity of Operations Plan*, the formal plan for keeping the government operating, even if at only a minimal level, during a time of severe national crisis. Looking around, the general shivered. He had never thought the civilian chain of command would be so severed that he would actually be in charge.

Twenty, maybe thirty, staff members manned the Command Center. Staring into their terrified faces, he realized that he was not alone. Like he, the junior officers and civilian administrators who had been roped into manning Raven Rock—in exchange for the promise of a top-notch job to follow—had never expected to actually see the day when the COOP would be put into place.

Now they seemed so young. All so young.

Or did he seem so old?

Swallowing the wad of dry spit caught at the back of his throat, he turned away. No way was he going to let them see his anguish. No way would he telegraph his despair.

The room was deadly silent, the air purifiers and cooling fans the only sound that he could hear. It was more than thirty seconds before he turned back to his staff. When he did, his gray eyes were expressionless, his face tight and as determined as any soldier's face should be.

Fine. The fates had willed it. Ugly as it was, this was his war. He would follow the procedures. He would do what he had been told. If, somewhere up above him, the world was coming to an end, it didn't matter. Who was dead, who was alive now, time would have to sort it out.

For now he had his orders. Follow the checklist. It was the law. He had no choice.

"All right, people," he commanded in a booming voice. "At 00:47:34 Zulu Time, the president of the United States directed a *White Wolf* operation. His orders have been formally confirmed by National Command Authority and my staff.

"We've prepared for and war-gamed this for more than fifteen years. You know all the procedures. Now it's time to get to work."

* * *

The ROE, or Rules of Engagement, for a *White Wolf* were extensive and complicated but unequivocally clear. In part, the war directive read:

CONTINUITY OF OPERATIONS PLAN (COOP) WHITEWOLF
IN THE EVENT OF A:
—DELIBERATE AND HOSTILE NUCLEAR

DETONATION OVER THE UNITED STATES, HER TERRITORIES OR DESIGNATED "SAFE HOUSE ZONES" (see OPPLAN Wilma for definition of possible criteria of designated U.S. Safe House Zones)

AND,

—ONCE PRESIDENTIAL AUTHORITY HAS INITIATED *WHITEWOLF,* THEN

—ALL NECESSARY CIVILIAN AND MILITARY ASSETS WILL BE DESIGNATED/ASSIGNED TO DETERMINE, WITHOUT DELAY, THE SOURCE OF THE HOSTILE WEAPON (see OPPLAN OUTBACK for information regarding possible fissionable material tracking and nation coding).

NOTE: *WHITEWOLF,* by definition, assumes the hostile detonation of a nuclear device by an unknown and/or non-recognizable organization/government-/nation-state. The initial thrust, and the most critical element, of *WHITEWOLF* is to aid in the identification of hostile parties by relying on the NMTD (Nuclear Material Tracking Database) so as to promptly and appropriately retaliate.

DURING THE IMPLEMENTATION OF *WHITEWOLF,* ALL INITIAL EFFORTS MUST BE DIRECTED TOWARD:

(1) PREVENTING FURTHER/SUBSEQUENT ATTACKS

(2) SECURING NATIONAL BORDERS, TERRITORIES, OVERSEAS MILITARY INSTALLATIONS, LOCATIONS OF NATIONAL INTEREST, STRATEGIC RESOURCES (OVERSEAS FOSSIL FUEL FIELDS, PORT FACILITIES), ETC.

(See Appendix 1A-3c for comprehensive list of known strategic assets.)

(3) WORKING WITH ALLIED NATIONS TO ASSURE MUTUAL SECURITY.

WHILE WORKING WITHIN THE CONFINES OF THE ABOVE, THE NEXT HIGHEST PRIORITY IS TO DETERMINE THE SOURCE OF THE NUCLEAR MATERIALS.

—ONCE THE SOURCE OF THE NUCLEAR MATERIALS USED AGAINST THE UNITED STATES HAS BEEN DETERMINED, *WHITEWOLF* WILL PROVIDE POTUS (PRESIDENT OF THE UNITED STATES) OR THE PRESIDENT'S SUCCESSOR WITH TARGET OPTIONS IN ORDER TO RETALIATE.

NOTE: *WHITEWOLF* RECOGNIZES THAT, AT THIS POINT, POTUS HAS DETERMINED THAT NUCLEAR RETALIATION IS THE LAST REMAINING OPTION. UNDER THIS ASSUMPTION, THE ATTACK MATRIXES (Appendix 1A-3e) WILL HELP TO DETERMINE WHICH MIX OF WEAPONS PLATFORMS AND FACILITIES WILL BE MOST EFFECTIVE. . . .

*　　*　　*

The plan, options, directions, summaries, and appendixes for *WhiteWolf* were more than four hundred pages long, but the general noted that some earlier officer, evidently figuring he could save a little time, had summarized the war plan on his own. Across the front page, he had written:

WAR PLAN *WHITEWOLF* SUMMARY:

Find out who did it.

Bring their world to an end.

And that was it, in essence. That was *White Wolf* at its core. Use every resource available to the United States to find out who had attacked them, then retaliate in kind.

So it was that, two hours after the attack on D.C., as the rest of the nation stalked through a mixture of hate and shock and dread, scrambling to deal with what appeared to be the loss of their national government, a group of men and women working deep within the underground complex in Southern Pennsylvania began to put the pieces in place so that the United States could strike back.

Against whom they were going to retaliate, they didn't know yet.

It would take them a few days to find out.

Then they would retaliate and kill them.

Because that was the plan.

*"And he beheld Satan; and he had a great chain
in his hand, and it veiled the whole face of the earth
with darkness; and he looked up and laughed,
and his angels rejoiced."*

—MOSES 7:26

*"Wo, wo, wo unto this people; wo unto the inhabitants
of the whole earth . . . for the devil laugheth, and
his angels rejoice, because of the slain of the
fair sons and daughters."*

—3 NEPHI 9:2

chapter three

The Great One looked out on the devastation that he had created in Washington, D.C. He stood alone, his callous face dull and lifeless. Even here, in the non-mortal world, the eyes were still the windows that looked into the soul—and his eyes, once so bright and full of joy, had narrowed to angry slits that boiled from the pollution in his being.

The problem was, he knew. He knew, more than anyone, what he had given up.

He would never have a family. He would never hold a child. He would never have the joy of knowing that, despite all the trials of mortal living, he had done the right thing.

He would never feel the peace of knowing that Christ was at his side.

There was no hope. No optimism. No light or sun in his life.

There was nothing left for him but emptiness and pain.

Yet he was alive. Like every other creature, he had no choice but to live.

So he stood alone, always angry, looking out on the putrid world he had made.

The smell of smoke from the nuclear explosion over D.C. hit his nostrils: burning trees, melting steel, scalded flesh, and smoldered clothes. The scent of destruction. His lips turned up at the smell. But there was more, something else, another scent in the air. Like a hyena smelling fear, he sensed the despair that filled the world.

He shuddered with delight.

How he cherished that smell.

The fires were still burning, the smoke thick and black as it billowed in the air. The very land seemed to wail. Portable hospital units had been put up everywhere. Washington, D.C., wasn't a city any longer, just a collection of hospitals and morgues. Lucifer cracked another smile. What horrible scenes did the men and women inside those hospital rooms endure! Bodies were being piled on the streets, waiting for disposal. And there was more to come. Much more.

Lucifer, the father of pain and lies, looked upon it all and growled. Lifting his hand, he raised his dark chain, swinging it easily. Flashing like a bullwhip, the last link *snapped* a clap of thunder through the air.

A dark murmur of expectation rose behind him and his angels crowded near. A few of them cowered, having felt the sting of the chain before, but most wanted to be closer to the smell.

He snapped the great chain again and the darkness grew more dense, the sun more distant, the day more dim. The horde of angels seemed to freeze, anticipating another snap of the chain.

Lucifer turned toward his servants, the great chain curling to his feet.

Silence.

Deadly silence.

No one breathed. No one spoke. No one moved.

The tendons in his neck pulled tight as he screeched. Shrill, cold, and piercing, the noise rolled toward the crowd.

To some it sounded like a scream. To some it sounded like a growl. But those few who knew him best recognized it as a laugh.

The bitter angels snorted around him, then added their jeers to the ugly sound.

ROYAL PALACE
RIYADH, SAUDI ARABIA

The king lay on top of his bed. The sun was setting now, and the enormous bedroom fell dim as the light faded against the desert sky, the failing sunlight that filtered through the forty-foot windows washing from yellow tint to dark orange to deep red.

Lying there, he shuddered, then sat up suddenly.

He didn't hear it, but he felt it.

He didn't see it, but he knew.

He felt the darkness laugh around him. He felt his master's cry.

Pushing himself from his bed, he reached out for his robe.

His master was in the battle.

So much work yet to do.

chapter four

Tucked between the rolling mountains, Front Royal was on the north end of the Shenandoah Valley, which was green and fertile and now full of people as tens of thousands of citizens had fled west, seeking the protection of the mountains, though none of them knew what the valley really had to offer or why they were there. The Appalachian Mountains ran south and west of the small southern town, providing an emotional wall if not any real protection from the devastation in D.C.

The Shenandoah River ran on the outskirts of the town. From where Sara Brighton stood she could hear the croaking frogs in the lowlands that fed into the river. It was a beautiful night, and from the balcony of the old hotel she could see the outline of the mountain peaks: dark, tree-filled mounds rising up to meet the light of the moon. Gentle and rolling, not like the Rockies, certainly not like the Alps, the rising shadows around her were still a comforting sight.

Front Royal was a typical western Virginia town, with beautiful old homes; narrow, tree-lined roads; and acres and acres of farms surrounded by spreading hardwood trees. Sara loved reading military history, something she had picked up from her husband, and she knew that at one time the infamous Stonewall Jackson had rolled through Front Royal, completely destroying the village as well as most of the countryside around it. Every town, every building, every farm had been burned to the ground, all to capture and secure the Manassas Gap Railroad and two stone bridges over the Shenandoah River.

Sara looked out on the countryside the general had fought so hard to capture.

Half an hour before, as the sun was just beginning to set, she and her two sons, Ammon and Luke, had lucked upon the run-down hotel at an intersection on Skyline Drive and checked in for the night, paying four times the normal rate for a single room. The boys had showered, wolfed some sandwiches from the café across the street, and fallen asleep on the floor, their sleeping bags rolled out against the far wall. Now she stood alone on the hotel balcony, her face bathed in moonlight. Behind her, the hotel door was open and she could hear the twins breathing in their sleep. She listened, finding comfort in the sound, then wrapped her arms around herself.

It was impossible to imagine what had brought them to this place, impossible to understand how much their world had changed. Inside her chest, she moaned, thinking of her husband's death.

It tore her apart, the fact that there hadn't been a funeral to note the passing of Neil Brighton's life. The stake president back in D.C. had wanted to hold a special service for him, but Sara wouldn't allow it. Hundreds of members had been lost in the attack; she wasn't the only widow in the stake, her sons the only children who had lost their fathers, and to have a special service for one person simply didn't seem right.

But the stake president understood the extraordinary role

her husband had played. "Sara, I think people appreciate how important Neil was to our nation. I think they understand how vital he was to the president, to our security. I think they understand how hard he worked, the sacrifices he made, the sacrifices of your family. We all know how much you missed him even before . . ." Here the stake president's voice had trailed off.

"How much I missed him even before he was killed," Sara completed his sentence for him, her eyes sad and tired.

"I mean that in the most respectful way, Sara. Neil sacrificed his entire life, while he was living and literally at the end, in order to serve his country. But he wasn't the only one in your family who sacrificed. You, your children, you paid the price too. I know how often he was gone, the hours that he worked, the burden that he carried. I think I understand."

Sara watched him, her eyes brimming. "President Willow, I love you, you know that, but I just don't think you do."

The stake president hesitated. "Can I tell you something?" he asked her.

She thought for a moment, then nodded.

The president cleared his throat. "You remember a few years ago, Neil came to me for a priesthood blessing. He was feeling overwhelmed with his responsibilities, his duty, the time it took, the time he couldn't be at home. Do you remember that, Sara? Do you remember when he came to see me?"

She raised her eyes and looked at him intently. "Of course," she said.

The stake president walked toward her and took her trembling hands in his own. "During that blessing, the Lord showed me—I think he showed us both—a glimpse of what lay ahead. During that blessing, for a moment I felt the responsibility your husband carried. I don't know if I can describe it, but for the one brief moment, I shared the burden that he felt. I think I had to have that experience in order that I could give him the blessing he needed to go forward. So yes, Sara, I think I understand just a little the burden and sacrifices that you and your family have endured, which is one of the reasons I would like to have some kind of memorial service for Neil."

"But we don't have a . . ." her voice grew slow here . . . "a body. Any remains. How can we provide a service without . . ."

"We can do it, Sara."

She seemed to think a moment, but the truth was, she had already made up her mind. "No, thank you, President Willow. Thank you for your offer, for your consideration, but I am not the only one who lost a loved one in this tragedy. I couldn't feel good about it. It just wouldn't be right."

So they had joined in a general service at the stake center for all those who'd been killed.

It was to be the only memorial she would ever have for her husband and the father of her sons.

"I think about all those pioneers who lost family members on the plains," she said to Luke and Ammon later on that night. "How many of the early Saints left their children or their spouses in shallow graves out on the prairie. They didn't love their lost ones any less than you or I, yet they didn't have a funeral service for them. We're not the first to have to go through this. I guess we'll be okay."

"Guess so," Ammon answered, "but I have to tell you, Mom, I didn't think it would end up this way."

Standing on the second-floor balcony of the Front Royal Inn, her arms growing cold, Sara considered the final service. That had been two days ago now. Seemed like two years. Two lifetimes. Too long.

She took a deep breath and held it, smelling the trees and

farms, then turned and walked into her hotel room. She knelt, said a short prayer—she had been praying all day and had very little more to say—and climbed into bed, staying on the right side, leaving the other pillow and the left side of the bed for Neil, just as she had done for more than twenty years.

Lying on her back, she stared up at the dark. The blinds were thin and bled some of the lights from the streets, casting distorted squares of yellow against the ceiling and walls. Sara could hear the frogs and swamp sounds through the old windows and thin walls.

She was tired. So tired. She felt like she hadn't slept in weeks. She closed her eyes. They were so heavy. It felt so good just to lie there, not to have to move, not to have to think. She didn't have to make a decision, she didn't have to pretend. For this moment, for right now, she didn't have to do anything.

Her mind started drifting, thinking of her husband. Funny—she couldn't quite picture his face. She thought of his smell: soap, shaving cream, Old Spice . . . there, she had it now, his face, his deep laugh and teasing smile . . .

Her eyelids were so heavy . . .

All she wanted was to sleep . . .

She heard his voice just as clearly as she had ever heard anything in her life.

"Sara, it isn't over."

She sat up on the bed.

"Sara, it isn't over," she heard him say again.

"Neil," she whispered softly, her voice catching in her throat.

"Listen to me, Sara." The voice was low but strong. *"I want you to stay right here. Stay here for two more days. Then get up and drive west. You will be shown what to do when it happens."*

"Neil," Sara called again.

"Stay here, then move west . . ."

And then the voice was gone.

She sat up on the side of the bed, staring at the darkness, then leaned back against the pillow, feeling full and warm. "Neil?" she repeated slowly before drifting off to sleep.

*　　*　　*

The sun was up and the room was bright when she opened her eyes. She had slept through the night without waking and she felt fresh and strong. Looking at her covers, which lay almost undisturbed across the bed, she realized she had hardly moved as she slept.

Glancing at the floor, she saw Ammon staring up at her.

"I had a dream, Mom," he told her.

Sara nodded slowly. "Your father?"

Ammon looked up at the ceiling. "We're going to stay here," he said.

"But why?" Sara answered. "It doesn't make any sense."

Ammon sat up on his sleeping bag and ran his hands through his hair. "Nothing makes sense anymore, Mom. Nothing at all. The only thing that makes any sense is what we know in our hearts, the things we know by the Spirit. That's the only way we'll be led. We can't look to anyone else right now, not our bishop, not other members. We're on our own for a while. But remember what the scriptures say about this day: Some pretty cool things are going to happen to those who will listen to the Spirit. Children will see visions. Children will have dreams."

Sara swallowed and looked away. "We will stay here, then." She paused. "Though I have no idea why."

"There has to be a reason."

"We will stay here two days."

"Two days," Ammon said, then lay back on his sleeping bag again.

* * *

Two days later, they paid their bill (Luke furious at the outrageous cost), packed their bags in the car, and were ready to go.

They waited until the sun was barely visible, its dull light shining down the narrow Shenandoah Valley, the sky red and blistery from high-altitude smoke and dust. Then they started the car, said a final prayer, and turned west.

Ammon drove, the oldest brother, if only by a few minutes. Sara sat in the passenger seat, Luke in the back.

Ammon stole a sideways look toward his mother as he drove. She had been forcing a sense of optimism ever since the attack, straining to make herself smile while reassuringly patting their legs. But he knew. He could see it in her eyes, her body language, the sadness of her mouth. She was hurting, dying with grief and pain. And fear. She was so fearful. She felt weighted down with the responsibility of her children in this upside-down world.

Ammon glanced at her again, then reached over for her hand. He took her fingers and squeezed them gently. "Mom, you are strong enough to do this."

Sara didn't answer.

Ammon gestured to the back. "Luke is strong enough. I am strong enough too. We're going to get through this. I promise you, we will."

She turned toward him, and for an instant he saw her for what she was, a frightened little girl. "I love you, Mom," he told her.

She nodded and pressed her lips together. "Thank you, Ammon."

"It's going to be okay, Mom. It really is."

She squeezed his fingers, then pulled her hand back and looked ahead.

Behind them, Luke was reading from a small set of red, military-issue scriptures that had belonged to his dad, the last thing he had taken from his father's bedroom dresser before walking out of their house.

Twenty minutes passed in silence. Then, without explanation, Luke started reading aloud:

"And I will also be your light in the wilderness; and I will prepare the way before you, if it so be that ye shall keep my commandments; wherefore, inasmuch as ye shall keep my commandments ye shall be led towards the promised land; and ye shall know that it is by me that ye are led.

"Yea, and the Lord said also that: After ye have arrived in the promised land, ye shall know that I, the Lord, am God; and that I, the Lord, did deliver you from destruction."

There was peaceful silence for a moment.

"Cool," Luke finally said.

Ammon nodded slowly.

For the first time in many days, Sara's smile was genuine.

DOWNTOWN CHICAGO, ILLINOIS

Azadeh Ishbel Pahlavi looked out through the dirty windows of the downtown office building, a five-story brownstone off Cage Park and Garfield Boulevard. The carpet under her feet was dirty, the walls cracked, the furniture worn, the wooden desks cluttered with papers and phones. There were a few pictures hanging haplessly on the wall but very little other decoration or office cheer.

Azadeh, trying her best to fit in, had taken on American fashion and was wearing a black skirt, white sweater, and leather belt. But she also wore a scarf covering most of her beautiful hair. A simple silver chain hung around her neck.

The American woman, a low-ranking member of the organization that had brought her to the United States from Iran, seemed friendly, but Azadeh didn't know. She was a stranger, after all, and Azadeh was constantly on guard.

Everything around her was so unfamiliar: the smells, the heavy sounds of traffic, the many different colored faces, the men who weren't afraid to stare, the towering buildings, the food, even the tacky feeling in the air.

She truly was a stranger. She was in a strange land.

A crushing wave of homesickness welled inside her. She missed her village. She missed her father. She missed her people and her home. She missed speaking Farsi, the eloquent words and velvet sounds of her native tongue. She missed the food, the great mountain that towered over her village, the peaceful wail as they were called to prayer, the woolen prayer rugs, the dark eyes of little children watching the Ayatollahs rise to speak. She missed it all, and, listening to the strange sounds that emitted all around her, she felt her heart begin to tear.

She tried to fight the feeling, but it seemed her faith was set to fail.

She thought of the short walk she had just completed along the sidewalk in Chicago, the angry stares and hurtful names. She did not know the words, but the sound of cursing was universal, and she knew that the hateful expressions had been directed at her. The Americans, perhaps warm and welcoming in another time and place, definitely had their ideas of Eastern people now. The fact that she was Persian, the fact that she was fleeing an oppressive regime, that fact that she was a victim, the same as they were, none of that mattered anymore.

She felt a single tear begin to well and quickly wiped it

away. She didn't want to start crying now, not after all she'd been through. She wasn't about to let it out. Not here and not now.

She took a breath and held it, fighting the homesickness, then forced herself to smile.

*　　*　　*

Balaam stood beside the young woman, whispering his evil thoughts into her mind. His voice was soft and smooth and tempting as he tried to draw her in. He had learned she wouldn't listen if he screamed, so he talked tenderly, gently, his voice like dry honey, sweet but slightly grainy against her ears.

Azadeh was a trophy. He wanted her so badly he could hardly look at her. So he gave his best effort, concentrating all his skill. *"They hate you,"* he whispered softly. *"They will always hate you. They'll never forgive your people for what they have done!"*

"But it wasn't *my* people," Azadeh countered in her mind.

Balaam kept his logic simple, his entreaties understandable, even reasonable. *"It doesn't matter. They are not smart enough to know the difference. All they see is the color of your skin and the darkness of your eyes. To them, you people are the same now, and they hate you all the same."*

Azadeh hesitated, her eyes falling to the floor. The woman from the rescue agency stared at her, her smile deceptively bright. Reaching out, she placed her hand on Azadeh's shoulder, but the girl drew back instinctively.

"Are you all right?" the woman asked her. "You look like you might not be feeling well."

Azadeh looked up with uncertain eyes. The woman spoke so quickly. All a jumble. All confusing. Why did they all talk so fast? It was impossible for Azadeh to understand them. She shook her head in despair. Yes, the woman appeared to be friendly, but Azadeh didn't know . . . lots of people came across as friendly when they wanted something from you. And everyone wanted something. Everyone had an agenda.

"*So does she!*" the thoughts continued in her head. "*The world is full of enemies. Haven't you learned anything? You are completely friendless here.*"

✻   ✻   ✻

Lucifer stood beside the angel Balaam, observing his work. The Great Deceiver wasn't a genius, even he knew that. (If he was so smart, how could things have turned out so poorly for him?) But he was old now, and experienced, and he had mastered his tragedies to a perfect art. He was a raging wolf with bloody teeth—there was no heart he wouldn't shatter, no lie he wouldn't tell to bring these mortals down—but he was a wolf in sheep's clothing, soft and inviting and so easy to believe. Seven thousand years of practice had shown him that such subtlety was the only way that some of the mortals, especially the young and innocent, would let him get close enough to really get inside their hearts.

"We have to do more than simply tempt them!" Lucifer often shouted to his flock. "Many times you can do far greater damage by whispering discouragements in their ears."

"*Why, God, if you love me, have you not blessed me when I needed you so? Why have you denied me the one thing that I need most?*"

"*Why, God, if I am worthy, do I continue to fail? I have done everything that I could think of, everything in my power, and yet I continue to fall short.*"

"*Why should I trust you? Why should I even try anymore?*"

"*I am not worthy of this blessing.*"

"*I am not worthy of your love.*"

"These are the lies that you must tell them! These are the deceits that they must hear!"

*　　*　　*

Remembering his words, Balaam glanced anxiously toward the master, then leaned toward Azadeh and kept on whispering in her ear.

"*This woman doesn't care about you. She might pretend, but it's not real.*"

Azadeh looked around, confused. No . . . that couldn't be. The woman seemed so nice.

"*Don't believe it, you fool. Do you really think she wants to help you!*"

Azadeh took a step back, looking around the cluttered office. Everything was so unfamiliar, so uncomfortable.

"*This will never be your home. No one here will ever care about you. The last person who ever loved you was your father, and your father is dead. You are alone now, by yourself, and you will never have a friend!*"

Azadeh shook, fighting the depressing thoughts in her head. "No, it will work out. I have my faith. I have my dreams."

"*No!*" the angry voice hissed. "*You will never feel at home here. You will never be happy. You will never feel joy again.*"

Balaam circled around her, his lips pulled back in a frown, his dark eyes glaring at her as he hissed from ear to ear. Then he stepped in front of her and stared into her face, taking in the long hair and slender arms. He hated all her beauty and the light inside her soul. He could see it. He could *feel* it. And it made him hate her more.

He had been waiting for these young ones for more than seven thousand years. He remembered Elizabeth and her brothers and all the things that they had done. He remembered them. He hated them. And the only thing he wanted was to reach up from his pit and pull them down into despair.

So he leaned toward the young woman and continued talking in her ear. *"They will always hate you. You will never be happy."*

He ranted on and on.

Lucifer smiled at Balaam as he listened. When it came to words of gloom and discouragement, this dark angel was pretty adept. Not all of the mortals would listen to such thoughts, but many of them would.

Staring at her, the Dark One had to wonder.

Would Azadeh listen to his angels? Could they drag her into hopelessness?

chapter five

The United States ramped up for war. No way would the country sustain a nuclear attack on its capital and do nothing about it. How could a quarter of a million people be killed, half a million left sick or wounded, a million more displaced, most without home or shelter, and the world not expect the United States to respond?

The Secretary of State eventually made it to Raven Rock. A few other cabinet members followed, then a couple of senior members of Congress and the Joint Chiefs of Staff. Sitting around the large conference table at the back of the Command Center, the remaining members of the government heard the cries for revenge.

They knew they had to act.

As a formal policy, retaliation didn't make a lot of sense. By definition, it happened after the policy of deterrence had already failed, and it lost a lot of punch with the policy makers who were far more focused on preventing the attack in the first place than in going after blood sometime after the fact. But as a practical matter, in the real world of human emotion, which is where the most critical decisions of nation-states have always been made, the thirst for blood was simply too powerful to ignore.

The first thing the acting president did was order all U.S. forces overseas to return to the States. The military began to withdraw. From the Middle East and Southern Asia to most of Europe and the horn of Africa, the U.S. pulled back its troops. In the greatest military redeployment ever undertaken, thousands of aircraft, military as well as commandeered civilian airliners, began crossing the Atlantic and Pacific oceans, ferrying U.S. troops and their equipment home.

The world watched in amazement, almost holding its breath.

Why was the U.S. pulling back from the fight?

To most, the answer was obvious.

*   *   *

Once the redeployment of the U.S. military forces was under way, the Raven Rock commanders turned their attention to the Office of Nuclear Forensics.

The key to a successful *White Wolf* operation was to properly identify who had attacked the United States. The organization tasked to do this was located in central Maryland. Small and little known, the Office of Nuclear Forensics (ONF) was suddenly the most important intelligence unit in the world.

Millions of people would live or die, depending on what ONF found.

*   *   *

By 2004, the Central Intelligence Agency was a broken organization desperately looking for redemption. It had been roundly thrashed for failing to prevent the September 11 attacks, then suffered an even greater hit to its credibility when it provided inaccurate intelligence regarding the threat of weapons of mass destruction inside Iraq.

In the following years, the agency faced an even more critical issue over nuclear proliferation. However, it quickly realized that nuclear forensics—the science of identifying and tracing the unique signatures of nuclear materials to their production sources—could provide the key to preventing a nuclear weapon from being transferred to a terrorist organization or hostile nation. Knowing that weapons-grade enrichment processes differ from one facility to another, nuclear forensic scientists believed they could identify the radioactive fingerprints left behind from a nuclear attack, in much the same way as it was possible to identify the perpetrator of a crime based on DNA evidence.

A small Office of Nuclear Forensics, code-named Snapper, was set up and tasked with a nearly impossible job: to successfully sample, define, identify, and isolate the unique characteristics of any nuclear material produced by a hostile government.

Russia and all of her former republics, China, Israel, North Korea, India, Iran, and later Saudi Arabia, Jordan, Syria, and Afghanistan, all were suspects who were added to the list of targeted governments from which Snapper tried to collect nuclear material samples. It proved extremely difficult, and in some cases virtually impossible, to collect viable samples from all of the sites, for Snapper had to rely on HUMIT, or human intelligence (i.e., foreign agents), to get the job done. Still, the working group was remarkably successful. Once a sample had been collected, the nuclear forensic specialists began the painstaking and time-consuming process of identifying and coding the fissile material, making it impossible for that foreign government, at least, to become an anonymous dealer of nuclear-weapons-grade material or nuclear bombs.

After the nuclear detonation over D.C., the small group of scientists inside Snapper worked literally twenty-four hours a day. Air and ground samples had to be taken from the bomb site, the material had to be broken down and analyzed, coded, and then matched to the existing database. The supercomputers, some of the most powerful in the world, spun through the computations, a billion calculations every second.

When they got their initial results, the director of Snapper shook his head in disbelief. "Do it again," he demanded. "That can't be right."

"We think it's right, sir," his subordinates answered confidently.

"Do it again. I'll give you another day."

"Another day! We need another week!"

"You have another day! I want the answer. Get to work!"

Back to the site of the destruction. More samples taken. More frantic work. Thirty hours later, they had the same results. There was absolutely no question where the bomb material had come from.

The scientists took it again to their boss, then stood back and watched as another shock wave blew through Raven Rock.

The nuclear weapon detonated over Washington, D.C., hadn't come from North Korea or Iran or Syria or any one of half a dozen countries the United States would have willingly bombed back to the Middle Ages.

The bomb that destroyed D.C. had come from Pakistan.

Pakistan. The nation's closest ally in Central Asia.

Not Jordan, not Tajikistan, not any of the former Soviet states.

Pakistan. The only nuclear power in the region with a pro-West and democratically elected (if only barely) government.

Pakistan. One of the United States' only friends.

The brains inside Raven Rock realized that although a

group within the Pakistani government may have provided the weapon, they couldn't have acted alone. And the Americans weren't completely clueless as to what had been going on. For years the CIA had been tracking the Pakistani scientist who had been working with one of the princes from the House of Saud.

Though they couldn't prove it, they were certain the attack had been coordinated and financed by the new king of Saudi Arabia.

And he surely had more weapons. This was not the end of his game.

Twenty-four hours after Snapper provided the nation's new leaders with their results, the orders were given.

Five nuclear warheads were targeted for the capitals of Riyadh and Islamabad.

Before sending nuclear-tipped warheads from the ICBMs buried in the barren plains of North Dakota, and from the hidden nuclear submarines a hundred miles off the coast of Oman, the provisional government inside Raven Rock warned the nations of Saudi Arabia and Pakistan to evacuate their capitals. They would give them three days; then the missiles would fly.

Three days to evacuate their cities.

Just enough time for the rest of the world to go insane.

Israeli satellites watched as Iran began to fuel its long-range missiles. The United States, China, and Japan watched as North Korea did the same thing. India went to the highest level of alert. The entire Middle East sat on the edge of a razor—Hezbollah soldiers moving to the southern Israel border; Hamas (or what was left of them after the previous nuclear attack against Gaza) declaring open war against Israel from the northern Gaza strip; Jordan and Syria forming an alliance and moving most of their military forces into Lebanon and the

Golan Heights; Egypt declaring (to everyone's amazement and despair) that they had developed their own nuclear warhead and would conduct an underground nuclear test; Chechan rebels attacking again in Moscow; twenty million Muslim citizens rioting throughout Western Europe's streets.

The list of crisis locations was pages long: a hundred years' worth of pent-up hatreds, imagined grievances, hostilities, jealousies, and darkening evil bursting like a rotted egg, the poison and decay finally rupturing the fragile shell.

Iran fired first, bent on reaping revenge upon Israel for attacking their fellow Shiite brothers in Gaza. For years the Iranians had threatened to wipe Israel off the map and they knew this would be their best chance to take their shot.

When Israel detected the Iranians preparing their long-range missiles, they launched their own missiles in a preemptive attack. Forty minutes later, the missiles passed each other in suborbital space. The difference between the outcomes was the fact that Israel had spent twenty years and more than five hundred million dollars on a missile shield defense. The Green Pine search and fire control radars saw the incoming Iranian missiles. The Citron Tree Battle Management Command and Control Centers targeted each of the seven warheads. High-altitude Arrow missiles killed the first four. The three remaining missiles penetrated Israeli airspace. U.S. Patriot missiles went after them once they had descended below 50 kilometers. Two of the remaining nuclear missiles were defeated, leaving only one to get through. Its target was Tel Aviv, but it had been knocked off course, missing the city by almost eight miles.

Tens of thousands of Israelis were killed when the nuclear warhead detonated, but nothing even remotely close to what would have been the death toll if the missile had stayed on track.

Iran, on the other hand, wasn't so well defended. All of the Israeli missiles reached their targets. The three largest cities inside Iran were gone.

Pakistan, bent on protecting its Muslim brother, began to fuel its missiles. Multiple warheads from India and Israel caught them before they could get in the air.

North Korea was just finishing fueling its missiles when the sky was darkened above the launching pads by sea-launched and air-launched Cruise missiles. All told, more than a hundred conventional missiles impacted the Korean launch sites, half of them South Korean missiles launched from just across the border. The North Koreans never had a chance, their first-generation launch and delivery systems too slow and cumbersome to compete in the twenty-first century of modern war. All of the launch facilities were destroyed, leaving a few missiles intact in their underground storage facilities but no way to get them in the air.

Then the world seemed to pause, a depressing and dark despair settling from one end of the earth to the other. Blackness filled the air. Nuclear rain fell in the deserts. Ten million people sucked up radioactive oxygen. The sunsets were dark red, almost purple, from the ionized smoke and dust that filled the atmosphere. Was it over? Just beginning? How far would it go? Almost a million people had died already. Gaza, D.C., Tehran, Isfahan, and Shiraz lay in heaps of smoking rubble.

It wasn't over.

The worst was yet to come.

And there was no way to stop the attack that would come from the blue waters off eastern U.S. shores.

chapter six

Short and fierce (all of the firefights they had were fierce now), the attack hit Sergeant Sam Brighton and his team at night, half a kilometer from the mud-and-brick wall that surrounded the small village.

After sending a false informant to accuse the village of hoarding a cache of weapons, the Syrian and Iranian insurgents had hidden in the desert, burying themselves under a thin layer of sand and breathing through reeds. There they had waited, knowing the American soldiers would eventually come.

When it came to killing Americans, the insurgents were very patient. A few days buried in the sand was a small price to pay.

Sam and his patrol had approached the tiny village on foot, avoiding the pathway from the main road, knowing it was likely mined. The attackers waited until they had passed, then shed their protective tarps and opened fire. Fortunately, they had waited too long, allowing enough distance between their hiding place and the American soldiers for Sam's team to drop and find protection below a small ravine.

One enemy team was positioned behind the U.S. patrols,

42

one team on the flank. They revealed themselves as one, break-ing cover and opening fire at the same time. Their tactics were effective if not particularly heroic: get a couple of thousand rounds toward the Americans, AK-47s and Rocket Propelled Grenades lighting up the night, then turn and run.

For the American soldiers, the firefight was like a burst of lightning: sudden, frightening, and intense. One moment they were stalking toward the village, three to five meters apart, hid-den by the darkness, moving silently across the sand; the next moment they were in the middle of hell, tracers and bullets and explosions all around.

For Sam, the battle came in a fury of dizzying sound and speed. Explosions. Flashes of light. Heat and compression. Calls from his buddies. A quick roll across the sand. Another punch of compressed air in his ears and chest. Screams from beside him. One of his men going down. The buzz of deadly bullets around him, above him, *one between his legs.* Falling again, pushing to his knees, rolling toward the ravine, return-ing fire behind and to the right. Calling in suppression fire from the U.S. A-10 fighters providing cover from overhead. The fighters screaming in. Dozens of frantic shadows all around him. Calibrated and careful fire from his team now. One . . . three . . . five or six of the enemy going down. The screams of a dying man beside him. Sulfur and smoke and the smell of vomit in the air. A medic rushing toward the wounded. An AirEvac chopper on the way.

The enemy fighters started running, their ghostlike images merging into the darkness up ahead.

One of the enemy soldiers nearest to him turned, shot one of his men at point-blank range in the face, then, *laughing,* turned and ran!

The sound of that guttered and bloodthirsty laughing snapped something inside him. In a rage, Sam grabbed his machine gun and went after the fleeing men. As he ran, the image of the battle began to blur again. Darkness formed around him. He ran hard and fast. The sounds of his buddies echoed far behind him. The ground rose suddenly, the desert becoming rocky, black boulders here and there. Sam kept on running, chasing after the enemy soldiers, ignoring the sound of Bono shouting in his earpiece, "SAM, DISENGAGE AND GET BACK HERE! I WANT YOU BACK HERE RIGHT NOW!"

The laughing soldier struggled to keep up with the others, not realizing that Sam was coming after him. Sam looked farther up the hill and saw two more enemy soldiers, twenty meters ahead of the last man, skulking images in his night-vision goggles.

He stopped and estimated the distance between them. Two hundred meters. Maybe seven hundred feet. A long shot . . . a very long shot, especially in the dark . . .

One of the men turned back, saw him in the darkness, and fired. Milliseconds later, Sam felt the buzzing rounds of red-hot metal flying past his head. Another shot and then another as the three men turned and fired.

Dropping to his belly, he extended the small legs on the barrel of his machine gun to form a tripod, took a breath and held it, and then tightened up his aim. More bullets popping into the ground around him, geysers of spitting sand around his face. An ounce of pressure on the trigger. Another breath. A bead of sweat dropping into his left eye. Another ounce of pressure on the trigger . . .

Phaat, phaaat, phaaat . . .

The three enemy attackers fell to the ground.

Sam pulled his head away from his weapon and stared across the barren landscape, studied the rising desert above him. The three attackers didn't move. Their limp bodies were sprawled at awkward angles across the loose sand. He watched them. They were dead, he was certain. His 7.61 shells—large enough to drop a buffalo—could make mincemeat of men.

He rested on his stomach, laying his head against the sand.

He felt so tired. So *consumed*. So empty and thin. A long moment passed. He didn't stand. He didn't move. The darkness grew around him. Thoughts were swimming in his head. A crushing moment of loneliness fell upon him. He'd never felt this way before. Confusion. Bitter disappointment. And a sadness so deep he thought it would crush his very soul.

His mind swirled. His heart raced. He rolled onto his back, overcome, his eyes misting, his nose wet. He thought of the man who had become his father, General Brighton. His birth mother, where was she? Snorting drugs in Atlantic City? Out in Las Vegas again? He thought of his adoptive mother and his brothers. Sara Brighton and her family were the best thing that had ever come into his life. Simply the best. Nothing else was even close. Where was she? Was she living? The entire city of D.C., two hundred thousand people, burned and dead. He thought of the citizens of Iraq. Iran. Syria. Afghanistan. None of them would have it. Freedom would never come to them. It was all coming down. It was falling apart. Everything they had fought and died for, everything every U.S. soldier who'd been hurt or killed for, the families who had suffered, the children without fathers, widowed women, mothers without sons, everything they had suffered . . .

All of it for nothing.

All of it was gone.

He took a breath, his shoulders shaking. Then he did something he had not done since he was a child, not since the first night with the Brighton family when he had hidden his head between the pillows and begged God to let him stay.

He took a deep breath and started weeping, the emotion spilling out in gulping sobs.

All of it for nothing.

All the sacrifices washed away.

He tried to hold it in, but he couldn't, it was just too powerful. So he cried, alone in the desert, his shoulders heaving. He struggled and he fought it, but it gushed out all the same. His face was wet with tears and sweat, the sand gritty against his cheeks, the salty teardrops rolling downward to sting the corners of his mouth.

He gulped the air. He cursed and swore.

And kept on crying like a child.

Royal Palace
Riyadh, Saudi Arabia

The king paced, his face contorted in rage. "That idiot Iranian should have waited," he hissed. "We could have done it together. We could have taken the pig-Jews down. But no, he wouldn't listen! He wanted the glory of killing all the Jews himself. He lost three of his cities! And the Jews, *not a one!* He should have waited. He should have listened. What a stupid, stupid man!"

The old man didn't react. A million people dead. Not a big thing to him.

The young king watched him, expecting some reaction, paced again, then fell silent, standing in front of the old man. The old man looked at him, his eyes cold and wet and bleary, his nostrils flaring as he breathed. Then he grabbed the king's attention and pulled him deep into his stare.

"The United States is getting ready to attack us," the king muttered bitterly. "They've warned us to evacuate our cities. But they'll never get that far."

"No, they won't, King Abdullah. You have the power to destroy them. I suggest you use it now."

The king looked away and blinked. "The United States is still a very powerful nation," he said, trying to mask his hesitation.

The old man sensed his timid heart. He hated the vacillation more than he hated anything. His face flushed with rage. "Do you finally understand why we have to do this?" he demanded, his voice low and mean. He resented being the instructor, always taking the lead. Didn't any of these mortals have the capability to think!

King Abdullah stood in front of him, his eyes low. It was getting harder and harder to look at his friend. The old man's skin had become so translucent that one could see the veins in his cheeks, and his eyes had grown so filmy that they almost looked dead.

The king didn't know who or what the old man was anymore. He didn't know where he had come from or why the man had chosen him. All he knew was that he had to follow, regardless of where he was led. He had made his decision to be the man's servant a long time ago.

The old man waited, his thin lips pressed together, his eyes boring through the pupil who was so slow to comprehend. "Do you get it?" he prodded angrily. "I want to know you understand."

King Abdullah was a tall man, a proud man, handsome by an earthly standard, with his dark skin and black eyes. He could walk into a room of world leaders and in minutes have them all eating out of his hand. But all of that slipped away when he was with the old man. And every time they were together, his groveling seemed to grow more and more pitiful, the old man extending his influence to the depths of his soul, twisting and turning the very breath out of him.

Abdullah turned away, unable to look the old man in the eyes. "I understand you want me to do this, and that is good enough, my friend."

The old man nodded slowly. "Yes, it *is* good enough. But I want to know if I can trust you. I want to know *what* you understand."

The king took a breath, his voice uncertain. "We must destroy them because they are the Great Satan . . ."

The old man lurched out of his seat and rushed toward the king with frightening speed. Getting right in Abdullah's face, he exhaled a foul breath. "Don't give me that!" he screamed. "You know, King Abdullah, who the *Great Satan* really is! You know the Master Deceiver; you have felt him in your heart. You know him. You have loved him. He is now your only friend. So get past all the stupidity and *tell me* if you can! If you can't, then shut up and listen once again."

Abdullah didn't answer, his heart thumping, a dew of perspiration forming on his brow. The old man glared, snarled like an animal, then returned to his seat.

"Listen to me, Abdullah." His voice was softer now. "In a world of lies and deceptions, this is the only truth you have.

"There are three reasons we must do this—three reasons we must destroy the United States.

"First, if we want to deny mankind their freedom, we *must* destroy the U.S. I don't understand it," the old man scoffed and spit, "but the Americans will sacrifice their lives, if necessary, defending the freedom of people they don't even know. It makes no sense—I know that, no one knows it more than I— but they will fight and die for others, even those who can't repay them or make them rich.

"That is the first reason we must destroy them. If we do that, we own the world. But as it is, the U.S. continues to be this obnoxious and glaring light on the hill. If we let it shine, the world will continue moving toward it like a moth to a fire. Simply put, we must remove that light before we can control the rest of the world. Once we have destroyed the United States, we can take our time, toppling the other democracies at our pleasure, for without the U.S. there to guard them, they are helpless as spoiled children."

Abdullah watched the old man, his dry lips spreading to a smile.

"The second thing, my dear king." The old man jabbed a bony hand toward the west. "The center of His people can be found in the U.S. Yes, their tent is wide, but the center stake is *over there*. They can't spread the truth if we force them to pull all their missionaries back. They can't spread the light if they are holed up in the dark."

Abdullah shook his head. He didn't understand.

The old man watched, then sniffed. "Forget it. That doesn't matter. Just trust me, it is important in ways you cannot comprehend.

"Now, the third reason. We must destroy the U.S. before we can take Israel down. If the Americans are around, they will defend it; we've seen it time and time again. They are nursing mothers to the Jews, protective fathers to their young. Will another nation step forward to protect them? No. Not a one. Anyone in Europe? Are you kidding! The Europeans now hate the Zionists almost as much as you do. China? Russia? Anyone? I tell you no. There is not a people or nation on the earth that will defend the Jews except the United States. So we must destroy their mothers before we can destroy the vile seed.

"And remember, King Abdullah, history is absolutely on our side, the side of your people and the Arab nations that you rule. *You are the chosen people.* Ishmael was the firstborn. Hagar was the first wife to bear. Isaac was a second son and a liar and his mother was no more. The birthright was stolen from you."

The old man spat in rage. *"He's the one who stole it from you . . ."* He jabbed his finger at some unseen enemy that seemed to linger near. "He stole the ancient birthright from you. *He stole it for His son.* But it is yours! And you must claim it! The time has come to set it right. Destroy the counterfeit covenant people and we destroy their counterfeit god! But you can't do that, King Abdullah, until you destroy the U.S.!"

The old man stopped to catch his breath, his eyes burning. He was an animal in a cage, consumed with fear and fury. "Five thousand years I've been waiting to wipe His people off the earth. We have a chance to do that now, and you must not let me down!"

Abdullah nodded, an overpowering sense of history falling on his soul, a massive weight that seemed to crush him to the center of the earth. No, it was more than just a sense of history—this was much larger and more powerful. A phrase slipped into his mind he had never heard before. He did not understand it, but still the words were clear. *"The plans were laid many years before there was even a house of Israel placed on the earth . . ."*

He faltered, stepping back, almost collapsing from the feel of it in his bones. The plans set in motion were as ancient as the stars. He was at the crossroads of eternal destiny and there was no turning back.

The old man watched him and reached out, placing his hands on the king's arm. Abdullah felt the dark power of his touch and seemed to gain instant strength.

"There is more," the old man whispered, "a final reason we must act. This is personal, I will admit it, but it's also the most important reason of all.

"We're going to kill them because I hate them. The years have left me full of *fury* and left them full of *light*.

"Before they cast me out, I warned them. Now they are in

my kingdom, and I will turn their lives into hell. I will center all my hatred on destroying their young faith."

The old man stopped and wiped the spit that stretched between his dry lips. His voice was low and soft now and the king struggled to hear it when he said, "That is my final reason, though you will never understand."

Abdullah seemed to shrink at the old man's last words. "But it is so great an undertaking," he mumbled in a frightened voice.

"You can do it," the old man said. "There are others who will join you. You don't have to work alone. Some will join you for our reasons, some for reasons of their own. *Why* they join us doesn't matter, so long as they do what I command."

chapter seven

Sam wiped his tears away.

He finally caught himself, embarrassed at his show of emotion. He pushed himself up into a sitting position on the sand. It was dark. He was exhausted. The firefight and chase up the hill after the enemy soldiers had left him hot and breathless.

The three enemy soldiers lying above him were dead, he was certain of that, and it bothered him that, unlike U.S. soldiers, their bodies would lie there for days before someone came to claim them—if someone ever did. The air around him still smelled like burnt gunpowder, but he knew it was only the barrel of his gun. Looking down from the small bluff, he studied the desert below where, minutes before, the firefight had taken place.

The night was cool. Fall was coming on; even in the desert there was some relief. The wind blew up from the south, humid and biting with tiny bits of sand.

He was dressed in full battle gear: Kevlar helmet, goggles, flak jacket and vest, desert cammies, leather gloves and boots. His weapon, a short-barreled Mk.48 mod 0 gas-powered

machine gun, was strapped loosely around him, and he had
pushed it to his back. The barrel was warm, too warm to be
accurate any longer (700 rounds a minute could scorch a barrel in short order), and he wished he had another barrel to
change it out. But it probably didn't matter—all the bad guys
were gone or dead. The sky overhead was as bright and clear as
only the remote desert sky could be. And it was quiet. Very
quiet.

He turned and listened to the wind, then pulled out the
tube for the flexible pack of water strapped to his back and
took a long drink.

*　　*　　*

Bono walked toward him through the darkness, coming to
a stop right in front of his man. "Looks like you got 'em," the
lieutenant said, nodding to the three dead men up the hill.

Sam grunted as he brushed the backs of his hands across
his cheeks. Had Bono seen him crying, heard his childish sobs?
He took a long draw of breath and shuddered in the dark.

Bono turned and sat down beside him. "You okay?" he
asked.

Sam nodded slowly. "It's all cool, man."

"It's okay," Bono answered, putting his arm around Sam's
back. "It's okay. You're okay. No big thing. It comes and
goes."

Sam didn't answer. He didn't know what to say.

The two men sat in silence, the great desert all around
them.

"Good work," Bono said, nodding up the hill again. "I'm
glad you got them."

Sam drank again. "I don't know, hearing the guy laughing
as he ran away . . . something about it kind of snapped me."

"Yeah. Makes you sick, some guy getting his kicks shooting another man in the face. But listen to me, Sergeant Brighton: If you ever take off like that again, you'll be peeling potatoes and handing out bedsheets for the next twenty years. I *will* have discipline on my fire teams, you understand me! I don't want any cowboys. You count on me. I count on you. That's hard to do when you go ponying out after all the bad guys. You got that, my friend?"

Sam nodded and pulled his night-vision goggles down to cover his eyes.

The sound of the AirEvac chopper filled the darkness as it landed beside the dusty road. "Who got it?" Sam asked, remembering their men who'd been hit.

"Viskosky," Bono answered.

"He going to be okay?"

"Tore his femur. Ripped the vein out. Lost a bathtub full of blood."

"Anyone else?"

Bono was quiet and Sam braced himself.

"A couple other minor hits. Nothing serious." He hesitated another moment. "Hastings was the guy who took it in the face," he finally said.

Sam shook his head and swore.

Bono nodded toward the hilltop. "That last guy, ol' smiley there, hid himself near the road. Shot Hastings from point-blank range right in the face."

Sam nodded sadly. "I saw that," he said. His emotions were under control now, pushed back deep inside him where it was all comfortable. "Viskosky be okay?" he asked.

Bono watched the chopper landing in the distance, its enormous rotors blowing up swirling vortices of sand in the landing lights. "He's going to make it. But it hurt him."

"I like him. He's a good guy. I guess he's going home."

Bono grabbed a fistful of sand and let it sift through his fingers, then lifted his eyes and looked up at the sky. "We all are," he announced. "They're pulling us back."

Sam didn't answer for a moment. "No surprise there," he finally said.

"Yeah, it's been kind of strange, the past couple days. I mean, here we are, pretending nothing happened. A nuke goes off in Gaza. A nuke goes off in D.C. Half of Iran gets hit. Yet for the past week, we keep soldiering on as if nothing's changed. Keep up our patrols, keep shooting at the bad guys, keep talking to the locals, trying to turn them into friends, when everyone knows it's all heading south. Another fireball is coming, there's no doubt about that. The U.S. can't take a nuke on D.C. and not retaliate."

Bono fell silent. The south wind kept blowing bits of sand against his face. "It's going to get ugly," he murmured, talking to himself more than to Sam.

The moon broke out behind a small band of high clouds, orangeish-red. Looking at it, Bono continued his observations. "Everything we do now is POF. Protection of Forces. Protect our own guys. That's all anyone is even thinking about anymore. The locals are getting restless, and so are the troops. No one wants to state the obvious, but we all understand. Things are going to change. None of these people are our friends any longer. They know what's coming, they just don't know when or where. We move here, they move there, but none of it matters. Our mission here is over. We've got to get out before it all comes crashing down."

Sam cleared his throat. "So now what?" he asked.

Bono shook his head sadly. "I don't know where they'll send us, but for a while we're heading back to the States."

Silence for a moment. "We're going home?"

"Soon as we can get airlift and transportation."

"What will we do then?"

"Wait and see, I guess." Bono pulled his flexible tube from his chest strap and took a long drink, then stood up and extended a hand toward Sam. "Come on, Lieutenant. Let's get back to our men."

Sam huffed as he pulled himself up. "Hey, what's this *lieutenant* thing? I work for a living, remember? You're the only officer here."

"Not anymore."

Sam stopped and stared.

Bono stepped toward him. Even in the faint moonlight, Sam could see him smile. "Got word this afternoon. A battlefield commission. You are now Lieutenant Brighton. Congratulations, friend."

"You're kidding me," Sam stammered.

"I wouldn't kid you, brother."

"But why? Out of all the guys, why me?"

Bono nodded up the hill toward the three dead insurgents. "It's pretty obvious to me."

Sam stared at Bono, his eyes growing suspicious. "You did this, right?"

Bono shook his head. "I didn't do it because I like you. And you also need to know that it didn't have anything to do with your father. You earned this, and we need you. It's as simple as that."

Sam didn't answer.

"Listen to me, Sam. It's important that you understand this. War is the great accelerator. It forces things to happen much more quickly than they otherwise would. It changes people, it changes nations, it changes *everything*.

"One of the things it changes is the opportunities that come in our lives. This is just one of many changes you are going to experience. Lots more is going to happen. We're just getting started, I'm afraid.

"So keep the faith and be a leader. That's your only purpose now."

chapter eight

The enormous palace outside Riyadh was the primary headquarters of the royal House of Saud. It was a warlike fortress, intimidating, almost evil looking, thick-walled and strong, a structure that provided an impenetrable bastion to the world and guaranteed there wouldn't be any outside interference in the affairs of the most powerful family on earth. Tall and brown, a little darker than the desert that surrounded it, the castle-palace was situated just a few kilometers from the capital city. One of the few mud-walled fortresses still in existence, the Riyadh palace was a reminder of the caliphs' greatest days. And it was clearly built for battle. Inverted-V-shaped slits were cut above tiny windows in the towers, and the walls were six feet thick. Though it was now surrounded by man-made lakes, green lawns, and a great garden that rivaled the finest in Europe, the palace was still imposing. One look was all it took to know that this was a place for business, a place of power, a place for taking care of the dirty work of the king.

Outside the palace, dozens of the royal children and grandchildren had gathered for a three-day celebration.

Between the east wall and the garden, they watched a display of warrior riding and Arab games. Wahab tribesmen from the east pounded drums and chanted in rhythm as veiled dancers swayed to the heart-quickening beat. The soldiers raised their curved swords while the children interlocked their arms and sang:

> *Allah loves His Prophet*
> *Allah loves His Home*
> *Praise to the King who loves the Prophet*
> *Praise to the land that guards The Stone*
> *Great King, we will defend you*
> *Even as you defend the Prophet's home*

Horsemen spurred their animals viciously through the trees, each of them carrying a flowing silk banner and raising a sword to reenact the charge of the fanatical Ikhwan holy warriors who had swept through Arabia to unite the individual tribes into the kingdom of the Saud. At one time, the Ikhwan were the most fearsome warriors on earth. Zealous, bloodthirsty, fanatical believers in Wahhabi Islam, the Ikhwan were the key to the royal family's early power.

The children watched the fearsome riders with delight. They danced and ate and laughed among the gardens, oblivious to the fact that the world was shifting right under their feet. For two hundred years the royal family of the House of Saud had ruled Arabia with obscene wealth and unchallenged power. But now that the father-king was dead, and his son King Abdullah had stepped into his place, the world was becoming a far more dangerous place.

Especially for these pampered young ones whose fathers had gathered behind the palace walls.

The next generation of royal children would bear the sins of their fathers.

And those fathers who wouldn't sin were just a few hours from death.

*　　*　　*

There were hundreds of lesser princes—sons of concubines, cousins, nephews, and such—scattered throughout the kingdom, but the eight most powerful princes had gathered in the palace Great Hall. Among the assembled men were the Minister of Defense, Minister of Intelligence, Minister of Government Affairs—the assembled princes ran virtually every element of Saudi life. Most of them were middle-aged, a few were older, none of them were younger than thirty-five. All wore the traditional *bisht,* a thin black cloak trimmed with gold thread. As they waited for their king, they poured thimbles of bitter cardamom coffee from brass pots. The princes were not used to serving themselves, and a few of them grumbled, not knowing that all the servants had been barred from the palace, indeed from the entire palace grounds.

Pushing back their white robes and adjusting their checkered head cloths, they talked among themselves in conspiratorial tones. They had assembled, they thought, to map a way forward in the post-nuclear-detonation world.

And though they *had* been brought together for a reason, they were about to find out that it was not for what they thought.

*　　*　　*

In a small waiting room down the hallway from the great chamber, King Abdullah al-Rahman whispered back and forth with the old man.

The old man's hair was white and long and thin, and it fell in a straggle off to the side of his head. His skin was blotched and wrinkled, but his eyes—those fearsome eyes—still burned like coals of red heat. They showed no real warmth or emotion—they didn't even seem human anymore—but they were hot with rage and the constant burning that emitted from his soul.

"You are ready?" the old man demanded of the new king.

The younger man nodded grimly. He did not appear excited or in high spirits. Though what he was about to do would consolidate his power beyond that of any single man on earth, he realized it wasn't that he was elevating his power so much as pulling all rivals down. But he also knew that didn't matter. The end result would be the same: He would stand atop the pile. Yes, the pile would be made of rubble, but he would stand atop it all the same.

The old man watched and then nodded, reading the passive look on Abdullah's face, knowing the king was beyond feeling now. Ironic, he thought, how the deadening of guilt seemed to kill the whole soul, robbing it of the ability to feel joy as well.

He leaned toward the king, searching for any signs of hesitation. "You will do this?" he demanded.

"I swear that I will."

"You swear it on our oath?"

"I swear it on my blood. The blood of my father. The blood of us all."

The old man gestured toward the chamber where the king's younger brothers were waiting. "You swear it on *their* blood!"

The king didn't hesitate. Instead, he moved toward the old man and took him in his arms. Locking his hands behind the old man's back, he squeezed tight, whispering the cold oaths in his ear.

The old man listened, then stepped back. Staring at the king, he pressed his dry lips in a cynical smile.

The king thought he understood all of the oaths that he had breathed. But the truth was, he didn't. He hardly understood them at all. He was nothing but a mortal; he could never really know.

But the old man knew. He knew how important it was to hide their counsels from the light. He knew how much the darkness was needed for their work. He knew that the source of the oaths stretched beyond the boundaries of time.

King Abdullah was not the first to share in the oaths and he would not be the last, but like all of the others who had known them, he had an exaggerated expectation of the part he would play. Yes, he was important, but how crucial could *one man* really be? Like all of the others, he would play his part and then fall away, his body placed in the ground to mold into rot.

Fools! the old man thought in disgust. Arrogant, suffering, self-important fools! They actually thought that they mattered. Short-sighted, condemned fools!

The old man hid his disgust behind a blank face as he studied the king. Was he worthy? Was he ready? Yes, he thought he was. How many of his family had he already killed? His father. His older brother. His brother's children and wives. All of them were dead now . . .

No, that was not right. There was one, a young child, who had escaped.

But they would find him. They *had* to find him. And they would kill him when they did.

* * *

The old man looked at his pupil and smiled.

The king had proven worthy. It was time to spread the

cult. He patted the young king on his shoulder. "You know what to do," he said.

The king swallowed, his Adam's apple bobbing against his tight throat.

The old man leaned toward him, his breath as dry as death. "The final attack, the most powerful devastation, is just a few hours away. You absolutely have to do this before your brothers find out what you've done. Some of them will help you. Some of them *are like you.* Go. Find out which of them is going to join you. Then take care of the rest."

The king frowned and started walking toward his brothers down the hall. He tried to keep his step up, but his feet still seemed to drag. He felt so empty and lonely, so frustrated and cold. He wanted to get it over with. He was growing weary of this war.

The old man watched, reading the look on his face. He called out, "King Abdullah."

The king stopped and turned around.

"After this thing against America, you know the next step, don't you?"

The king stared, his face blank.

"Your filthy half-brothers, all those Shia, they will have to be put in their place. Claiming the authority of Allah when we all know that Ali, their first leader, was a filthy liar and nothing more. They've become chaotic and impossible, a pock upon you all. Your job won't be over until we've taken care of them as well."

The king took a step back. Yes, it was true he hated the Shia; he'd hated them since he was just a child. Every Sunni hated Shia. *Ahl al bayt. "People of the house [of the prophet]"* was their claim. How insulting! How absurd! All of them were liars and imposters.

But they were also Muslim brothers!

His heart sank again.

"How far . . . how long will this go on?" he muttered desperately, the hopeless thought escaping his lips before he could call the words back.

The old man considered the question, then smiled a wicked grin. "All the way," he answered softly. "All the way until the end."

chapter nine

They stood in the foyer on the first floor of the public housing building, a dreary high-rise identical to the four dozen other buildings around it. A blight on the city for more than three generations, the complex of poverty might have been the pride of some government bureaucrat back when it was built in 1960, but it was nothing but a fester of drugs and violence and criminal activity now.

In the lounge, half a dozen men spread out on a pair of stained couches, dropping heroin, playing cards, and calling filthy names to every girl who walked by. One of them tossed a knife, dropping it again and again on the floor, the curved tip sticking through the soiled carpet to the floorboard underneath. Another cleaned his gun, a Saturday Night Special with the serial number filed off and loaded with illegal armor-piercing bullets. A Chicago Housing Authority security officer stood near the front door. The men seemed to ignore him, and he ignored them as well. A long-standing agreement stood between them: He looked away; they cut him in on the action. Sometimes they paid in cash, sometimes in women.

Almost every night since the nuclear detonation in D.C.,

there had been riots in the ghetto, but the police had finally retaken control and the smell of pepper spray had begun to dissipate, though a faint whiff of smoke still drifted in the air. To the men's right, one of the elevator doors was jammed open—it had been a long time since it had worked—and the other elevator door opened and closed with regularity as it moved the building's occupants up and down.

Azadeh Ishbel Pahlavi stood before the older woman. It was the first time in her life she had ever seen a black woman this close, and she couldn't help but stare at her beautiful skin. The woman's hair was braided and wrapped in silver beads. Her eyes were as dark as her hair, but they smiled with a dazzle that somehow made Azadeh feel good. Azadeh was taller than the other woman by an inch or two, but both were slender and small-boned. Each of them fidgeted anxiously as they stared.

Then, without any apparent reason, the black woman broke into a smile. Leaning toward Azadeh, she pulled her close and held her a moment longer than two strangers would have normally embraced.

Mary Shaye Dupree, the older woman, pulled back. "Welcome, Azadeh," she said.

Azadeh bowed, an overly dramatic move that bent her almost in half. "Miss Dupree," she answered, her English almost perfect, at least these few words, for she had practiced the introduction a hundred times. "My name is Azadeh Ishbel Pahlavi. Thank you for inviting me here."

The woman smiled again, white teeth and full lips. "You call me Mary, or Mary Shaye, but not Miss Dupree, all right?"

Azadeh nodded slowly. "Yes, ma'am," she said.

"Not ma'am, now. It's just Mary."

Azadeh nodded. "Just Mary," she repeated, her face growing confused.

The black woman laughed, then lifted a small present she

held in her hand. "I got this for you, Azadeh. It isn't much." She hesitated, gesturing to the crumbling surroundings around her. "I don't have much, you understand, but I wanted to give you something."

Azadeh stared at the gift, her eyes growing bright. She had been given a gift only one other time in her entire life and, thinking of the silver mirror and brushes from her father, she shuddered. She thought of the night on the mountain, the night she had been driven from her home, the rain that turned to snow, the cold, being lost, the hopelessness and despair. She thought of her father and the stranger and how the precious gifts had reappeared. She trembled as she remembered, then turned toward Mary. "For me?" she asked haltingly. "But Miss Dupree . . . Mary, I don't have you anything."

"That's okay, baby. I didn't expect you to."

"For me? You are certain?" Azadeh repeated.

"Yes. For you, baby. But don't get your hopes up, it isn't much, all right."

Azadeh bowed again. "Thank you, Miss Dupree." She spoke slowly and carefully, struggling to pronounce every word.

Mary Dupree reached out and lifted the young woman, tugging on her shoulders. "You don't do that," she told her. "Don't you bow to me. You've got no reason to bow to any-one. You understand me, girl."

Azadeh nodded, though she didn't. She didn't understand at all. Mary Dupree might as well have been asking her to quit breathing as to ask her not to bow. She had been bowing at the waist since she was a little girl. Her father had insisted. It was how it was done. "Persians are gracious people," he had told her. "We are not too proud to bow."

She stared blankly at Mary, her mind racing, suddenly con-fused. "Yes," was all she answered.

Mary nodded, watching Azadeh's face closely, then pointed to herself and said, "Mary, okay? You call me Mary. And you don't bow to me. I'm not your master. I'm your mother now . . ."

Azadeh took a sudden breath. She had never had a mother, not since the day she was born. It was a nice thought, and she appreciated it, but this woman would never be her mother, no matter how she tried.

Mary continued to watch her closely. "I understand," she said as if she had read Azadeh's mind. "Maybe not your mother. But that's okay. I'll be something. We'll worry about that later." She nodded to the present. "Go ahead," she said.

Azadeh glanced at the small gift. Mary followed her eyes. "Really, it isn't very much," she repeated. "I get along, but it isn't like . . . you know . . . the good Lord has blessed me in many ways, but not with a lot of money. I mean, look at this place." She tilted her head toward her surroundings, the peeled wallpaper, the cracked linoleum, the dirty floor.

Azadeh looked around. "It is beautiful," she said.

Mary stared, then broke into a smile. Could she be serious? Could this be beautiful to Azadeh? Could this place be that much better than the place she had left?

The look on Azadeh's face assured her it was.

Oh, girl, Mary thought, *where did you come from? What was it like over there?* She pressed her lips together, then nodded to the present. "Open it," she said.

Azadeh lifted the small package. It was wrapped with plain white typing paper and tied with a small bow made of blue string. She carefully pulled back the paper, taking her time so as not to tear it, then pulled out a small velvet box. Mary smiled as she watched her, almost squealing with anticipation. Azadeh sensed her excitement and started bouncing, moving from one foot to the other.

She flipped the velvet lid open. It contained a small silver ring. No stone or other ornament, just a simple silver band.

Mary lifted her own finger to show an identical ring on her right hand. "Twinners," she said happily.

Azadeh hesitated. She didn't understand the word, but she clearly got the meaning. And Mary's excitement was infectious. Azadeh couldn't help but laugh. Gently she pulled the ring out of the velvet box, glanced to Mary's hand to check which finger she wore it on, then pushed the silver ring onto her pinky finger too.

She looked up and smiled. "Thank you," she said.

Mary nodded, clearly very pleased with herself. "You're welcome, Azadeh," she answered, nodding at the open box again.

Azadeh looked down and noticed a piece of paper tucked inside. Lifting it, she unfolded the paper and spread it out. Mary looked away for a quick moment, seemingly embarrassed. "I didn't do all that good in school," she said in a soft voice. "It's not like I'm a famous poet or anything. But sometimes I write. Sometimes it's the only way I have of expressing myself. I wanted to tell you something and this seemed to be the best way."

Azadeh looked at the quarter-sheet of paper and started reading slowly. The script was small and written in a delicate hand.

> *Your mother kissed your soft skin*
> *Before God called her home to rest*
> *Now at night I'll kiss your forehead*
> *And try to do my best*
> *Because she's watching from the heavens*
> *Hoping I can fill her part*
> *So I will love you like your mother*
> *And mend your broken heart*

Azadeh finished the poem and then just stared at the paper, keeping her face toward the floor. When she looked up, she smiled weakly.

"I know it's no good," Mary explained shyly. "I only wrote it last night. I could do better if I had more time. But, I don't know, it seemed to say what I wanted it to. I just hope you understand."

Azadeh nodded. "Thank you, Mary."

Mary nodded. Azadeh smiled again, her dark eyes wide. Looking at her, Mary realized once again how startlingly beautiful she was. She moved toward her, took her by the shoulders, and looked into her face. She studied the dark hair flowing out from under the scarf, then moved her gaze down to the beautiful eyes and soft skin. The oval face. Thin arms and slender fingers. "Oh no, child," she muttered as she stared. "This isn't good. Not good at all." Glancing over her shoulder, she shot a deadly look at the men who were lounging on the dirty couches. "We're going to have to be careful, Azadeh. Really careful. Understand?"

Once again Azadeh had no idea what she was talking about.

Mary stared at her another moment, then took her by the hand, moved to the elevator, and punched the button for the fifth floor. "Come on," she said. "Let me show you your new home."

*　　*　　*

Mary led Azadeh into the apartment. The young girl carried two worn pieces of luggage—one over her shoulder, the other one in her hand. Together they contained everything she possessed in the world. Reaching toward her, Mary took the bags and placed them on the floor as they passed through the front door.

The apartment was warm and clean. A small window over the kitchen sink looked out on the next high-rise building and a narrow alley five floors below. The furniture was worn and covered in assorted brown fabrics, none of which really matched. The linoleum was clean and slippery from polish, the kitchen chairs chrome with plastic coverings, the table just large enough for two people. The entire apartment smelled like cinnamon and coffee, and Azadeh drew a deep breath as she walked in.

But there was something else in the air, a smell that seemed faintly familiar although she did not immediately recognize it. A harsher smell, more tart . . . something like the disinfectants they splashed on everything back at the refugee camp in Khorramshahr. The smell propelled her back, and she stood without moving, her face blank, her eyes suddenly focused in the distance, her mind flashing through the memories: the constant mold and cold at Khorramshahr, the flapping tents, always being hungry, always sick, always coughing, always lonely, having no family, no village, no friends.

But the worst part had been the unending boredom; mind-numbing and spirit-breaking, it had sucked the life out of her like the moisture from a peach left too long in the sun.

Azadeh stood near the front door of the apartment, unaware of her surroundings, swallowed up completely in powerful memories. She thought of her old friend, one of the very few friends she had ever had in her life and certainly the only friend she had made in Khorramshahr. *Bânu* Pari al-Faruqi was dead now. She didn't know how she knew that, but she was certain that her Christian friend had finally passed through the Great Veil. And though she grieved for Miss Pari and the illness from which she had died, there was still a softness to her sadness that she couldn't deny.

She didn't really understand what the Christians meant

when they talked about heaven, but surely Pari's husband had been there waiting for her. Surely they were together now, after so many years of being apart.

Azadeh had to smile as she thought of her friend, remembering the brightly colored murals Pari had painted on the walls of her tiny wooden hut at Khorramshahr, the flowers she had kept near her window to soak up the sun, the small bushes she had nursed along the muddy path that led to her front door. She was a breath of fresh air in a very stale world, a world that was concerned only with moving people on, one way or another getting them out of the way. Azadeh didn't know if she would have survived Khorramshahr without Pari. If it hadn't been for her and the U.S. soldier . . .

Her memories shifted to the young American who had saved her life. She remembered the first day she had seen him in her burning village, her father's martyred body behind her, tearstains and mud creating tracks on her cheeks. He had stared at her and smiled, then approached her as he would a wounded animal, softly, holding his hands out, kneeling in the dirt. He was the one who had told her to go to Khorramshahr. Then he had remembered and come to rescue her, risking everything to save her life.

She thought of him all the time now. His face. His kind smile. To her, he was more than a hero. He was . . . he was, well, he was much more than that.

* * *

"*Azadeh,*" Mary repeated. "Azadeh, are you all right?"

Azadeh shook her head and looked around. "I'm sorry," she answered quickly.

Mary watched her, then smiled. "I lost you for a moment."

Azadeh blushed. "I was just thinking . . . I was just think-ing of Khorramshahr."

"Where?"

"Khorramshahr. The refugee camp. I had a good friend there. I was thinking of her."

"Would you like to talk about it?"

"About Khorramshahr?"

"Yes, dear."

"No. No, certainly not. Why would I want to talk about the camp?"

"I don't know, Azadeh, I just thought . . ."

"No, ma'am. I do not want to talk about Khorramshahr." Azadeh moved away. "I am sorry. I do not mean to sound rude. There is . . . not much good to talk about."

Mary nodded, her expression growing soft. "That's fine. We don't have to talk about it. We don't have to talk about anything you don't want to."

Mary moved to the window. From one side, she could look past the corner of the closest building to the city streets below. Traffic was heavy and there was still a hint of smoke in the air. Her neighborhood, her city, the entire world had changed in the past couple of weeks. She drew a deep breath and stood in uncomfortable silence for a moment. "Do you realize how close it was for you?" Mary asked Azadeh as she turned around.

"What do you mean?"

"A few more days and you would never have made it here to the States. How many foreigners from Muslim countries do you think the United States is allowing into our country right now? Not very many, I guarantee you."

Azadeh nodded slowly, biting her lip.

"After what has happened in the Middle East and Gaza, and now here in the United States, do you have any idea how difficult it would have been for you to get a visa, to get permission to stay here? Virtually impossible. No way. No how. Besides all the political implications, there is chaos everywhere. The government . . . everything is at a standstill. I know you had been waiting already for months, but I don't think that would have mattered. Another few days and you would never have made it here."

Azadeh shrugged her shoulders weakly. "I was very lucky."

"No, I don't think it was luck, baby. Things like this don't happen because of luck or pure chance. There was a reason, I'm certain. There is a reason you were sent here. You may not know what that is, but I promise you, Azadeh, there is a purpose for you being here, in this place. You have a mission. You have a purpose. The good Lord works in mysterious ways, and you are one of his great mysteries, it would seem."

Azadeh hardly moved. She didn't know what to say. Truth was, she had little idea what Mary was even talking about. Her perception of Allah, who was her god, was that he was not overly involved in the affairs of men, certainly not involved on any personal level. It was impossible to imagine that he would care about or intercede in the affairs of a single individual. To her, there was no Father in heaven, certainly no loving God. Her god was powerful and demanding of her loyalty, but that was about all he was.

Mary leaned against the counter. "Someone is watching out for you," she concluded.

Azadeh shrugged again.

Mary waited for an answer, then pointed toward the hall. "I want to show you your bedroom. And there's someone else you need to meet."

Azadeh hesitated. "Of course, ma'am," she said.

"Mary!" Mary pleaded, gently punching Azadeh's arm.

"Mary," Azadeh repeated, then started laughing. "I promise, Mary, that is the last time I will make that mistake."

Mary led Azadeh into the living room. Small and clean, it reminded her of her home back in Iran. They moved down a narrow hallway to the first room on their right. Mary pushed the door back and Azadeh saw a twin-size bed, a freshly painted white bureau with a slightly broken leg, and an empty closet. "This will be your bedroom," Mary explained. "It is your space, your getaway, if you will. Feel free to do what you want with it. If you want to paint it, wallpaper, whatever, I'll help in any way I can."

Azadeh looked around in amazement. "Really! This is mine?"

"Yes, baby. This is yours."

"It is . . ." Azadeh struggled for the words. "It is . . . very wonderful. It is . . . too large for me. It is . . . I am grateful."

Mary patted her arm. "That's so great, Azadeh. Believe me, gratitude is a lost art here in America. But you are too kind. Now, come on. There's something I need to show you. You may not know this, but it won't be just you and me living here."

Azadeh followed Mary back to the small living room. Mary nodded for her to sit down, then took a seat on a small wooden rocker across from the flannel-covered couch. Azadeh sat, her knees bent to the side. The two women were only a few feet from each other, and Azadeh could see Mary's hands tremble slightly as she rested them in her lap.

"I'm so glad to have you here, Azadeh. Do you know that?"

Azadeh held Mary's eyes but didn't answer.

"Do you believe that I'm glad to have you with me?" Mary pressed.

"I think so," Azadeh finally answered.

Mary compressed her lips and played with one of the silver beads at the end of her tightly braided hair. "It's all right if you're not sure. I don't worry too much about that right now. You'll know soon enough how I feel. It won't take long for you to believe me when I tell you that I didn't agree to take you in for the money that they give me, or because I needed someone to clean the floors. I didn't do it because I wanted someone to talk to or someone to care for me when I get old. I brought you here because I want to help you. That's it. Nothing else."

Azadeh concentrated, her brow furrowed, and Mary realized that she had to speak more carefully if she wanted the girl to understand.

She started again, this time more slowly. "I know that you have been dealt a very hard start in life," she said.

"Oh, no!" Azadeh answered. "I have been very blessed. Yes, I lost my mother. But my father was wonderful, the most wonderful man in this world. He blessed me. He blessed my life. I have been very happy."

Mary smiled and edged to the end of her seat, moving closer to Azadeh and reaching out for her hand. "I understand that. I really do. I've been told enough about you to understand what a good man your father must have been. But all I want to do is help you. Be your friend. I want us to be a family if we can. I think, in time, you will believe me and know that is true."

Azadeh watched her for a thoughtful moment. "I believe you," she finally answered.

Mary squeezed her hand. "Thank you." Looking away, she glanced toward the window, then turned back to Azadeh. "Did you know that I have another daughter?"

Azadeh shook her head.

"She is a special little girl. The love of my heart. When you meet her, you will feel the same, I am certain. Come on. I want to show you."

Mary pulled on her hand and led her down the hallway to the second bedroom at the end of the hall. Putting her finger to her lips for silence, she slowly pushed the door back.

The smell hit Azadeh in the face. Disinfectant. Medicine. It smelled like the infirmary at Camp Khorramshahr, a smell she would never forget.

The room was dimly lit, the drawn shades allowing just a little light to seep into the room from around the edges of the window. There was a double bed against the far wall, then another mattress placed on the floor beside it. Blankets, medical instruments, and medicines seemed to be everywhere.

A little girl was sleeping on the mattress that had been placed on the floor. Mary moved toward her and knelt down on the mattress. She reached out and lifted the little girl's hand, but the child didn't wake or stir. "Hey there, little princess," Mary said in a soft but cheerful voice.

The child kept on sleeping. Mary sat for a long time, simply holding her hand. Azadeh waited at the doorway, unsure of what to do.

chapter ten

The lieutenant turned in a slow circle, scanning the desert around him. The sand was brown and as fine as talcum powder. Slow to move, it seemed to paste itself to the bedrock, the oldest sand on earth. Here and there small bluffs of black, craggy rock penetrated the rolling desert, the flinty hunks of lava glinting in the angled sun. From a distance, the bluffs appeared to be covered with dark bushes and low vegetation, but Bono knew that wasn't true. He knew that as they got closer the dark patches would emerge as small hunks of stone that jutted from the ground, not vegetation. Above his head and to his back, opposite the setting sun, the sky changed color as it rose above the far horizon. Near the ground it was solid white from reflecting off the sand, but it deepened to greenish-silver and then dark blue directly over his head. The sand and rolling mounds (they weren't high enough for Bono to quite call them hills) seemed to go on forever, and the air was so clear that the details of the dismal landscape didn't seem to fade, no matter how far off he looked.

Sam stood somewhere behind him, quiet, unseen, and unmoving, but Bono knew he was near. A soldier, especially a soldier who spent much of his time in the desert, developed his senses, and Bono could smell the other man's leather boots, the detergent on his uniform, the spearmint gum in his pocket, the aftershave he had put on a few days ago.

Bono turned in two full circles, his feet treading lightly across the brown sand, years of moving without leaving a trace instinctive to him now. Then he held still and listened as Sam moved quietly to his side.

"So this is it?" Samuel Brighton shook his head as he looked around in disbelief.

Bono noticed the single lieutenant's bar that had been sewn onto Sam's lapel. He nodded toward the barren desert. "That's what they say."

Sam squinted through the setting sun at the utterly barren landscape around him. "What did Adam grow here? Snakes and sand fleas? Help me understand this, Lieutenant, because I'm not so sure you've got your geography right."

Bono hunched his shoulders. "It might have changed a little bit over the years."

"Changed a bit. Yeah, I guess so." Sam's voice was sarcastically lighthearted. "If this *was* the Garden of Eden, and if this is what it looked like, I'd say Adam got the better end of the deal. Getting tossed out of this hunk of burning sand couldn't have been the worst thing that happened to him that day."

Bono smiled but didn't answer as he continued looking down from the bluff.

It was so quiet he could feel the atmospheric pressure in his ears, the air perfectly calm as evening came on. His neck tingled from a light sweat that evaporated in the rapidly cooling air. The sun was low now, a huge, blood-red ball sinking toward the western horizon. As he watched, it began to fall so quickly its movement was perceptible.

The thought that this land of rock and sand and black

scorpions searching desperately for some warm-blooded prey had once been the Garden of Eden was almost laughable. But it really didn't matter. Bono knew it wasn't true. "This isn't it," he said to Sam after a long pause. "Not literally, I mean, not the Garden of Eden. Yes, it's true that most scholars and historians believe the Garden had to be somewhere near this place, but we know that's not the case."

"Do we?" Sam sounded surprised.

"True that, my friend."

"This isn't where Adam and Eve strolled among the animals and chomped down a couple apples?"

Bono shook his head and smiled. Sam was on the right track, but his understanding of the gospel still had a long way to go. That was what made him so interesting. He had so little knowledge, but his emerging faith was so strong. It was as if the death of his father had turned on the switch of faith inside.

"No, this isn't the location of the Garden," Bono finally repeated.

Sam waited, then turned toward him. "And you know this because . . . ?"

"It was revealed. So we know."

"Hmmm . . ." Sam thought. For the first twenty-some-odd years of his life, he would have thought that that was foolish. But it was enough now. "Where is the real Garden?" he asked.

"America, my bushy-haired friend."

Sam shook his hair from his eyes. He had the longest hair in the unit now; it hung down past the bottom of his neck. The blond had to go—he had dyed it black so as not to stand out—but it still curled and was more fine than a Middle-Eastern man's, and he didn't quite fit in with the locals around him. Still, it was better than the blond that immediately branded him as different.

"America? That makes sense," he answered after thinking awhile. "Not geographically, I guess, but something in my gut says that is just right. America is the chosen land. Why wouldn't the Garden be there?"

Bono lifted a hand toward the horizon, pointing south across the short bluff where they stood. "At one time, the sea must have reached up to where we are standing now," he explained. "The Euphrates and Tigris merged just to the north, then dumped into the Persian Gulf somewhere near here, I would guess. Even if this wasn't the literal Garden of Eden, it certainly was the cradle of civilization. The fertile lands between the Tigris and Euphrates . . ." he shot a look at Sam . . . "I'm sure you can tell me their Arabic names, can't you, stud?"

"Dejla and Furat."

Bono shook his head in disgust. "How do you *do* that! Come on, man, I can't remember my wife's maiden name or how to count to ten in Spanish despite sitting through at least three thousand episodes of *Sesame Street* as a kid, yet you hear an Arabic word a single time and you can remember it forever!"

Sam smiled, satisfied. It was true. He really could.

"I just don't get Arabic," Bono muttered. "It's like running water through a sieve. The words go in. They flow out. I can't remember anything."

"Hey, you got a beautiful wife and great aim. It wouldn't be fair if you got everything."

"Still, I don't know how you do it."

Sam shrugged. "It just comes. It doesn't mean anything."

Bono cocked an eyebrow. "But you can't remember any history?"

"Dead people and lost cities. Not my thing, I guess."

Bono swatted at a circle of biting sand flies that hovered

above his head, then continued his instruction, even though he knew that Sam wouldn't remember and really didn't care. "This place gave birth, if not to Adam, certainly to the first cities and civilizations of man. Nimrod, the great hunter mentioned in Genesis, was the founder of Nineveh, the capital of ancient Assyria, which was up on the Tigris north of here. And Nineveh wasn't some insignificant desert village. It was a massive city, taking three days to walk around. An entire library of clay books was found there, probably the oldest on earth. The Prophet Jonah, of course, preached in Nineveh. He was a funny guy, ol' Jonah. Got all ticked off when the entire city repented and was saved. Wanted to see some falling meteors and blazing fireworks, I guess." Bono pointed slightly west. "Babylon, the most famous ancient city in the world, was the capital of ten Mesopotamian dynasties starting almost four thousand years ago. Of course, Nebuchadnezzar built his amazing cities on the backs of his slaves, many of them Jews. Muslims believe the prophet Noah—they call him the second father of people—lived in Fara, which is just north of here. The Prophet Azra lived in Auzayr, Hizkael in El-Kifl."

Sam listened, watching Bono as he moved his finger across the horizon, pointing at different spots in the desert that looked identical to Sam. Sand. Low bluffs. Lifeless dunes. Nothing else.

Bono turned east. "Ur of the Chaldees is out there, birthplace of the prophet Abraham. It was a spectacular city until the Euphrates changed its course, leaving it to shrivel in the desert, suffering a slow but certain death."

Bono quit talking and wiped a dark sleeve across his brow. "I know it looks barren—"

"Barren!" Sam interrupted. "That's a pretty generous description, I'd say. *Barren* indicates a happenstance lack of life. This desert is one step beyond that. It seems to be *sterile,* as if a great cosmic hand had intentionally wiped away every form of life."

"Maybe," Bono answered slowly, "but there is still beauty here. The openness. The endless sky. The heat turning the sand into shimmering waves. The horizon that glitters in the distance. The colors of silver and dark blue overhead. The deep quiet. The clean air. It's really beautiful."

Sam looked around and nodded slowly. The wind shifted and, behind them, they began to pick up the sound of human voices as the man-made sounds of clicking metal and gas-powered generators signaled their base camp's coming to life.

The American soldiers, a small group of elite Cherokees, were tearing down their camp, getting ready to bug out. Sam turned, knowing this would be the last time he would see the base camp in the light. By morning, they would be gone. He studied the camp. Three kilometers south of them, the ancient town of Eridu jutted up against the desert sky. Forty meters to his right was a double strand of razor-wire fence—behind that, a small minefield, then another double strand of wire. Unseen guards watched the perimeter of the base camp from various buried locations. HUMVEES and the other machines that the men used to kill the enemy were tucked away at the center of the camp. There were no tents, only bunkers, and the camp was set back twenty-four hundred meters from the main road, just beyond the range of the insurgents' most powerful rocket-propelled grenades. An unpaved trail, heavily barricaded, made its way though the desert from the highway to the camp.

The evening light began to fade, turning dull yellow and then hazy orange as the sun disappeared. The two men sat down, resting on the warm sand. "You heard about Rodriguez?" Bono asked.

Sam closed his eyes and didn't answer. Months before, a scout patrol from their old Ranger unit had been hit by a roadside incendiary bomb. Both Sam and Bono knew the men who had been injured; all of them were close friends. Mercilessly, all four men inside the HUMVEE had been severely burned. No more hair. No more skin. No more eyes. Over time, months of agony and anguish, each of the men had slowly died. The first to pass away, a young lieutenant, had been the lucky one—he had lived only a few weeks. One man lived for three months. Another for more than six. All four men were now gone, Rodriguez being the last man to give up the final fight, a little more than nine months after being exploded in a burst of fire that had burned him from head to foot.

It sickened Sam to think about them. Nine months of battle. Nine months of anguish and pain. "Please, just kill me," he mumbled as he considered the horrible fate of the men.

Bono heard him and nodded. "Yeah. I'm with you, baby."

Sam ground his teeth.

"Rodriguez was what, twenty-one?" Bono asked.

"Yeah." Sam took a deep breath as he answered. Twenty-one was barely old enough to marry. It was too young to die. Then he thought of his father, General Brighton, who had also been too young to die.

He thought of the pictures he had seen of D.C. after the nuclear detonation. Charred buildings. Hunks of burned concrete, the oil boiled from the blacktop on the streets. A few scattered trees, black and lifeless, nothing more than dead trunks and drooping branches that looked like witches' hands reaching up from the ground. The spot where the White House had once stood had been identified, but there was nothing there. Four days had passed now and he knew that his adopted father, the only man who had ever cared anything for him, the person who had taught him what it meant to be a man, who had sacrificed everything for the only things he had loved, would not be found there. Like the others, he had gone up in smoke and ash.

The two soldiers were silent as the darkness came on.

Sam turned to Bono. "Things haven't gone too well, have they?" he asked.

Bono shook his head, discouragement softening his icy-blue eyes. "It ain't going swimmingly, I suppose."

"They've been saying it for years now. This place is not worth the price we've paid."

Bono thought of Rodriguez and didn't say anything.

Sam stared at Bono, then turned back to the growing darkness around them. "So we're leaving here tomorrow?"

"The air transports are lined up down in Basra. We'll be out of here in a day."

"Think we'll ever come back?"

"I don't know," Bono said.

Sam thought a long moment. "Would you die for this place?" he asked as the moon started to rise at their backs.

Bono shrugged his shoulders. "For this place or this cause?"

"I don't know. Take your pick. Our cause. Our mission. The things they tell us to do."

A light breeze began to move the night air. "All we're trying to do is help them," Bono answered from the dark.

Sam kept his eyes on the horizon, staring at the spot where the sun used to be.

"Just trying to help them," Bono repeated as if he were trying to convince himself.

Sam grunted and asked, "Does that mean yes or no?"

Bono slowly nodded. "Yes, I would die here. I would die for this cause. Good men die here every day. Some Americans. Some Iraqis. All are children of God."

Sam nodded, his face determined, then turned toward the

lieutenant. "I want you to know something, Bono. I tell you now as my friend.

"I would die for this mission. It's a magnificent cause. My father died for this duty. So have others I have loved. I want to live—you know we all do—but I won't turn away from this fight. Every generation has its battles, and this is the fight of our time.

"You remember that, Bono." He touched the lieutenant on the chest. "If you have to, you go and tell them. I did what I had to do."

chapter eleven

As the afternoon wore on, the children of the royal family spread across the great lawn and green gardens. A few were standing on the shore, dipping their feet into the man-made lake; a few were chasing the camel riders through the trees. Many of the younger children had gathered near the back wall of the palace where an ice cream fountain oozed ice cream and chocolate and sent it cascading down four tiers of silver plates.

The king's security agents, large men in black robes and gray turbans, moved through the crowd. They had divided up their assignments, and they moved among the offspring of the princes very quickly, taking up their charges one by one.

The largest of the security men moved toward Prince Saud bin-Alquana, the Foreign Minister's oldest son. Eighteen and proud, he stood above the other children, watching his younger cousins play. The king's man moved toward the princeling and touched him on the elbow. "*Sayid,* I need you to come with me," he said.

The young prince turned. He was dark, determined, and stout like his father. "Who are you?" he demanded.

The agent nodded, lifting his bearded chin toward the palace. "Your father sent me for you."

"My father?"

"*Sayid*." The agent bowed.

The princeling hesitated. Something didn't feel right. He didn't know what it was, but his gut seemed to crunch. "Who are you? Where is my father?"

"Young prince, I am to take you to him."

The prince wanted to pull back. He wanted to run away. The sudden fear made no sense, but he knew that something was horribly wrong. "What does my father want?" he demanded, trying to force a strong voice.

"I do not ask, my *Sayid*." The agent put a little pressure on the young man's elbow, his grip firm.

The young man didn't move.

"Come," the agent said, his voice lower now. "I have my orders. You will come with me."

Tightening his grip, he pulled the young prince along.

Around him, the king's other men gathered up the oldest sons of the princes who were meeting in the Great Hall.

chapter twelve

Small for an oceangoing craft, the 1,600-ton cargo ship *Ab Tayyib* (previously called the *Cristi,* previously called the *Sunna,* previously called the *Ali bin,* which was what the ship was called when it first raised suspicion as being an al-Qaeda-operated vessel) had been re-flagged and re-registered at least a dozen times in its life, three times in the past month alone. Presently flagged in Cambodia as the *Ab Tayyib* (a good name and good omen, God willing, the captain thought), the ship was owned by a Greek shipowner, Dimitris Kokkos, and a Pakistani-American, Rifat Muhammed. More or less permanent residents of Croatia, both Kokkos and Muhammed were wanted by the Greek authorities for smuggling, an inconvenience that required a couple of hundred thousand dollars in annual bribes to keep the government at bay.

The *Ab Tayyib* was black with red striping, freshly painted but rusting underneath the thick paint that had been carelessly slapped around. Barnacled below the waterline and poorly maintained, the *Tayyib's* two huge diesel engines kept the dual propellers pounding at the sea, but it was becoming more and more common to have to shut down one of the engines for maintenance as the ship chugged along. The deck was worn, the grating torn in places, and the cavernous hold smelled of diesel, grease, mold, salt water, and filth. The ship had been at sea for several months now, having stopped in Malaysia before moving on to Cambodia, where it was re-flagged a final time before sailing back to Yemen, through the Gulf of Aden and the Suez Canal.

Ten weeks after leaving the expanding ports at Jeddah, the ship had traveled the equivalent distance of a trip around the world. It would have been impossible to have tracked it even if it hadn't been repainted, re-flagged, and renamed.

There was simply no way to know or be suspicious when the ship showed up off the eastern coast of the United States.

Had the Coast Guard had any reason to board the vessel, it would have taken only seconds for the mission of the *Ab Tayyib* to become painfully obvious. The ballistic missiles and elevator-controlled launcher built into the hold were pretty hard to disguise.

At 04:43 local time, the improvised communications center inside the rusting *Ab Tayyib* got the highly encrypted strike instructions. The exact altitudes, flight azimuths, trajectories, and yield settings for the warheads had already been programmed into the flight computers, but still the captain reviewed the final flight instructions very carefully, comparing every line of code against the numbers burned into his memory.

His first officer hovered over him, his hands moving nervously.

"Praise be God," the ship captain finally said.

The first officer forced a quick smile, though inside he had to hold down a cry of grief.

He didn't want to die. No man really did. But he would

die now, he knew that, and though he had been preparing for this moment since he was a child, the reality of having just a few hours to live still left him cold.

He thought of his wife. He thought of his children. Would they know? Would they remember? Would they honor his death as much as he hoped that they would?

THE *CHOUN OHMONEE* (THE GOOD MOTHER)
NINETY-THREE MILES WEST OF SAN FRANCISCO

The *Choun Ohmonee* was a smaller ship than the *Ab Tayyib*, but more seaworthy, faster, and ten years newer. Flagged in North Korea, a society more secretive than any other nation in the world, it hadn't gone through the painful exercise of re-registering and re-flagging to hide its movements and identity, although it had been renamed as a concession to the Arab masters.

The arming and deployment of the *Choun Ohmonee* had been a straight-up operation. No subterfuge or deception had been involved; it simply loaded up the missiles at the military port in Cho'ong jim, then headed east across the open Pacific toward the United States.

Now, sitting off the western coast, it waited for the same message as its sister ship to the east.

chapter thirteen

Mary Shaye Dupree held the sleeping girl's hand while speaking to her softly. She wiped her brow, which was pale and clammy, then pushed aside a stray strand of dark hair as she caressed her cheek. The girl's face was bony, her lips tight, her thin hair matted to the side on which she slept. Azadeh noted the intravenous line sticking into the child's left arm and the monitor attached to her middle finger, but she wasn't certain what they were for.

When the child didn't wake, Mary leaned across the mattress and kissed her, tucked the soft blanket around her neck, stood, and turned to Azadeh, motioning toward the hall. Closing the bedroom door quietly behind her, she walked with Azadeh into the living room again.

"Her name is Kelly Beth," Mary said as they sat down. "I adopted her when she was just a toddler, which was some eight years ago now."

"A toddler?" Azadeh wondered.

"I'm sorry . . . a young child . . . not a baby, a little older."

Azadeh nodded, understanding. "She is . . . very sick?"

"Yes. Very sick." Mary turned her eyes toward the window.

It had started raining and the day had turned gray. "She isn't going to live, I don't think. I used to hope. I used to pray. But I don't think any of it mattered."

Azadeh studied her hands. "She has a sickness?"

"Cancer. Inoperable bone cancer."

Cancer. One of the very few English words that Azadeh would have recognized even as a child. It translated to *saratán* in Farsi. She nodded sadly. It was a dreaded word, a deadly sickness, a sickness that, based on her experience, didn't offer much hope. When someone got *saratán* in her small village back in Persia, that person was almost certain to die. No such thing as insurance. No real money. No good doctors. They might die in a short time or a long time, they might die in a lot of pain or maybe quickly, but they almost surely wouldn't live.

"I'm sorry," she offered quietly.

"We caught it really late," Mary continued, her voice pained and measured now. "I know that it was my fault. I'll have to live with that for the rest of my life. But at the time, I just didn't understand, I didn't realize, I had never dealt with anything like this before. She hurt all the time, deep in her legs, and I took her to the doctor, but the people down at the clinic, you know . . . they're inexperienced and way over-worked. It wasn't their fault. I think they did the best that they could, but by the time I got a referral down to Cook County Hospital, there wasn't a lot they could do. They tried a few things, some new things, they experimented with some new drugs and procedures, but like I said, we were . . . you know . . . way too late to help her . . ." Mary's voice trailed off.

Azadeh watched a single tear roll down each of her cheeks, which Mary quickly wiped away. It pained Azadeh to see her suffering, and she instinctively wanted to reach out and take her by the hand.

Someone moved down the hallway outside their front door. The rain dribbled against the kitchen window, trickling down from fifteen stories overhead. The old refrigerator hummed. But other than that it was silent as Mary stared across the empty space. "I love her," she finished. "I would have done anything for her. I would do anything now. If there was *anything* I could do . . ."

Azadeh reached out and took Mary's hand, holding it inside her own. "I'm so, so sorry," she repeated.

Mary coughed, then turned to face her. "The good Lord, he is out there. I have to learn to trust him. It will all be okay."

Azadeh nodded back toward the bedroom. "*Insha'allah*. If it is God's will."

Mary nodded. "*Insha'allah*. God's will."

Azadeh was a sensitive girl by nature, and her upbringing had only made her more so. She knew that Mary wanted to talk about her child. "Tell me her name again," she asked.

"Kelly Beth."

"Kelly Beth. That is beautiful. If you were to translate my middle name, Ishbel, from Farsi into English it is very close to Elizabeth. Elizabeth and Kelly Beth. Two good names. Very similar." Azadeh paused a long moment, looking off. "My last name, Pahlavi, goes back many, many generations in Iran. It is royal blood. And my given name, Azadeh, means 'Freedom is my oath to God.'" She folded her arms, almost defiant, and her eyes flashed. "I have always been very proud of my names," she said.

Mary smiled and touched her shoulder. "Ishbel is almost the same as Elizabeth?" she asked.

"Yes, very close."

"That is beautiful."

Azadeh nodded down the hallway toward the bedroom. "How old is Kelly Beth?"

"Almost ten. She will be ten next month."

"Then we will celebrate her birthday."

Mary pressed her lips together. "If she makes it that long."

"You said that she is . . . I do not remember the word . . . she is not your own . . . flesh? Your own child?"

Mary stood and walked into the kitchen. There was a small coffeemaker beside the sink, and she poured herself a cup. "Would you like some?" she asked Azadeh as she lifted the half-empty pot.

"No, thank you."

"You do not like coffee?"

"Not American coffee. It is too . . . weak. Like water. We have a much stronger drink. I miss it. It is good. But," she laughed a little, "very bad for you, I think. It stains our teeth and makes us . . . ah, quick to temper. I am glad to be away from it, I think."

Mary brought her cup back and sat on the couch, folding her legs underneath her to keep her feet warm. "I adopted Kelly Beth when she was just a child. Her father had abandoned her before she was even born. Her parents never married. Her mother was strung up . . . do you know what that means, Azadeh?"

Azadeh shook her head.

"Oh, that is so beautiful," Mary laughed with delight. "You don't know what *strung up* even means. You've never had to fight it. You've never had to watch what it can do to those around you. That is very good, Azadeh." She reached toward the young woman and patted her knee. "We want to keep it that way, girl. We're *going* to keep it that way."

Mary leaned back against the couch and sipped the warm coffee. "*Strung up* is when you have ruined your life on hard drugs. Heroin. Cocaine. You know about them?"

Azadeh squinted as she thought. "No," she finally said.

"That's all right, baby, we can talk about that later. Let's just say that Kelly Beth's mother wasn't able to take care of her anymore. She didn't want her baby, at least not sufficient to keep herself healthy enough to care for her. I had a chance to take Kelly Beth and help her. It was supposed to be only for a couple of weeks, a couple of months at the longest, but it went on and on, and it ended up that I was able to adopt her, you know, make her my child."

Azadeh nodded.

"Her mother is dead now," Mary concluded. "No one knows about her father. No one even knows who he is."

"I understand," Azadeh answered. But the truth was, she didn't. It was all so strange. So different. There was much to learn in this new country, and she felt lost and insecure.

For a moment she almost wished she were back in Khorramshahr. It had been hard there, but she had understood it, unlike so much of this new home.

chapter fourteen

ROYAL PALACE
RIYADH, SAUDI ARABIA

King Abdullah walked into the Great Hall. The thirty-foot ceiling towered over his head and the room was dark, illuminated mostly by a row of dim lights along the ancient walls. Four huge, wrought-iron chandeliers hung from enormous beams that crossed the ceiling, but the room was built deep inside the palace, and there were no outside windows or natural light. The thick walls, heavy brick and ancient mud, stifled every sound from outside. Four over-stuffed leather couches were arranged around a circular depression in the floor, part of an old fire pit. A low oak table trimmed with gold sat where the fireplace used to be.

Abdullah moved to the center of the room. His eight brothers fell silent and the room seemed to suck them up, making them feel even smaller than they were. Abdullah raised his hand, indicating for the ministers to sit down, which they did, dividing themselves up among the four couches.

Abdullah studied them without saying anything, assessing the mood in the room. Yes, they were some of the most powerful men in the world, but each of them stared up at him with dark, submissive eyes.

The king knew that some of his brothers were furious at his sudden rise to power. Some resented the death of their father and their oldest brother, the crown prince. Most suspected that Abdullah had killed them, but they couldn't prove it, even if they had wanted to. None of them did—far better to leave that filthy stone unturned—but they resented the fact all the same.

They also realized that Abdullah had turned the kingdom away from their father's path toward democracy. None of them were disappointed by that, though some might have wished it hadn't been so bloody. And although they were grateful the king had secured their royal power, they were also furious about the nuclear attacks in Gaza and D.C. The entire world had been thrown into utter chaos. Things were so messy now, so much more difficult to control.

As the eight ministers took their seats, Abdullah almost smirked. If they had any idea . . . any idea what he planned to do.

"Brothers," he started slowly, "let me get right to the point."

The princes watched him carefully. They hardly seemed to move as a heavy air settled over the room.

Abdullah paced, his eyes cold and sullen, his skin tight, the hollows of his cheeks deep and dark. He seemed to cast a spell upon them as he moved, drawing them in to his world. "Some of you are wondering," he started, "so I will tell you. Yes, I killed our father. Yes, I killed Crown Prince Saud. I killed his wife, Princess Tala. I killed their children. I killed them all."

The men sat in stunned and open-mouthed silence. Not a sound penetrated the ancient walls. Only their breathing and a few croaking swallows could be heard in the enormous room.

"I killed them," Abdullah went on, "but that is not

everything you need to know. I also arranged for the nuclear attack in Gaza. I arranged for the attack on D.C. as well. And we are just beginning." The king glanced down at his watch. "The most deadly attacks will take place a little less than three hours from now."

The senior prince bowed his head. Abdullah watched him carefully, then went on. "Believe me, dear brothers, I have just started my work. I killed our father. I killed our brother. Now I will kill you as well. You are either with me or against me. There is no middle ground. You either join me or I kill you. It is as simple as that.

"What is it going to be? You have two minutes to decide."

The senior prince stood up, his face contorted with rage. "Join you! You're a madman! You killed my father. You killed my brother. I will never—"

Abdullah reached under his robe, took out a Colt .45 from a shoulder holster, and shot his younger brother in the head. The power of the bullet propelled the prince's body, almost lifting his feet off the ground before sliding him across the wooden floor. By the time he hit the ground, he was already dead. The sound of the gunfire echoed through the enormous chamber and then was swallowed up again. The air filled with the acidic tartness of burnt gunpowder, and blood began to seep from under the dead prince's head.

King Abdullah took a step back, eyeing the other princes in the room. They stared at him aghast, too shocked to speak or move. "Don't underestimate me," he told them as he fingered the warm barrel of his gun. "I am absolutely committed to my course. This isn't something I dreamed up in the past week or so. This goes back much further. I have been planning this for years."

Standing before his brothers, the king thought back to his first meeting with the old man, so many years before. He thought of their introduction on the beach, the airplane trip to the city, sitting in the Mercedes outside the United States Embassy in Paris, learning he had to kill the people inside the embassy before he could take the next step.

He could hear the old man's voice as it hissed in his ears. *"You must kill them if you will join us. I will give you thirty seconds to think about it, but that is all the time you will have to decide!"*

It was a good test. Abdullah knew that now. Catch them off guard. Make them decide! Who were they? What were they? What was really in their hearts? Would they kill or would they hesitate? Would they wash their hands in blood?

The results of the test would be immediate and nearly flawless. There was no cheating, no second-guessing, no faking the results. They were either with him or against him. And they had to kill to join his cause.

And not just any blood was going to satisfy him. The king was more demanding than that now. It would take more than a simple murder after all that he had learned.

Abdullah turned to his brothers and took a step toward them. "Are you with me? Then you must do this! I want to know what's in your heart. Will you bloody your hands to join me! Or will you choose to die right now?"

"Join you?" one of his younger brothers muttered, his eyes gaping wide in rage and fright. "Join you, King Abdullah? What are you talking about?"

"Join me as I bring the Great Satan to its knees. And if you think that I've already done that, let me assure you, you are wrong. There will be another attack before the day ends, an attack that will destroy them as a nation, send them back two hundred years. Tens of millions are going to die. And then we will rise up with our brothers as the most powerful people on the earth." Abdullah stopped and caught a breath. His face was drawn now, his eyes blazing, his lips pulled tight. He looked almost like an animal: bared teeth and glowing eyes, his heartbeat racing through the pulsing vein against his neck.

"*Christianity! Freedom! Human rights!*" He spat the words. "These are foul and loathsome things. *The spirit of their god is found in freedom.* But with one attack, we kill them both!"

"Tell me, my younger brothers, and I want you to tell me now! I will need your help to establish the world order after the U.S. has been destroyed. There is too much work, too much responsibility to be carried by just one man. I need your allegiance. But I need to know right now. Will you join me? Will you help me destroy the Great Satan! Are you willing to help me kill a hundred million of our enemies, to completely bring them down! Or do you seek a weaker peace, a weakened nation, a weakened order, a weakened state!"

The king took another breath. The muscles in his face relaxed and he lowered his eyes. He paced back and forth once again, then glanced down at his watch. "Twenty seconds and counting. What is it going to be?"

The seven men sat in stunned silence. Their mouths gaped open as they stared with dry and unblinking eyes. It had been less than three minutes since the king had walked into the room. Three minutes to learn that he had killed their father, the crown prince, a hundred thousand Palestinians in the Gaza Strip, all the people in D.C. Three minutes to watch him shoot their older brother!

One of them looked down at the dead prince, who lay atop a spreading pool of dark blood.

It had to be a joke. It could not be real!

"King Abdullah," he started, lifting his eyes to the king, "what are you saying?" His voice was high and rasping, panic rising with the wad of spit in his throat.

"Are you with me?" Abdullah demanded, his eyes blazing again. "Are you willing to work with me as we reorder the world?"

"I don't know! I don't know! I don't even know what you are talking about!"

Abdullah lifted the Colt and shot him.

The prince fell over dead.

chapter fifteen

The first night that Azadeh was in her home, Mary lay in her bed without moving, listening to the dark. She could hear Kelly Beth's deep breathing just beside her and she suddenly panicked as she counted every breath.

How many precious breaths did her baby have left?

She lay there in near terror for an hour, but no matter how she tried she couldn't help but count the breaths. Finally, in dark frustration, she pushed herself out of bed. Moving down the hall, she quietly opened the door to Azadeh's bedroom and looked in on her. She could see only the girl's outline in the dark, but it appeared she was asleep. Mary closed the door and walked quietly into the kitchen, moved to the window, and looked out on the night.

Just in front of her was another brick wall, another tenement building, dirty and blackened from a generation of soot. Five floors below her, a homeless man slept on the grate. Steam rose around him, but still he shivered from cold. Mary watched him, then turned her gaze to the only patch of night sky she could see from her valley of mortar and stone; there were no stars in East Chicago and she could not see the moon.

She reached out to open her dirty kitchen window, pushing up against three or four coats of white paint, but the window held tight. How long had it been since she had opened it up? She pressed upward again and the thin pane finally moved a few inches, allowing the cold air to blow inside.

She stood by the sink, letting the air chill her bare arms, and took a deep breath to savor the smell. The air came up from the park and carried a faint scent of trees and wet brush. It was quiet outside, at least as quiet as Chicago could be. With the taxis and MLK Highway, the elevated train on its track, music from the bars, and the thugs on the streets, she never heard actual silence, just a lessening roar. She glanced down at the drug dealers on the street corner. They were there every night, come heat, snow, rain, or shine, a permanent part of the sidewalk, like the cracks in the cement. The coming storm meant absolutely nothing to them. Nuclear war in the Middle East, even nuclear war in their own country, none of that mattered to these men on the streets or the addicts who lined up to get another hit.

At forty-three, the black woman was petite, with a thin face and small nose. *Mary Shaye Dupree* was an old southern name that went back three hundred years, back to the mistress of an old French plantation owner on the outskirts of New Orleans. But that was a long time ago, and Mary Shaye had no sense of her southern roots. Four generations before, her kin had migrated north, looking for jobs and freedom from the cotton fields, but she hardly knew about them or appreciated what they did.

Mary was a strong and fine-looking woman, but her strength was fading fast, for the world and its burdens were bringing defeat. Wrapping her arms around her shoulders, she shivered from the night air. She studied her reflection in the window, staring into her own eyes. Seeing the defeat, she turned quickly away.

Walking down the narrow hallway, Mary made her way back to her bedroom and stared at her daughter's gaunt face in the dim light. The child was beautiful still, though her hair had grown thin and her lips had drawn tight. She was sleeping in pain; that was clear from her groans. As Mary stared at her, she felt the helpless pangs of despair. She was no longer angry—she only felt empty now.

The best thing she had ever done in her life was to take this little girl and bring her into her home. Some of her happiest moments had been when she held this child in her arms. For almost eight years she had loved her as if she were her own—maybe more, she didn't know—all she knew was that she loved her until she couldn't love any more.

And now her little girl was being taken, piece by piece, day by day. The vibrant laugh, the soft hugs, the wonderful smile—all of it fading, all of it dying away.

Kelly Beth opened her eyes and looked up at her mom.

"I didn't mean to wake you," Mary said quietly.

"I had a weird dream," Kelly Beth answered, her voice dragging out from fatigue.

"Tell me about it." Mary sat down on the edge of the bed.

"I don't know, Mom. It was so real. So clear. But I don't get it."

"That's the way of dreams," her mother answered softly.

Kelly Beth waited, catching her breath. "I was watching a funeral," she began. "There was a horse and a wagon, and lots of military guys around, and this beautiful little girl, the funeral must have been for her dad. And when it was over, she looked up at the sky like she was talking to God."

Her mother listened, then nodded. "Is that all?" she asked.

"No, Mom, and this is the part that I don't get. While I was watching this funeral, it felt like it was for someone I knew, someone almost like a brother, I think."

Her mother smiled, then pulled her close. "But you don't have a brother, Kelly."

The girl relaxed against her pillow. "But the feeling was so clear."

Her mother patted her hand, then kissed her cheek. "Think about it," she said, "and maybe you'll figure it out."

The little girl closed her eyes, exhaustion overcoming her again. Seconds later, she was asleep.

*   *   *

Mary watched her daughter for a long time, then wiped her eyes, stepped across the mattress, and lay down on her bed. Resting on her pillow, she stared up at the dark.

She was relieved and happy to have Azadeh here, but Kelly was fading quickly now, and Mary felt like it wasn't fair to bring Azadeh into this situation after all that she had been through. But it was what it was, and there was nothing she could do.

Rolling over, she thought of the young men she had seen on the street. The two young preachers looked ridiculously out of place, like baby-faced monks in their white shirts and ties. "Go back to Utah!" one of the tenement neighbors had mocked them as they had walked down the street. The boys had smiled and waved to her, then continued on their way. That was two weeks before, and she had not seen them since.

The worried mother thought about them, then rolled across the mattress once again.

The night passed in silence, but sleep didn't come, for the faces of the strangers seemed to haunt her somehow. Why couldn't she forget them? It made no sense at all! Who were they, these preachers? And why did she burn inside?

"Find them!" a quiet voice seemed to cry in her soul. *"I have a great work for your children. Go out and find them so they can save Kelly's life!"*

chapter sixteen

Mary got out of bed long before anyone else was awake. The sun was barely up and the city was still coated in dark hues. She checked Kelly Beth's drip line, felt her face, then pulled on a T-shirt, sweatpants, and some old leather shoes. She wrote Azadeh a quick note, then let herself out of the apartment and headed for the stairs—easier and faster to walk five floors down than to wait for the elevator.

Crossing the noisy, six-lane street that ran in front of the housing complex, she dodged a dozen yellow cabs and police cars. The riots had subsided, but the tension was still as thick as the smell of exhaust in the air and it seemed the cops were everywhere. Walking through the screen door at the old corner market, she headed immediately to the cooler, looking for some milk and eggs. The cooler was almost completely empty: A few sodas and some hot dogs were all it contained. She walked back to the counter and forced her most commanding voice. "Marlo, you swore to me that you'd have some dairy products by this morning."

The large black man looked at her regretfully. "I'm sorry,

Mary, I really am. They promised they'd send us a truck yesterday, but you know the gig, we're the last ones in line. You think they're going to bust their butts to get some stuff down here to East Side? I don't think so, dear. We'll get it when the white folks in midtown and Naperville are stocked up and fat."

Mary leaned into the counter. "Marlo, you got to help me. You know what I'm going through with Kelly Beth. She has to have some milk with her morning medicine or she gets sick to her stomach. I'm not exaggerating, Marlo, she gets sick and throws up. You can't do that to her. Please, isn't there something you could do?"

The store owner shook his head. "I can't turn water into milk. I can't just make it appear. I'm not hiding anything in the back cooler. I just don't have anything right now."

Mary clenched her jaw in sadness and frustration. "So a bomb goes off in D.C. and the entire world falls apart. A bomb goes off in D.C. and all the milk and dairy products in Chicago disappear. It isn't right, Marlo, I'm telling you it isn't right."

"Tell me about it, Mary. I haven't slept in five days. Four nights in a row, I've had to stand guard by my front door. Do you know how many thugs I've had to scare away from my place?" He reached beneath the counter and stroked the shotgun he had hidden there. "I'm the only joint on the block that hasn't been completely looted."

Mary glanced behind her at the nearly bare shelves. "I don't know, Marlo, it looks pretty well looted to me."

The man only huffed. "The cops don't care about any of us black store owners. The Koreans and Pakistanis up in Gary, they get taken care of, but us folks down here in the projects, we got to fend for ourselves."

Mary shrugged and looked around. "Any bread?" she said.

Marlo seemed to stop and think before reaching down

below the counter. Feeling beside the shotgun, he pulled out two loaves. "My last two," he said, then nodded to the back door. "There's a couple dozen eggs in the back room. You better get them, too."

Mary squinted. "Thank you, Marlo. I mean that. Thanks."

She started walking toward the back-room cooler and Marlo called out to her. "You could take some of those eggs and mix them with warm coffee. Give that to Kelly with her medicine. That'll help keep it down."

Mary went into the back room, then returned to the counter with the eggs. "Hey, Marlo," she said as he rang up her small sack of groceries. "There are a couple guys around here. I haven't seen them in a while. Young kids. One's a white boy, but the other one is black. White shirts and ties. You know them?"

The store owner shook his head. "I don't know. You talking cops?"

"No, no, no. Preachers. Real young preachers."

"Jehovah Witness. I thought they abandoned this miserable place."

Mary hesitated. "I don't think that's them," she said. "They're always together, always the same two young guys . . ."

"Mormons," Marlo answered.

Mary thought and then nodded. "Yeah. I think that's right."

Marlo glared at her. "You don't want to be talking to those Mormons. A bunch of racist white boys. You don't want to be talking to none of them."

"Really?" Mary answered. She didn't know what to think. "But one of them was black."

"Yeah, trust me, Mary, you don't want to go talking to no Mormons. They're only trouble, okay? I got a friend down in

Hobart. His daughter joined that church. One night they pulled her into their church, beat her up, then threw her out on the street."

Mary shook her head. Marlo believed lots of things that seemed unlikely, and this sounded like another one of them.

"Swear to you," Marlo answered, seeing the disbelieving look on Mary's face. "Besides, it doesn't matter. They're all gone anyway. Their prophet, Joe Smith back in Salt Lake, called all their missionaries home. I heard it on the radio a couple days ago. Right after the attack back in Gaza, all the Mormon missionaries around the world were called home. Guess they figured it was time to shine their guns, protect their stored-up food, and go hunting for some wives."

Mary shook her head. She had absolutely no idea what he was talking about. "They are gone?" she pressed with disappointment. "Are you certain they're not here anymore?"

"Sure of it. I see everyone who walks into this neighborhood, and I'm telling you they haven't been here since ol' Israel dropped the big one on the Palestinians over there."

"And there's no Mormons around here but those missionaries, no church or anything?"

"Not in this place."

Mary nodded sadly, bitter disappointment seeping deep into her soul. *You told me to find them!* she thought sullenly. *But how can I find them if they're not here anymore!*

*   *   *

Mary waited in the lobby for the elevator, grocery sack in hand. Minutes passed. The elevator never descended— apparently it was broken again—so she headed up the stairs, grateful she lived only five flights up.

Letting herself into her apartment, she kicked her leather shoes behind the door and headed for the kitchen. Azadeh was sitting at the small table, the newspaper spread out, reading the front page. A large picture of blackened D.C. took up most of the space above the fold. Mary glanced at it. "Anything new?" she asked.

"I don't understand most of it," Azadeh answered. "I read to help me with my English."

"That's good," Mary said as she placed the small sack of groceries on the narrow counter next to the refrigerator. Glancing over her shoulder, she asked, "Have you looked in on Kelly?"

"She is asleep," Azadeh answered. She hesitated, then added, "She seemed cold. I put another blanket on her and sat with her for a time. I did not try to wake her, but I just wanted . . . you know . . . I just thought she might like someone there, even if she was asleep. I hope that was okay. I sat by her on the mattress and sang a little song."

Mary turned to face her. "That's sweet, baby. You are kind. And you're right, I sometimes think she's asleep but then I'm surprised to find out that she was awake and hearing everything that I said."

Azadeh pressed her lips together, thinking of Miss Pari. "My father used to sing me a song when I was young," she said. "It is a beautiful song, a little sad, but in a nice sort of way." She started singing in Farsi, the words gentle and slow.

Mary closed her eyes as she listened. "That is beautiful," she said when Azadeh was finished.

Azadeh looked away, embarrassed.

"Will you teach me the words? Will you translate them into English?"

"My father tried to make a translation once," Azadeh answered. "I'm not sure I can remember it exactly."

"Try. Please. Do the best that you can."

Azadeh thought a long moment, then started singing.

The world that I give you
Is not always sunny and bright.
But knowing I love you
Will help make it right.
So when the dark settles,
And the storms fill the night,
Remember I'll be waiting
When it comes,
Morning Light.

Mary smiled. "So beautiful. I love that!"

Azadeh let her eyes fall to the floor. Mary watched her closely. The young woman was dressed in a black skirt that rested on her knees and a red blouse with a matching tie around her waist. Her thick black hair fell past her shoulders and was tied with a ribbon at the back. Her skin was a perfect bronze, her eyes large and bright. She didn't have on any makeup, but she didn't need any and never would. Staring at her, Mary realized she was as naturally beautiful as anyone she had ever seen before.

"Gosh, it's so good to have you here!" she exclaimed.

Azadeh smiled shyly.

Mary stared at her a moment longer. "You don't have any idea how beautiful you are, do you, Azadeh?" She sat down at the small kitchen table as she spoke.

Azadeh lowered her eyes but didn't answer.

Mary leaned toward her. "You really don't understand, do you?"

The look on Azadeh's face assured Mary that she didn't. Mary thought for a long moment. It was going to be hard. And it almost seemed wrong. But she had to tell her. She had to warn her. She had to strip away some of her innocence if she was going to survive in this place. She had to lay it out to prepare her to live in this new world. It was a wonder, an absolute modern-day miracle, that someone as old as Azadeh could be so innocent. It was . . . she didn't know how to describe it . . . renewing and beautiful. Many of the children around her had little babies of their own, yet Azadeh seemed to be completely innocent of such things. "Azadeh," she started, "you are a beautiful young lady. I know that all this is new, but you're going to have to be careful."

Azadeh looked at her. "Careful," she echoed.

"Careful, baby. There are people around here, people in this city, in this neighborhood, in this building even, who will hurt you or take advantage of you in very bad ways. Some of them will try to fool you. They'll pretend to be your friend. They'll act one way one day, then turn on you, baby. Do you understand anything I'm saying?"

Azadeh met Mary's eyes. She remembered the Iraqi who had come to fetch her from the camp, the man who claimed to be an agent for the uncle she didn't have. She remembered the way he had looked at her, the way he had summed her up with his eyes. She remembered other men, some old, some young, who looked at her the same way. So yes, she understood. She understood much more than Mary thought.

Mary waited, intertwining her fingers nervously. "We'll talk more a little later," she finally said. "Now, did you get some breakfast?"

Azadeh's forehead furrowed.

"Breakfast. You know . . . did you get something to eat?"

"No, not yet, but I made myself some tea if that's all right."

"Sure. Anything. This is your home; you can have anything you like." Mary stood up, went to the counter, and started putting the little bit of groceries away. "Azadeh, I have to go down to Columbus tomorrow," she said as she worked. "Kelly has an appointment with a doctor at a special clinic down there. It's been scheduled for months. She has seen him a couple of times, but this will probably be her last visit. I really hate to leave you, but it's a long drive, about four hours each way, so I'm going to leave tonight."

"I will be fine," Azadeh answered. "You do not have to worry about me."

"Really? You'll be okay?"

"Of course, Mary."

Azadeh heard a child's voice calling from down the hall. Mary heard it too. Both of them stood and walked toward the bedroom.

*   *   *

Mary went in first while Azadeh stood near the doorway, unsure of whether she should go in or stay out. Mary knelt on the mattress, lifting Kelly's hand. "How you doing, baby doll?" she asked.

Azadeh noted Mary's cheerful voice. She knew the woman was forcing herself to be so positive, and she admired her ability.

"Good morning, Mom," Kelly answered.

"You slept in this morning."

"I was tired, I guess." Kelly didn't notice the stranger standing at the door. Mary leaned over and kissed her forehead, then stood and pulled up the heavy Venetian blinds. The sky was clear, and sunlight flooded into the crowded room. "Kelly, remember we talked about the young lady who was going to come and stay with us."

The child's eyes immediately brightened. She slowly turned her head and looked toward the door. "She's here! You're here!" She reached for Azadeh's hand. "Azadeh. You're here! My mom and I have been waiting! My name is Kelly Beth." The little girl struggled to sit up.

Azadeh moved toward her and dropped to the floor. She took the girl's hand and held it. "Hi, Kelly Beth," she said.

The two young women stared at each other. "Oh my gosh, you're so beautiful," Kelly said. "Even more beautiful than your picture. Isn't she beautiful, Mom?"

Mary had to laugh. "Funny you should mention that," she said.

Azadeh held her hand more tightly. "Miss Kelly, you are the beautiful one."

The little girl shook her head and smiled. "No, Azadeh. Not since . . ." She shot a quick look toward Mary. "You *have* told her, Mom?"

Mary moved back toward the floor mattress and sat down beside Azadeh. "Yeah, baby. She knows."

Kelly turned back to Azadeh. "I used to be beautiful like you. Well, maybe not so beautiful, but I was pretty. But not now. Not anymore."

Azadeh shook her head. "No, Miss Kelly, I can see it. I can see through the sickness. You are still beautiful."

The younger girl looked uncomfortable. "I hate for people to see me anymore. It's embarrassing."

Azadeh whispered something to her in Farsi.

"What was that?" Kelly asked.

Azadeh repeated the phrase, this time in English: "*Beautiful is the soul that looks out from my eyes.*"

Kelly listened and thought a moment. "I like that," she said. She looked away, her forehead furrowed, then slowly turned to Mary. "Mom, last night I woke up. I told you about my dream? That's true, right?"

"Yes," Mary answered.

Kelly turned back to Azadeh. "She was in my dream," she said, pointing, her voice animated now. "I remember it all perfectly now. There was a funeral. A little girl. Lots of soldiers.

But Azadeh was there too. She was standing in the back. And she was . . . she was crying."

Kelly looked into Azadeh's eyes. "Why were you crying, Azadeh?" she asked. "Why were you in my dream?"

chapter seventeen

It took less than five minutes for King Abdullah to know which of his brothers were going to join him.

Soon after he had shot the first two men, the remaining six began to see the light. Later, when two more faltered upon understanding what he intended to do, they were quickly taken care of. The four remaining princes had agreed to join him, swearing allegiance to his cause.

King Abdullah had known that two of the four would join him. The third one, he had been uncertain about. And the fourth prince who had chosen to support him had come as a complete surprise, proving once again how difficult it was to truly judge a man's heart.

After getting their agreement, the king had given the four conspirators two hours to ponder, sending them to their rooms under guard. Once the sun had set and left the desert to swallow up the yellow light from the moon, once the hot wind had quit blowing from the dry lands to the south, the four princes had come together in the Great Hall and waited on their king again.

* * *

Abdullah looked at them through a gap in the bricks where the mortar had cracked away. The old man stood beside him, his hot breath in Abdullah's ear as they watched the four men mill together, their faces drawn and tight.

"Do you see them?" the old man whispered.

Abdullah shook his head.

"They are there," the old man assured him. "Believe me, they are there. Now that the sun has set, they are more free to move about. They hate the light, any light: the light of the sun, the light of freedom, the light of the truth. As it is they love the darkness, and there is plenty of darkness now."

Abdullah stared, shaking his head. If they were there, he couldn't see them, but he believed the old man.

The old man pulled away and folded his arms defiantly. "You know that what you are about to do is not original," he said.

King Abdullah continued staring through the gap, not saying anything until the old man placed his cold hand upon his shoulder and turned him around. "This thing that you are asking has been done a thousand times before. The Great Enemy, in his hypocrisy, asked it of his own prophet. The ancient Jews, in their apostasy, required it of their own. There have been altars built for this purpose on every continent in the world. It has been a sign and device of Master Mahan since the first blood was spilt upon this world."

Abdullah looked at his own hands, remembering the evil things that they had done. "I understand," he offered simply.

The old man waited, then pushed against his shoulder, edging him toward the hidden door. "Go then. I will be watching. You will not let me down."

*　　*　　*

King Abdullah entered the Great Hall and stood before his brothers, reading the looks on their faces and the darkness of their eyes.

"Brothers, we are almost finished," he said. "Our greatest enemy, the Great Satan, is within a few hours of being brought to her knees. Once she stumbles she will die, suffering a long and violent death, ripped to pieces from the inside as she seeks to right herself. We will propel her to that moment, let there be no doubt in your minds, but we will only push her. She will finish the job herself.

"When she is dead, you and I will be the most powerful men on earth. Then we will turn toward the Little Satan. She will not last a week. The entire world hates the Zionists and will gladly see them destroyed. Then we rise again, the chosen people, and lead our Arab brothers into a Pan-Arab world."

The four princes were silent. Deep in their hearts, they believed every word that he was saying, for they could hear the dark spirits around them whisper the same lies into their minds.

Abdullah watched them, satisfied. One more step and he would have them. One more oath, and they were his.

Anything they could conceive of, it would be given to these men.

But the power and the glory that he offered was far too great to merely give away. There was a price to pay.

Of course they would agree to join him when a gun was pointed at their heads. That had been a simple exercise to weed out the weakest of the men.

And they might agree to join him for the promised wealth and power.

But it was time now to find out what was really in their hearts. It was time to find out if they were driven by simple brainless lust or greed, or if they could be driven by something else. Something even more powerful. More eternal. More compelling and wonderful.

They had sworn a sacred oath to him, but was their loyalty real? Would they pay the price to join him, or would they cut and run? Would they do what he had done? Would they spill the blood of their family? The blood of their own kin?

He didn't know. He didn't know.

But he was about to find out.

He clapped his hands, and a hidden door opened at the back of the room. Two of his agents came out holding the oldest son of the Minister of Defense between them. The boy was bound, his hands tied behind his back. And though his eyes were wide in terror, he didn't struggle against his bonds.

Abdullah walked to a couch, reached under the cushion, and pulled out a ten-inch, serrated knife. He turned toward his brother and placed the long knife in his hand. "Brothers," he said, his voice low and raspy, "it is time to prove your oath."

chapter eighteen

Mary carefully helped Kelly into a chrome wheelchair and pushed her to the elevator in the middle of the hall. Azadeh followed her out of the apartment. "Remember, Azadeh," Mary said for at least the third time, "you have my cell phone number right there."

"Yes," Azadeh replied.

"You remember how to call me?"

"Yes, ma'am."

"The clinic is in downtown Columbus. Northridge Children's Cancer Center. It is well-known. If you have any questions, you can ask almost anyone."

Azadeh nodded, smiling as she hovered under Mary's protective worries.

Mary stood and thought, going through a checklist in her mind. "I've got the keys, the map and address . . ." She glanced at Azadeh. "Can you drive, baby?"

Azadeh shook her head, amazed at the thought. Teenage girls didn't drive in Iran. Neither did their mothers—at least, few of them did. "No, Mary," she answered, almost laughing. "No, I do not drive."

"Okay, okay. I was going to tell you that I've borrowed a car from Yevonie, she's a good friend of mine. I don't think my old beater would have made it, but hers is pretty good. Anyway, I was going to tell you that you could take my car if you needed anything or had to get somewhere, but I don't suppose that's going to happen."

Azadeh laughed again. "No, ma'am, I do not believe I will be driving around Chicago."

Mary smiled. "Of course not. But someday. Someday soon we'll help you get your license."

It was a terrifying thought to Azadeh. Still, she smiled and muttered "yes, ma'am" in reply.

Mary had given up on the ma'am thing and didn't correct her. "Okay, I think I've got everything," she said, closing her purse. "Remember, we'll be back tomorrow night. It might be late. I don't want you to worry, okay? If anything comes up, I'll call you . . ."

"I will be fine," Azadeh said.

Mary reached for the elevator button, then pulled her hand back. "I wish you could come with me," she said again, "but there's no place for you to stay. They won't let you sleep at the clinic. I'm *really* sorry."

"It is all right. It really is."

"I just hate to leave you alone on only the second night you are here. But it won't always be like this. This is the last time we have to go clear down to Columbus."

Azadeh lifted a hand to cut Mary off, then walked toward Kelly, who was waiting in her chair. Azadeh knelt down beside her. "You will be okay?" she asked.

"Sure," Kelly answered. "I like Doctor Ryan. He always has . . ." she had to stop and turn her head to swallow . . . "a treat for me." Her voice was weak from talking to Azadeh for so long that morning.

Kelly looked up with her dark eyes and Azadeh felt her heart melt. There was so much about this little girl that was so easy to love.

Azadeh smiled at her, but inside she seemed to panic. Kelly looked so weak, so drawn out, as if at the end of a battle that had gone on too long. "Have a good trip," she added quickly to push the thought away. "When you get back, I will teach you how to speak more Farsi. You never know, it might come in handy sometime."

Kelly smiled. "See you tomorrow night."

Mary and Kelly stepped into the elevator, leaving Azadeh alone in the hallway. As she watched the elevator doors close, a thought leapt into Azadeh's mind.

Smile at her, Azadeh. You may never see her again.

She raised her hand and smiled quickly. "Good-bye, Kelly. I'll see—"

The metal doors rolled shut.

Mary and Kelly were gone.

Azadeh stood for a moment in the hallway, thinking sadly, then turned to the open apartment door.

She cleaned and straightened, took a bath, unpacked her clothes, hanging them in the closet (everything she owned hardly filled one half of one side), then stood alone in the middle of the bedroom, unsure of what to do.

chapter nineteen

THE *AB TAYYIB* (THE GOOD FATHER)
EIGHTY-SEVEN MILES EAST-SOUTHEAST OF CAPE HATTERAS,
NORTH CAROLINA

Starting as early as 2005, the Iranians had paved the way for the EMP attack upon the United States when, early in the spring, they completed a series of missile tests over the Caspian Sea. Firing from a freighter very similar in size and weight to the *Ab Tayyib,* they sent their Shehab-3 missiles climbing upward on steep trajectories, exploding them 150 to 180 miles above the water.

After monitoring the missile tests, the United States had concluded that they were an utter failure. "Missile Tests Fall Short of Expectations," the classified reports had read.

But the missile tests hadn't been a failure. In fact, they had been a rousing success.

Further testing in 2006 revealed that the high-altitude nuclear warheads might be better launched using the more powerful and updated Scud missiles. Because of this, King Abdullah had made the decision to replace the Iranian Shehab missiles inside the hull of the *Ab Tayyib* with the more capable and powerful Scuds.

Developed by the Soviets in the mid-1960s, the Scud missiles were the grandchild of the German V-2s that haunted

England at the end of the Second World War. Originally designed to carry a 100-kiloton nuclear warhead, the updated missiles had been sold and shipped to dozens of nations throughout the world. Modified from its original nuclear role, the Scud was capable of carrying a 2,000-pound conventional warhead up to 180 miles. Later, Pakistani and Iranian scientists had taken the Iraqi Scuds and improved them to provide even greater range. The warhead and fuselage weight had been reduced, the fuel tanks expanded, and the engines modified in order to burn most of the fuel during the launch phase of flight, a technique that developed a far greater launch velocity, pushing the missile even higher into the upper atmosphere.

Known as *Al Abbas,* the newest Scuds had a range of 800 kilometers, a long way to go, especially when flying almost straight up.

But the Scuds did have one problem. Because their warheads were permanently attached to the missile bodies, they were notoriously inaccurate—acceptable when tossing a nuclear weapon, but completely unacceptable in conventional war.

Still, the military officers on board the *Ab Tayyib* weren't concerned about the *Al Abbas* missiles' weakness. Tonight they needed altitude, not accuracy, and the Scuds were very good for that.

* * *

The final launch orders had been received and confirmed. Preparations complete, the captain of the *Ab Tayyib* turned to his first officer, who stared back with dark, empty eyes. "Are you ready, my friend?" he asked.

The officer nodded slowly but didn't say anything.

The captain took a deep breath. He had enough Valium and opium in his bloodstream to keep his emotions in check. "Launch the missiles," he ordered, his voice tight and dry.

The officer stared at him a long moment, then turned and walked away.

*   *   *

Darkness had settled over the rolling ocean. The skies were almost clear, with scattered layers of thin cirrus at twenty-one and twenty-six thousand feet. Operating in the starlight, their navigation lights turned to dim, the weapons crew set to work. The ship was turned to put its tail into the wind and set at 12 knots to match the south wind, minimizing any airflow over the deck. The hold was opened, the dual-plate doors folding back on huge, hydraulic rods, and the elevators raised, lifting the two side-by-side missiles and their launch rails into the dark night.

Eleven minutes after the captain's order, the launch deck was ready and clear, the final navigation updates input into the missile launch computer, the ship stabilizers below the water-line extended to their maximum length.

The captain gave a final word. Standing at the weapons control panel, the first officer turned his key and stepped back. The captain moved toward the panel, inserted his own key, and punched in a final code.

The gelled fuel moved through the high-pressure lines inside the Scud missile engines, the fuel flow tripling every half-second. Then the deck lit up with white light, turning the darkness into day. Ignition. Smoke. Furious noise and vibration.

The first missile lifted into the air. It hung there half a second, the nose cone moving in the breeze, then thrust skyward into the dark night, the enormous exhaust nozzle blazing white-hot flame. Ten seconds later, the second missile also fired.

The missiles flew in trail, the second missile mimicking the flight path of the first until passing through fifty-five thousand feet. There the second missile turned slightly south, heading for the southern states. The first missile continued northward and climbed, both of them reaching for 285 miles above the earth.

285 miles. 1,504,800 feet. The perfect altitude.

Any higher and the electromagnetic pulse would have been weakened by the distance to the ground. Any lower and the range of exposure wouldn't have been maximized.

Three fishing vessels were within ten miles of the freighter when the missiles fired into the night sky. Half a dozen eyes watched as the missiles climbed upward, the white fire illuminating the smoky trail that followed. But no one knew what it was, and no one knew what to do.

As the missiles climbed, they also became visible along the east coast, their smoky contrails and burning engines illuminating the night.

Higher. Higher. Almost straight up they flew. Crossing the shoreline, they followed their intended flight path to the east.

Seventy thousand feet below the first missile, a ten-year-old boy stood on the beach. To his right, the ocean lapped, the whitecaps illuminated by the low moon and stars. Above him, he watched the tiny trail of moving flame.

"What is that?" he asked his brother.

"I don't know," his brother said.

It was eleven minutes, nineteen seconds from missile launch to the highest arc in the parabola, where the warheads would explode.

THE *CHOUN OHMONEE* (THE GOOD MOTHER)
NINETY-THREE MILES WEST OF SAN FRANCISCO

Three hours behind the Eastern Time Zone, the North Korean frigate, the *Choun Ohmonee,* got the launch codes for its missiles when the sun was barely setting. Still, the crewmen didn't wait until it was dark to launch. Once they had received the codes, they knew they had only a few minutes to get the missiles in the air.

The modified cargo doors were pulled open, the launchers raised, the missiles readied to go.

The North Korean freighter launched her two Scud missiles a little more than forty seconds after her sister ship in the North Atlantic Ocean had fired hers. The two missiles burned their way upward, piercing the glowing sky. Like their predecessors, the missiles followed each other until passing through fifty-five thousand feet, then separated, the first one taking up a northern heading, the other tracking almost straight east.

NORTH AMERICAN AEROSPACE DEFENSE COMMAND (NORAD)
INSIDE CHEYENNE MOUNTAIN, EAST OF PETERSON AIR FORCE BASE
COLORADO SPRINGS, COLORADO

The Combat Operations Center came instantly to life, the huge screen at the front of the room illuminating the two missiles climbing over the east coast. A low growl filled the air from the warning buzzer overhead.

"Oh no, oh no . . ." the chief controller mumbled as he stared at the screen.

"What is it? What are they!" the commanding general demanded.

"I don't know, sir."

"Where did they come from!"

"Launch point was . . . they share the same launch point . . . looks like eighty, maybe ninety miles off the coast . . ."

"Submarine-launched missiles. You've got to be kidding me!"

"It could be. They are ballistic . . ."

"What are their targets?"

Five seconds of hesitation. "We don't know for certain, sir. The missiles are still in their climb phase. Their flight paths are not matching any of our parabolas. They're going high . . . going high."

The general thought a second. "Check your systems," he said, his voice low and cold.

Another long moment of silence. Every eye in the Combat Operations Center watched the senior controller. "Sir," he finally answered, "self-check complete. We have two confirmed bandits. Both of the missiles are still climbing."

"That can't be right," the general answered. "Not when they were launched so close."

The controller moved his cursor across his screen. "Final self-check complete," he announced, finishing the last step in his checklist to confirm the missile launch.

The general's face was utterly calm, but his mind raced ahead. "Get me Raven Rock," he said as he turned to his chair.

Another warning chime. The enormous screen of the United States lit up again.

Two more missiles. Off the west coast. Climbing. Always climbing. One turning north, one heading east.

Twenty seconds of silence as the controllers and computers worked.

"The four missiles have taken up headings to hit our four major quadrants," the lead controller said.

And that was all it took. The general finally understood.

Falling back in his chair, he gripped the armrest, realizing that the world, as they all knew it, was about to end.

chapter twenty

The missiles reached their target locations: 285 miles above the Earth and spread out evenly across the United States, the coordinates roughly correspon- ding to northern Idaho, the Four Corners, Detroit, and Nashville. Once the missiles had reached their preprogrammed coordinates, they exploded at almost exactly the same time.

Each of the missiles carried a fifty-kiloton warhead, the equivalent of fifty thousand tons of TNT, one hundred million pounds of explosive power.

Inconceivable heat and overpressure spread across the lower reaches of space from the growing fireballs. But the heat and radiation were not the purpose of the explosions, for they were not dangerous to human life, not at such a high altitude.

No, this attack wasn't designed to kill Americans from either heat or an explosion. It was designed to kill Americans by starving them to death.

As the warheads exploded, an atmospheric tsunami swept across North America. From the southern edge of Canada to central Mexico, extending as far south as the Gulf of Mexico and the Caribbean Sea, four crashing waves of electromagnetic power burst across the sky.

* * *

In addition to heat and overpressure, a nuclear explosion also generates a massive burst of electromagnetic energy known as an electromagnetic pulse, or EMP. When such a surge of X rays and gamma rays are unleashed at the edge of the earth's atmosphere, they interact with the air molecules, creating an enormous burst of highly charged electrons that are magnified by the magnetic field around the earth. The final result is an enormous pulse of energy.

The electromagnetic shock wave generated by the four simultaneous nuclear explosions was unimaginably intense, a hundred million times more powerful than any radio signal ever before created by man. This massive wave of energy raced toward the surface of the earth at the speed of light, destroying every unprotected electrical circuit in its path.

A thousandth of a second after the explosions, the destruction was complete.

* * *

Sometime in the spring of 2005, the United States government came to an incredible conclusion. Almost entirely unreported (which didn't really matter since there was very little anyone could do about it anyway), the findings of the Senate Judiciary subcommittee on terrorism, technology, and homeland security were synopsized in the *Washington Post:*

An electromagnetic pulse (EMP) attack on the American homeland . . . is one of only a few ways that the United States could be defeated by its enemies— terrorist or otherwise. And it is probably the easiest. A single Scud missile, carrying a single nuclear weapon, detonated at the appropriate altitude, would interact with the Earth's atmosphere, producing an electro-magnetic pulse radiating down to the surface at the speed of light. Depending on the location and size of the blast, the effect would be to knock out already stressed power grids and other electrical systems across much or even all of the continental United States, for months if not years.

. . . The loss of power would have a cascading effect on all aspects of U.S. society. Communication would be largely impossible. Lack of refrigeration would leave food rotting in warehouses, exacerbated by a lack of transportation as those vehicles still work-ing simply ran out of gas (which is pumped with elec-tricity). The inability to sanitize and distribute water would quickly threaten public health, not to mention the safety of anyone in the path of the inevitable fires, which would rage unchecked. And as we have seen in areas of natural and other disasters, such circumstances often result in a fairly rapid breakdown of social order. . . .

Those who survived . . . would find themselves transported back to the United States of the 1880s.

This threat may sound straight out of Hollywood, but it is very real. CIA Director Porter Goss recently testified before Congress about nuclear material miss-ing from storage sites in Russia that may have found its way into terrorist hands. . . . Iran has surprised intelli-gence analysts by describing the mid-flight detonations of missiles fired from ships on the Caspian Sea as "suc-cessful" tests. North Korea exports missile technology around the world; Scuds can easily be purchased on the open market for about $100,000 apiece.

A terrorist organization might have trouble putting a nuclear warhead "on target" with a Scud, but it would be much easier to simply launch and detonate in the atmosphere. No need for the risk and difficulty of trying to smuggle a nuclear weapon over the border or hit a particular city. Just launch a cheap missile from a freighter in international waters—al Qaeda is believed to own about 80 such vessels—and make sure to get it a few miles in the air. . . .

Today few Americans can conceive of the possibility that terrorists could bring our society to its knees by destroying everything we rely on that runs on electricity. But this time we've been warned. . . .

(Senator John Kyle, "Unready for This Attack," *Washington Post*, April 16, 2005)

Microseconds after the four warheads exploded, all across the United States, electrical conductors and generators were destroyed. Transmission lines were rendered useless. Computers and microchips were instantly burned through. In a fraction of a second, the United States of America was transplanted back to the preindustrial world.

Electronic banking as well as the financial information on 300 million Americans was instantly vaporized, disappearing in a puff of digital smoke. With a flash of unseen light, the United States became a cash-only world.

At the time of the explosions, there were a few more than 3,400 civilian airliners in the sky. (Had the explosions occurred just a few hours earlier, at the height of the afternoon aviation rush, the number of airborne aircraft would have exceeded five thousand.) None of the electrical circuits inside these aircraft were designed to withstand an electromagnetic pulse. As a result, the flight controls, navigation equipment, GPS, radars, cockpit displays, and electronic engine controllers were rendered useless. Most of these aircraft crashed.

Thirty-two hundred aircraft. On average, 150 passengers apiece.

640,000 Americans dead.

But tens of millions of other deaths would follow, for the entire nation was now just a few months away from mass starvation, completely incapable of feeding itself. The ability to plant, harvest, or transport food, the ability to purify and provide clean water, the ability to provide for the most basic needs had been instantly stripped away.

And that was just the beginning.

Medical instruments, hospital power generators, electronic ignitions inside semis and family automobiles, controllers inside the diesel engines on locomotives, cell phones, televisions, refrigeration units, the infrastructure for handling power, fuel, energy, banking and finance, telecommunications, emergency services—all of it was gone.

Four simple warheads—none of them more sophisticated or any larger than those designed during WWII—were all it took to bring the greatest nation on earth to her knees.

chapter twenty-one

They headed west. Luke drove, his right hand on the wheel, his fingers nervously tapping it. Sara sat beside him, her hands resting calmly on her lap. Ammon crouched in the backseat of the Honda, leaning against the window, his eyes closed. He hadn't spoken in a couple of hours, but Sara knew he was awake.

Traffic was heavy, the interstate clogged in both directions, though the heaviest line of cars was heading west. A long, slow, and discouraging day's drive was behind them. The setting sun was directly ahead, the slanting rays burning through the front window. They didn't talk as they drove, the Honda tires humming over the smooth interstate. Sara reached up and turned off the radio; every station played nothing but the news, repeating the same information again and again. The president was dead now, the vice president as well. The Speaker of the House of Representatives and president pro tempore of the Senate were both alive but critically injured, leaving the Secretary of State as the acting president. Occasional riots still flared up in Chicago, New York, and L.A., but most of the other major cities had calmed down.

Millions of people, with no real explanation, were fleeing the east coast. Everyone had a grandparent, a sibling, a distant relation, or a friend who lived away from the major cities, and those people were extraordinarily popular right now.

Behind them, almost four hundred miles to the east, Washington, D.C., one of the greatest cities in the world, lay in a smolder, the smoke hanging over the area in a black, inky cloak. Thousands of volunteer firefighters had converged on the city, but there wasn't much they could do. Downtown had nothing left to burn. The outskirts of the city still smoldered, but it was impossible to fight the fires with all the radioactive dust and contamination in the air. Most of the firefighters didn't have anti-radiation suits and so they stood guard, waiting for the all clear to move in. Same for the rescue teams. Little they could do, but they did what they could.

As the sun dropped, the sky before them turned a deep crimson, the upper atmosphere having been choked with thick dust from the nuclear explosions over Gaza, D.C., and Iran. Luke moved both hands to the wheel and stretched his back against the seat. Sara leaned over to check the fuel gauge for the second time in the last five minutes, then sat back and closed her eyes. "We don't want to go below half a tank," she said.

Luke only nodded.

Most of the service stations they had passed were closed. SOLD OUT, NO VACANCY, and CLOSED signs seemed to be everywhere. The lines of cars at the few open stations back at Columbus had been blocks long. Four hours, five hours in line were the norm there, though it didn't seem to be as bad once they got away from the population centers.

American society was as fragile and interconnected as a spider's web; every hurricane, every snowfall, every hot summer day that pressed the electrical grid had the potential to bring an entire region to its knees. The transportation infrastructure was completely incapable of handling the sudden and massive migration that was taking place. Sara suspected many of the service stations that were closed still had fuel in their underground tanks but were unwilling to sell, hoarding for the next day when the prices would be higher and they could make even more.

She shook her head at the greed.

"Stay at home. There's no reason to panic. Save your fuel and your resources," was the official word out of Raven Rock. But the advice from the government spokesman didn't mean a whole lot. No one trusted what was left of the federal government. It seemed like it was every man for himself now.

As they drove, Sara thought through their situation, considering their location and inventory of supplies. They were two days' drive out of Washington, D.C., heading west. The protection of the Rocky Mountains was still at least thirty hours of driving away—*if* they could get gas, and if nothing else went wrong. They had enough food for a couple of weeks, but their water would last only a few more days. The 72-hour emergency kit had been a lifesaver, but they could only stretch it so far. She glanced nervously over her shoulder to the trunk of the car. Ten thousand dollars cash—all that the bank had allowed her to withdraw at one time—was hidden under the spare tire in the trunk. They had wrapped the hundred-dollar bills in an old plastic bag and shoved it in the space where the tire jack had been stored, but she knew if someone were suspicious—or hungry, or angry, or greedy or mean, or desperate, or any of the dozens of emotions they had witnessed over the last two days—they could find the money. The package was just too big and awkward to hide it inside their little car. She thought of the cashier's check tucked under her seat, another ten thousand dollars, good as cash in normal times, but who knew what it was worth right now? From what the radio said, it was 1929 all over again. Many financial institutions were refusing to hand out money, and the lines at the banks were almost as frenzied as the lines at the service stations and grocery stores.

The trunk was crammed with what remained of their 72-hour emergency kit, extra food, their last case of bottled water, two ten-gallon red containers of fuel, winter clothes, sleeping bags, a tent, winter boots, rock-climbing equipment (Ammon had insisted on bringing the ropes, although Sara didn't know why). The backseat held their suitcases, another bag of extra clothes, a set of scriptures . . .

There was a sudden *thump,* and the car shuddered. Sara jerked and looked quickly to the road, her hands gripping the dash anxiously.

Luke reached out to calm her. "It's cool, Mom," he said. "There was a shredded tire in the road. Nothing to worry about."

Sara looked back, saw the next car roll over the piece of tire, then turned around in her seat.

Leaning over, she rechecked the gas gauge, then let her eyes drift toward her son. A Beretta 90-TWO handgun was hidden under Luke's seat. 9mm. Ten round clip. Black and gray. A full box of ammunition was stuffed in the glove compartment. She pictured the handgun's beveled grip and shivered, hating the fact that it was so near.

She rested against the console between the two front seats and considered the gold coins hidden underneath her arm. Using their small toolbox, Ammon and Luke had removed the plastic console and hidden a metal box containing forty gold coins, each weighing one ounce. Two weeks ago the gold would have been valued at something like $25,000. Today it was worth ten or twelve times that, maybe even more.

She didn't know what made her more nervous, the hidden gold coins or the gun. The gun might keep them safe, she could accept that, but the gold—that could only bring them problems. If anyone knew they had it, if anyone even suspected . . .

She shivered, almost wishing they had left the gold back in their home in D.C.

Home . . . home . . . her mind drifted back. The great old house in D.C. The wide, rolling lawn, Kentucky Bluegrass with Bermuda mixed in to keep it green against the southern heat. The enormous sycamore and oak trees, some of them dating back to the Civil War era. Ah, those beautiful trees, tall and broad and strong. She leaned against the headrest and closed her eyes.

The lawn . . . the old house . . . a popping fire in the fire-place in the winter . . . summer nights, warm and fragrant with honeysuckle . . . the sound of cicadas . . .

She drifted away . . .

The lawn was wet with dew. Neil was walking across the heavy grass in the darkness of the predawn light. The sun was an hour yet from rising, but the light from the streetlights illuminated his outline as he walked. He was tall and broad-shouldered, and his hair, wet from his morning shower, stuck to the middle of his forehead. He was dressed in his Air Force blues, an old leather briefcase tucked up under his arm. A government SUV and its driver were waiting for him at the curb. He stopped to pick up the newspaper, then turned. She was standing in the light of the kitchen window, and he smiled at her.

"I love you," he mouthed, placing his hand at his heart.

"Neil, come back to me," she whispered slowly.

He looked at her, flipped the paper up and caught it, then turned.

"I need to talk to you," Sara called out. "I need to know what you want me to do."

The general kept walking toward the waiting car.

She turned from the window and ran toward the front door. "Neil, I'm not ready," she cried, her voice choking. "I'm not ready for you to go. I don't know what to do without you! I don't know what to do!"

* * *

She felt a warm hand on her shoulder. "It's okay, Mom," Ammon told her from the backseat. He was leaning forward. "It's okay," he gently assured her again.

She opened her eyes and shook her head. Luke split his attention between the road and his mother. "You okay, Mom?" he asked.

She shook her head again. "I'm fine. I'm fine. I must have fallen asleep."

Ammon watched her carefully. "That's good, Mom. I don't think you've slept in days."

She shrugged. "I've had plenty of sleep."

Luke and Ammon glanced at each other. They both knew that wasn't true.

Sara pushed a strand of hair from her eyes and stretched. Luke glanced at her as he drove. She was still beautiful—the years had been more than gracious—but it was clear that she wore a certain sadness now. A deep remorsefulness had settled into her eyes, and he wondered if it would ever go away.

She looked at him and smiled, then glanced into the backseat. "Ammon, could I have some of your bottled water?"

He reached to the cup holder between the front and back seats and handed her a plastic bottle. "Here you go, Mom."

She took a shallow sip, then handed the water back.

"Go ahead, Mom, you should drink it all."

"No, we need to be careful . . ."

"We've got plenty of water, Mom. Enough for at least a couple of days. We're going to be able to get more, I'm certain." He pushed her hand back. "Go ahead. It's okay. You can't be silly. You've got to take care of yourself."

Sara smiled wearily. "Thank you, Doctor Spock," she joked. But he didn't take the water, and she finally drank it down, swallowing half the bottle in one long gulp.

*　　*　　*

The road seemed long and lonely. A roll of low clouds, black and menacing, began building in the west. Occasional flashes of lightning illuminated the core of the thunderstorms, but without the summer's heat they rose quickly and then faded, scattering into low but light-absorbing clouds. Minutes later, the car passed a green highway sign suspended over the freeway: Indianapolis 22 miles. There, the highway split, Interstate 65 heading northwest toward Chicago, I-70 turning slightly south, bending toward St. Louis, then Kansas City, then the great Kansas plains, then Denver, and finally the towering Rocky Mountains to the west.

An exit with a couple of gas stations and a rest stop loomed ahead, glowing lights comforting against the cloudy afternoon. They continued on the freeway, coming after a short time to where the highway split, the two right lanes turning north toward Chicago.

Sara sat up suddenly. She stared, her mouth open, hesitating. Suddenly she cried, "Turn here!"

"No, Mom," Luke answered, "we need to stay on I-70 heading west."

The exit was coming fast and they were in the wrong lane.

"Turn here!" Sara repeated, almost reaching for the wheel. "Turn, Luke! Turn now!"

"But that will take us to Chicago. It *isn't* the right way . . ."

The exit was almost upon them. The car on their right began to drift, taking the exit at highway speed.

"Take the right lane, Luke. Take 65 toward Chicago . . . *Please* turn . . ."

It was too late. The exit was moving past them.

"Do it!" Ammon shouted from the backseat.

"*Please, Luke!*" Sara cried.

Luke jammed the wheel to the right. A screech of tires and car horn sounded from behind them. He felt the rubber on his wheels give, losing their grip on the road. He backed off, his left wheel almost dipping off the pavement, then pulled the car more gently through the turn. They made the exit, but barely, Sara gripping her seat belt at the shoulder while holding her breath.

A few seconds passed in silence.

"Why'd we do that, Mom?" Luke asked at last, glancing at her.

His mother didn't answer.

"Mom, are you okay?"

Still she didn't answer.

"Mom . . . ?"

"I'm fine, Luke."

"You know we're driving north now. We're heading toward Chicago. This isn't taking us any closer to where we want to be."

"I know that, Luke."

Another moment of silence.

"So . . ."

"I don't know, Luke. I just had a feeling. I almost heard a voice. *Turn here. Go toward Chicago.* It wasn't something I came up with. I have no reason to head up here. I tried to fight it, it made no sense, but the feeling was so *urgent*."

Ammon leaned forward from the backseat. "You did the right thing, Mom. No worries. We'll just head north for a while and see what happens, then decide what to do from there."

Luke scrunched his face. "It doesn't make any sense."

Sara stared out her window, then turned. "Look around you, Luke. Does *anything* make any sense anymore? It might be that the only things that *do* make sense are the things we can't make sense of. I heard the voice. I felt the Spirit. We have to trust the warnings. That's the only thing we really have anymore."

Luke nodded. "All right, then."

Sara reached over and touched his shoulder. "We'll do the best we can. It'll be okay."

*　　*　　*

They drove for almost two hours. The sun disappeared below the distant horizon. The moon rose over the flat plains, blood-red and full. Sara turned and watched. It looked like an evil, bloody eye staring down from the sky. The night grew dark. The North Star drifted into view, slightly off to their right.

Sara stared at the red moon as she thought.

The landscape around them glittered with lights from farms and small towns tucked among the great Midwest plains. The clouds had blown and scattered and the sky was deep and full of stars. A dim light began to glow before them from the Chicago metroplex. Although it was still twenty miles in the distance, the massive cluster of lights lit up the entire northern sky.

"We ought to stop for gas," Luke said. "The closer we get

to the city, the harder it's going to be to get it without having to wait for hours in line."

Ammon pointed from the backseat. "The next exit. I see some lights. There's two or three stations up ahead."

Luke saw them, half a mile east of the exit. He started to slow. "Looks like there's only a couple dozen cars in line."

Sara nodded as he steered toward the off-ramp.

The flash was sudden and bright, white-hot, blazing and intense. It burst down from the night sky, leaving a yellow glow that quickly faded and then disappeared.

Everything fell silent. Their car stopped suddenly. No chug. No cough or sputter. It was as if someone had reached over and turned the key off. The Honda slowed, and Luke had to use both hands to steer it toward the side of the road.

Sara's heart leapt into her throat. "What's wrong?" she asked anxiously.

"I don't know, Mom," he answered.

The Honda coasted to the bottom of the off-ramp and rolled to a stop. Ammon sat forward in the backseat, staring at the instrument panel, which was completely dark. "How much gas did you have?" he asked.

"A little more than a quarter tank."

"Try it again," Sara said, her voice tight.

Luke turned the key. Nothing. Not a click. Not a sound. The engine didn't turn.

"Could the gas gauge be wrong?" she wondered.

Ammon pushed himself farther forward. "You don't have any headlights," he said.

Luke turned the key again and again. Nothing. He sat back in exasperation.

"We're not out of gas," Ammon said. "If that was the problem, the battery would still turn the engine over. The battery would give us headlights. Maybe the alternator failed."

Luke slapped the steering wheel in frustration. Sara fought to keep her stomach under control. Would they be able to find a mechanic? How much would it cost them? How long would it take?

Ammon looked around, then swallowed in sudden fear.

Something was wrong.

Really wrong.

The darkness around them was complete.

The lights from the gas stations had gone out. The street-lights at the bottom of the off-ramp, all the lights in the parking lots, the entire countryside had grown dark. No twinkling lights in the fields. Nothing to the east or west. He looked around desperately.

The glow from the distant lights of Chicago had also disappeared.

It was as if the entire world had fallen dark.

A power outage? Maybe. But if it was, it was a huge one, spreading across the entire area.

He sat back and thought.

Why would a power outage have affected their car?

He stole a glance ahead, expecting to see a long line of car lights on the road before them, but the whole freeway was perfectly dark. Turning, he looked behind them, peering through the back window. He could make out the shadows of the other cars in the moonlight, but none of them were moving. They were all at a standstill.

No headlights. No movement. The radio had gone quiet.

His heart began to pump like a hammer in his head. He leaned over, grabbed the handle, and pushed the door back, listening in the blackness.

Nearly perfect silence. The only sound a gentle breeze.

It was as if the entire world had gone away . . .

He thought some more and then groaned.

Sara turned in the seat to look at him. "What is it!" she demanded, her voice steady but thick with fear.

"Try your cell phone," he commanded.

Sara pulled her cell phone from her purse and flipped it open. "It looks like my batteries are dead."

"Try yours, Luke."

He reached into his pocket. "I've got nothing." He pushed and held the on switch. "That's kind of weird," he said.

Ammon didn't answer. Instead, he climbed out of the backseat. His mother and brother followed, meeting him at the front of the car.

Perfect darkness. Perfect silence. Not a light in the distance. No sound of passing cars.

Ammon's face turned pale in the red moonlight, and Sara moved toward him. "What is it?" she pleaded. "Do you know what has happened? Do you know what's going on!"

Ammon slowly nodded. Luke reached out for his arm. "What is it, Ammon?" he whispered.

Ammon leaned against the bumper, then lifted his hands to his face. "We're not going west," he told them. "We're not going anywhere."

Luke turned and looked around him, taking in the total darkness. The night was so quiet it was eerie. He shuddered and hunched his shoulders. "What happened, Ammon?"

"An EMP," Ammon answered slowly.

"EMP. What is that!"

Before Ammon could answer, they heard a voice calling out from the darkness. Behind them, forty or fifty yards down the freeway, a car door slammed and a woman's voice called again, "Please, can someone help me?"

Her voice was high and panicked. She was clearly terrified.

Ammon hesitated, staring at the emptiness behind them, then turned to Luke. "Come on," he said.

They started moving toward the voice that was sounding from the darkness. Sara grabbed Ammon's arm as he moved away from her, slipping her fingers down to grasp his wrist. "Be careful," she said, squeezing his arm. "You don't know who it is or what they want."

Ammon turned toward her. "We'll be fine, Mom." He nodded to Luke and started walking. Luke followed him. Ammon stumbled, almost tripping over the shoulder in the road where the asphalt dropped away to meet the gravel, the darkness deep around him, cavelike and complete. "Hey," he shouted. "Hey there, can you hear me?"

"Yes! Yes! I can hear you. Can you help me?"

The voice was not far away now, just ten or twenty yards. He slowed and waited. "I'm here," he said. "There are two of us. Can we help you?"

A small black woman emerged from the darkness, a fragile shadow in the starlight. "My car has stopped . . ."

Ammon shrugged. "So has ours," he answered carefully. "I'm sure everything's going to be okay, though. Sometime soon, they'll send some help." He was lying now and he knew it and his voice cracked because he wasn't any good at it. "Don't worry; I'm sure everything will be just—"

"No," the woman interrupted him. "Look around you. Everything has stopped. No cars. No lights. It's like there's nothing out there." She gestured around her with her arms. "It isn't right." She was silent a long moment, then took a step toward him, looking at his face. "I don't know what to do now. Please, I have two daughters . . ."

Ammon looked past the small woman, searching for her daughters, but there was no one there.

Mary Shaye Dupree reached out to him. "I was coming

back from a special clinic down in Columbus when my car stopped." She looked around. "I have a little girl. She is sick. I've got to get her home."

Luke bit his lip as he moved to her side. "I'm sorry, but that's going to be a little difficult right now. But I'm sure—"

"She's got to have her medication. I only brought enough for two days. If I don't get her home, if she doesn't get her medication . . ." her voice slowly trailed off.

Luke shifted on his feet, a heavy weight seeming to fall on him. Things were bad enough with just the three of them. What could they do for her? "Your daughter, is she okay?" he asked, sensing Mary's anguish.

"No. No, she's not. Please, can you help me?"

Ammon's jaw tightened up as he turned to Luke. His brother stood back, unsure of what to do.

Mary watched them hopefully. Then, sensing their helplessness and indecision, she reached up, covered her mouth, and breathed deeply, her shoulders shivering with despair.

chapter twenty-two

EAST SIDE, CHICAGO, ILLINOIS

It was early evening and the sun had just set outside. Azadeh walked into the living room and stood again. She turned toward the television, but couldn't figure out how to turn it on, the remote control far more complicated than anything she had ever worked before. She sat down and read through the remains of the newspaper, reading aloud to practice, pronouncing every word as carefully and correctly as she could. From time to time she came upon a word she didn't know and pulled out an English-Farsi dictionary to look it up. *Legislator.* She didn't know that one. She turned for her dictionary again . . .

The lights went out suddenly.

She sat without moving at the kitchen table. The apartment was dark. Completely dark. No light bled in from the streetlights outside.

She waited, unsure of what to do.

Five minutes passed.

She heard voices in the hallway. Angry voices. Shouting voices. Somewhere in the rooms above her, she heard the pounding of heavy footsteps running back and forth.

Still no lights. The room was quiet.

She stood up and moved toward the window that looked out on the city.

She saw the brick-and-mortar wall before her. Standing to the side, she looked from the corner of the window past the brick wall to the city streets below.

All she saw was utter darkness. No streetlights. No car lights. No light at all.

Everything around her, for as far as she could see, was an absolute black hole.

"And the time speedily cometh that great things are to be shown forth unto the children of men."

—DOCTRINE AND COVENANTS 35:10

chapter twenty-three

Sam Brighton stood in the aisle of the D.C. Metro, holding the overhead bar that ran down the center aisle of the train. Bono stood beside him, his head down, completely lost in his thoughts. Every few minutes, Bono glanced at his watch.

Sam watched him. "Dude, you really didn't need to do this," he said for the third or fourth time. "Go on. Go home to your family. They need you a lot more than I do."

Bono looked up and forced himself to smile. "This won't take much time," he said.

"You're crazy, man. Stupid of you to stay here when you could be on your way home to your wife."

Bono didn't answer.

The Metro train hummed along, sixty feet under the ground, heading to the northwestern suburbs. The two men were quiet. Sam read the advertisements above the seats. *Wicked* was scheduled at the Kennedy Center downtown. The Washington Wizards were playing at home for the weekend. *Not anymore,* he frowned to himself.

Upon their return to the United States just a few hours

before, the two men had been given two weeks' leave. Sam needed the time to try to find his family. Bono planned to hop the train up to Baltimore (the closest place he could find where he could still rent a car), then drive like a madman to his in-laws' place in Memphis, where his wife had taken their little girl after the explosion in D.C. He glanced at his watch again and calculated in his mind. A three-hour train ride to Baltimore. A fifteen-hour drive from there. Eighteen hours to get to his family, *if* he didn't run into problems and if he could find the gas.

Eighteen hours to get home, leaving a little less than twelve days to be together with his beautiful wife and the little girl who was the spitting image of her mom.

Sam read his friend's thoughts by the faraway look in his eye. "Listen, dude, I don't need you to baby-sit me," he said. "Go on. Your wife is waiting!"

"She understands," Bono said.

"You've been gone for months! You've only got a few days to be with her. What are you doing here!"

Bono lowered his head and didn't answer.

Sam tried a final time. "I really don't need you—"

Bono cut him off with a sudden lift of his eyes. "Listen, man, you don't know anything about your family. You don't know if they're alive or if they're dead. Now, do you really think I'm going to leave you here to do this alone? Do you think I *could* do that? Come on, give me a little credit. My wife's okay. She's alive, man, I know that, same for my little girl. You don't know about your mom or your brothers. Do you really think I'm going to take off and leave until we know if they're okay? I'm not like that."

Bono's voice was firm, almost hard, and Sam knew it was time to back off.

The two men rode in silence. The train was quiet and

smooth and it was easy for Sam to lower his head and lose himself in his thoughts.

Half a minute passed.

Bono kept his head low. "She understands," he said again.

Sam looked up but didn't say anything.

"My wife understands I have to help you." Bono seemed to be talking to himself. "She wouldn't leave you to do this alone. Neither one of us would."

Sam looked away and swallowed as he watched the passing subway tunnel's cement walls and flashing blocks of yellow light.

"Thanks, Bono," he whispered after a minute had passed.

"Sure thing, dude."

Sam glanced at the rows of multicolored plastic benches on his left and right. The subway car was clean and almost completely deserted. Most of the outlying Metro lines that ran around D.C. were still operating—only the lines that ran to or through what used to be downtown had been destroyed—but few people had the guts or a reason to ride the subway anymore. Sam shook his head, amazed at the fact that the Metro ran at all. Mussolini would have been proud: The downtown district was destroyed, a quarter of a million people had died, the government was hardly working, but the trains were running and were running on time. He laughed at what he considered a fairly pointless gesture of public relations, knowing it was a fabrication mostly for the benefit of the citizens who lived outside of D.C.

Give us a few weeks and we'll have everything back in order. Things will be the same soon. Just give us a little time. That was the government line.

But no one was buying it.

Everyone knew things would never be the same.

He shifted his eyes to the back of the Metro. A large black

woman sat near the door, her dark eyes closed, her hands clutching a leather handbag. Sam could see a bulge from the inside of the handbag and guessed what it was—many of the people who dared to venture out now were armed—and he touched the 9mm Glock strapped under his military jacket. A black man stood on the other end of the Metro car, his dark suit a striking contrast to the dirty running shoes on his feet. Walking had become the norm for the survivors of D.C. and no one wanted to hike for miles in dress shoes.

So it seemed that the people were adjusting—walking shoes or boots with suits, backpacks and briefcases with food and water instead of laptops and business reports, cash in their pockets, white masks across their faces to keep back the smoke and dust.

The train rolled gently into a turn, the underground tunnel lights slipping by. Although the car was nearly empty, Sam was happy to stand; he'd been sitting for most of the past fifty hours, in military terminals, on board crowded aircraft, inside military vans. The last thing he wanted to do was sit.

Bono looked up and asked, "How far is it from the Metro station to your home?"

"Couple miles." Sam nudged the military backpack at his feet. "Nothing but a brisk walk through the park."

An identical backpack rested against Bono's knee. Sam and the lieutenant were prepared for pretty much anything. They had food, water, guns, passports, military orders, nightsticks, a change of clothes; they could get by on their own. At the next Metro stop they would hoist the backpacks, start out at a gentle jog, and be at Sam's parents' house within sixteen minutes. An eight-minute-a-mile pace, loaded with guns and packs. No problem for either one.

Sam adjusted his combat fatigues. The camouflage design was tight and small and much greener than the pattern on the camouflage uniforms that the soldiers used to wear. He reached up and fingered the single lieutenant's bar on the right lapel of his jacket.

Bono watched him. "How's it feel?" he asked.

"About the same," Sam shrugged.

"But it isn't the same, Sam. You're an officer. You're the leader. Your men will be watching and following you."

"I'll do the best I can, Bono."

"I know you will. Which is why I pushed for the battlefield commission. The men already follow you."

Sam pulled again on the lieutenant's bar.

"Your dad would have been proud."

Sam nodded slowly. "Roger that," he said.

"Your mom's going to be proud too. When we find her and your brothers, they're going to freak. *Lieutenant* Samuel Brighton. She's going to think that's cool."

Sam pressed his lips together and nodded. "I think you're right," he said.

The train pitched suddenly and the locomotive engine rolled back. The cars decelerated, and the men had to grab the handhold to brace themselves.

The train continued slowing.

Then the lights went out.

It grew very quiet.

Pitch dark spread around them as the train rolled to a complete stop.

chapter twenty-four

The emergency lights kicked on, illuminating the Metro car in yellow light. Sixty feet underground, the electrical circuits on the train had been protected from the enormously powerful surge of deadly power that had just burst down from the upper atmosphere, leaving the Metro's batteries and emergency lighting circuits intact to illuminate the cars.

For a moment, no one moved. The train was still as stone. The woman kept her seat, looking around in bewilderment. She clasped her bag even tighter, and Sam wondered briefly what precious thing she kept inside. The black man at the back of the Metro car turned toward them. Sam and Bono stood in place.

Five . . . ten . . . twenty seconds of silence. Everyone expected the normal car lights to come up and the train to lurch forward and resume traveling again at any moment.

A full minute of silence passed before Bono turned to Sam and asked, "How often does this happen?"

Sam shook his head. "Never," he answered quickly,

nodding toward the emergency lights. "This isn't a delay or traffic problem. This train shut completely down."

A recording started playing through the speakers over their heads. "We are experiencing a momentary delay. Please remain in your seats. DO NOT EXIT FROM THE TRAIN. We will be moving shortly. If necessary, there is an emergency telephone to the conductor at the back of the car."

The black man swore and thrust his hands into his pockets. Sam turned to him. "You from around here?" he asked.

The man hesitated, then nodded.

"You always ride the Metro?"

"Every day until the big one."

"You ever had this thing shut down like this before?"

The man shook his head.

Sam turned to Bono, then moved toward the emergency telephone at the back of the car. Bono followed him and listened as he spoke. The conversation was very short.

"What's up?" Bono asked when Sam replaced the red handset.

"Conductor says it's just a momentary delay."

Bono shook his head and looked at the dim emergency lighting around him. "I don't think so," he said.

Pushing by Sam, he picked up the phone receiver. No numbers or buttons to push, just a direct line to the conductor's station at the front of the train. "This is Lieutenant Calton," he said, his voice commanding, "United States Army Special Forces. You've got two soldiers back here on official leave and we need to know what's going on."

Sam turned away and pulled out his cell phone. Flipping it open, he saw there was no signal. He turned to the black man, who had pulled out his phone too. "Can you usually get a signal here?"

"Yeah," the man grunted. "They put cell relays through

most of the Metro tunnels. Some of the tunnels out in Maryland, you can't get a signal, but here in Virginia you always could."

Sam looked at his cell phone again. *Searching for signal* flashed across his screen.

Bono hung up the phone, moved toward him, and lowered his voice. "Conductor says they've lost all electrical power."

"On just this train?"

"No. The entire grid." Bono looked around. "The whole system has shut down." He leaned a little closer. "He says he can't get a hold of anyone upstairs . . ."

Sam shook his head in rage. "Another nuclear detonation!"

Bono caught his arm. "I don't think so. It makes no sense to bomb a bunch of rubble. And we would have felt it, some kind of vibration, a noise, our ears would have popped from the surge of pressure through the tunnel. No, we would have had some indication if there'd been another detonation. This has to be something else."

Sam was moving to his backpack. Bono turned to the other people in the car. The black woman was standing now, her eyes dark and pleading. "Listen to me," he started, "I don't know what to tell you. I don't know what you should do. The conductor told me they have lost all power through the electrical grid. Right now, he can't get in contact with anyone up top. You probably ought to just stay here. Someone is going to come along eventually. If they can't get the train moving, they'll send rescue units down."

The black man watched Sam hoist his pack onto his back. "You're telling us to stay here," he countered, "yet I see you're bugging out."

"I'm not telling you to do anything," Bono answered. "I

don't know any more than you do, and I don't have any authority to tell you what to do anyway. I'm just saying if I were you I'd probably stay."

The man looked suspicious. "What *aren't* you telling us!" he demanded.

Sam slid Bono's pack across the floor, and he reached for it. "I'm straight up with you, buddy. I've got no reason to lie. And I'm not telling you what to do or even giving you advice. But think about the situation. We're, what . . . three or four miles from the next station? We're underground. It's going to be dark. I don't know what the track does up ahead. Does it narrow? Will another train come? If they restore power and we're touching the third rail, are they going to find us smoking like a barbecue on the Fourth of July? You make your own decision; I'm just saying that if I were you I'd probably stick it out here."

Sam tightened his pack and moved toward the door. Prying with his fingers, he forced one of the doors back. A warning chime started sounding overhead. He held a flashlight in his hand.

The man's forehead creased into a scowl. "You say it's too dangerous out there to make it on our own?"

"I'm saying you should do whatever you think is best."

"But you're going out there."

Bono shrugged. "We're Army Special Forces."

The man stared, but didn't answer.

Bono didn't need to say any more.

*   *   *

Sam held the flashlight, keeping the beam low enough to illuminate the way for both him and Bono, allowing them to move with only one light. They stood on a narrow, blackened, cement walkway that ran parallel to the heavy tracks. They looked left and saw nothing but a black hole as the subway tunnel extended behind them. None of the other passengers had gotten out of the cars. They turned and started walking toward the front of the train. The curb was narrow and the wall scraped Sam's shoulders as he walked. He pointed the flashlight forward. The train extended into the dark, each car illuminated by the emergency lighting. Sam noticed that the boxy lights built into the walls of the cement subway had grown dark. A few of the passengers saw them and pointed as they walked by. Seven cars ahead, they reached the electric locomotive. The engineer sat in a small booth behind a thick window. Sam stopped beside the engineer's station and the conductor pushed the window back. "Get back inside the cars. Help is on the way," he said.

"You've talked to someone?" Bono asked.

The engineer hesitated. "Not yet. But it's just a matter of time. And let me tell you something, boys, you don't want to be in the tunnel when the trains start to run. You know how many idiots get killed like that every year?"

Sam nodded down-track. "How far to the next station?"

"Farther than you can walk before the trains start running again."

"How far might that be, sir?"

"Don't be stupid," the train driver shot back. "You go wandering off down the tracks and you screw it up for all of us. If we've got people on the tracks I have to report it. That means they shut the whole line down. Which means we'll all have to sit here until Metro Security runs you two boneheads down and gets you off the tracks. Now go on, get back inside the car, and we'll be out of here in no time."

"You really think so?" Bono asked him.

The driver hesitated. "Of course I do."

"I think you're kidding yourself," Bono answered. "I think

you know we're in deep do-do here. I think you know we're going to have to find our own way out. You just haven't quite come to grips with that yet. But think about it, sir. No communications with anyone upstairs. No power of any kind anywhere on the grid. Your entire system shut down. This isn't a matter of changing a circuit breaker and getting back on our way."

The engineer grunted but didn't say anything.

"How far to the station?" Sam asked again.

The driver thought, then answered slowly. "Three miles. Maybe a little more. Hope I don't run you over as I go speeding by."

"We do too. Now good luck to you, sir."

The soldiers turned, tightened the chest straps on their backpacks, and started running. Sam held the single light and they stayed close together, sharing the narrow beam as they ran.

Their breathing was heavy but evenly paced as they settled into stride. Sam checked his watch, estimating the time until they emerged at the station.

chapter twenty-five

Sara moved through the deep darkness toward the black woman and put her arm around her shoulders. The silver beads at the tips of her tightly braided hair glistened in the moonlight. Ammon and Luke stood back, relieved to have their mother there. "My name is Sara Brighton," Sara said, holding Mary's arm. "Can you tell me who you are?"

The black woman stiffened under Sara's touch, glanced toward her quickly, but kept her head low. Her guard instinctively up, she took a suspicious step back, aware of Sara's pale skin shining in the dim light. Her mother, a good Christian woman, had taught her from the time she was old enough to walk that all were God's children and she had no room to judge. But a lifetime of hard conditioning and bad experiences had also taught her to be careful when it came to people not of her race.

Then she thought of her sick daughter, and her fear of the strangers was quickly swallowed up. "My name is Mary Dupree," she answered softly.

Ammon stepped forward and shook hands, introducing

himself with a smile, feeling the weak tremble in Mary's fingers. Luke waved a hello.

Mary studied them: Luke in his baggy shorts, sandals, and T-shirt; Ammon in Levi's, hiking boots, and dark jacket. Nice-looking boys, she thought, but not city kids, that was certain.

"I was down in Columbus," she explained as she turned back to Sara. "I have a little girl. She's very sick."

"Sick? You mean like with the flu or something?"

"No, ma'am." Mary stopped and cleared her throat. "I wish that's all it was. You don't know what I would give . . ." Her voice was very quiet now. "No, ma'am," she repeated, straightening her back, "my baby's suffering with cancer. We were down at a special clinic for her last treatment, but the doctors wouldn't even do it. They said that it was too . . ." She stopped once again, looking off. "Too late," she concluded.

Sara listened, understanding, her mouth hanging open in shock. Ammon turned to Luke and gritted his teeth in sympathy, unsure of what to say.

"Where's your daughter now?" Sara asked.

Mary pointed behind her. "Back in my car."

"And your husband? Is he with you?"

"My husband passed away ten years ago last Tuesday."

Sara noted Mary's immediate remembrance of the date. She now knew from experience what that meant. "I'm sorry," she answered quickly before turning to Ammon and Luke. "Guys, we need to help Mrs. Dupree, don't you think?"

Luke shot an uncomfortable look at Ammon and hesitated before answering, "Of course, Mom."

"Let's go check on her daughter. That's the first thing we need to do."

"Cool, Mom. For sure." He turned to Ammon. "I'll get a flashlight."

"I doubt it will work now," Ammon said.

"Why's that?"

Ammon shot a glance toward the timid-looking woman at his side. "Later," he whispered.

Luke hesitated, still not understanding. "Won't hurt to try," he said as he moved around the car and reached into the backseat. Working his way in the dark, he found a flashlight and pulled it out. He pressed the switch and got nothing.

"Come on," Ammon said.

Luke flipped the switch again and again, then started unscrewing the lightbulb end of the flashlight.

"Come on," Ammon repeated and started walking.

The four adults moved through the night, walking slowly, their hands reaching out in front of them as they walked toward Mary's car.

*   *   *

Later, they stood in conference outside the car. The moon, bloody and red, had climbed toward its southern apex and the wind was picking up. Enough time had passed that their eyes had adjusted to the dark and what before had been only darkness was revealed now in shadows of gray and black.

"All right, what we gonna do?" Luke asked. He spoke softly, afraid of waking the little girl who was sleeping in the backseat of the car. Sara looked through the window, a worried expression on her face. The child should have been in an ambulance. It was ridiculous that, weak and sick as she was, she had been transported by private car. Sara raged at the sight of the fragile child hunched against the backseat, her knees pulled up to her chest, her shoulders trembling weakly from the cold. Mary had placed a small sweater over her, but that was all she had.

"She's a beautiful little girl," Sara said as she stared at the child.

"She's an angel," Mary answered. "You just don't know what kind of girl she really is."

Sara nodded to her sons. "My kids are hardly babies, Mary, but I think I understand how you feel about your daughter."

Mary looked at the young men standing beside their mother. "They look like good boys," she said.

Sara opened the back door and reached in, tucking the small sweater more closely around the little girl's shoulders. "What's her name?" she asked.

"Kelly Beth."

Sara stood and turned to Luke. "How cold is it right now, do you think?"

"I don't know, Mom, somewhere in the fifties, I would guess."

"How cold's it going to get tonight?"

"Colder. Not too bad, but it won't be comfortable."

Sara turned to Mary. "Do you have anything with you, blankets or whatever?"

Mary shook her head. "I don't know. I don't think so. It isn't even my car. I had to borrow it from a friend to get down here. My car is such a beater, I didn't think it would make it. I brought that sweater, but I wasn't planning on . . . you know . . . I wasn't thinking we would have to . . ."

"I understand," Sara said, placing her hand on Mary's arm. "Don't worry, Mary, we'll work this out."

Ammon moved toward her. "Have you got the key?"

"It's in the ignition," Mary told him. Ammon walked around the side of the car, opened the door, and reached in. Just for grins he turned the key, getting nothing. He pulled it out and moved around to the trunk. Feeling for the keyhole with his fingers, he inserted the key and turned it, and the trunk lid popped open. Luke pushed it up. They stared for a moment, unable to see anything in the dark. Ammon reached in and started feeling, announcing what he touched: "An old tire. What's this? Feels like a wheelchair. Lots of dirt. A rusted jack, I think. Couple empty grocery sacks. A little garbage." He stood. "I think that's it."

"Nothing we can use?" Sara pressed him.

Luke pushed the trunk closed. "I don't think so, Mom."

Sara thought. "Okay," she said. "What does everyone think?" Her two sons huddled close around her. Mary stood apart, but Sara turned to draw her in. "Mary?" she asked.

Mary hesitated, unsure. She didn't feel like she belonged inside the circle of the family; that was obvious from the uncomfortable expression on her face.

"Mary, listen to me, okay?" Sara said as the small woman held back. "I don't know what's going on here. We're just like you—we were driving down the road when the same thing happened to our car. I think that Ammon," she nodded toward her son, "has an idea what has happened, but he hasn't even had time to explain it to us yet. We'll get to that soon enough. But I want you to know that, no matter what has happened, or what's going to happen after this, we will not leave you alone here. You understand that? We're not going to leave you alone. We're not going to leave Kelly Beth. We're going to stay with you, take you with us—whatever we do, we can stay together as long as you need. I mean that, Mary. We're not the kind of people who would just leave you and Kelly Beth out here by yourselves."

Mary stood in the dim moonlight, her face tight, almost stunned. "Do you really mean that?" she asked.

"I really do."

"You don't even know me. You don't know Kelly. Why would you even care?"

Sara shrugged.

Luke patted the dead flashlight against the palm of his

hand. "My mom's the kind of person who's been dragging lost puppies home all her life." He shrugged. "She's just a good person."

Mary lightened, her face relaxing just a bit. "You a church-going family?" she wondered.

"Every week," Luke smiled. "Rain or shine. Super Bowl, hurricanes, typhoid fever, whatever, Mom's got us there."

"You are . . . ?"

"We are Christians, Mary," Sara answered. "That's all that matters. We believe in and follow Christ."

Mary hugged her arms around herself and lifted her eyes toward the stars. "Thank you, Goodly Father," she said out loud. "Thanks for sending these people here to help me. Thanks for not leaving me and Kelly Beth alone."

Sara waited a moment, then turned to Ammon. "Tell us about the EMP," she said.

He hesitated. "I don't know that much."

"Then just tell us what you can."

Ammon shifted from one foot to the other. It was getting late and colder now. As they stood, they heard occasional voices up and down the freeway and saw, or really sensed, faint gray movement against the starlight. Luke kept turning toward the shouting voices, but no one came their way.

Ammon cleared his throat. "Okay, it's called an EMP. Electromagnetic pulse. It's caused when a nuclear warhead is detonated high in the air, almost out in space, I think. Dad and I talked about it a couple of times. Then I read a little about it. I could tell it was one of the few things that really scared him, so I wanted to know. There's tons of information on the Internet, but I don't remember all that much. I do remember Dad telling me he thought it was the most likely and most deadly thing that could happen to the United States. Remember last winter when we were skiing up in Vermont, that one night he and I stayed up and talked, looking at the Northern Lights? He told me then that he thought an EMP could kill half of the people in the United States."

"Half!" Luke answered. "Come on, dude. Really? Half!"

Ammon shrugged his shoulders. "I'm pretty sure that's what he said."

"Are you saying that half of all Americans are dead right now? I mean, what happened to us? Why didn't any of us die?"

"No, no," Ammon answered. "That's not how it works. The nuke goes off in space, really high up there, somewhere over the country. It sends out a powerful force of electrons or protons or magic stuff, I don't know, all I know is the electromagnetic pulse reaches down to earth and fries all the electrical circuits in everything we have, from toasters to computers to electrical cables, cars . . ." he nodded to the dead flashlight in Luke's hand . . . "pretty much everything is gone."

"But it doesn't kill anyone? That seems kind of pointless as a weapon, then."

"No, dude, think! If that's what really happened, then we just got sent back to the preindustrial world. Look at us! Is there any better illustration? We're stuck out here on the freeway. Our cars won't work. We've got no cell phones, no radios. What are we going to eat . . . I know, I know, we've got a little with us, but enough to get us through the winter? I don't think so. Where are we going to go? How are we going to get there? Water? Sanitation? At least the pioneers had cows and horses and oxen and stuff. We've got nothing, Luke, nothing but what we stuffed in our car. What if this has happened all over the country? Can you see it? You get the picture? How are we, how is America, going to even feed itself?"

Luke swallowed. "No kidding." He was whispering now.

"Yeah, no kidding."

Sara put her hand to her mouth. "Is it really that bad, Ammon?"

Ammon shook his head, his blond hair catching the moonlight. Standing beside Sara, he towered over her. "I don't know, Mom, but it kind of looks that way."

Mary's face hadn't changed. She simply didn't understand. EMPs? Electrical circuits? It made no sense at all to her.

"What are we going to do, then?" Sara asked.

Ammon looked around. "We've got to change our thinking, and we've got to change it right away. This isn't a matter of trying to figure out how to make it through the night. It isn't going to be any better in the morning. No one's going to send out the cavalry to help us. We need to plan. We need to think. And we have to realize that we might have to get through this alone."

Sara walked two steps away and stared into the darkness before turning back. "But it might not be that bad, right? I mean, we don't know for sure it was an EMP. We don't know for certain. It could have been something else. It might be something as simple as—"

"What, Mom? What else could it be! The entire countryside is dark." He gestured toward the glowing lights of Chicago that were no longer there. "Our car, our cell phones, our flashlights. Every car around us . . ."

"No, Ammon, I'm just not ready to believe that we are completely alone in this. Help will come. There might be other parts of the country that weren't hit. There are other countries, other nations . . ."

"Help is months away, Mom. Weeks away, at the *very* earliest. Consider what we're asking! It's an impossible task. How do you feed three hundred million people? How do you get them water? How do you even keep them warm? And the truth is that real help might not *ever* come.

"Think about it, Mom. Think about Hurricane Katrina. That was *one* city that was hit, a couple hundred thousand people. The rest of the nation was unaffected except for some other areas along the Gulf Coast. The federal government was functioning—it hadn't just been hit by a nuke over Washington, D.C. Yet look what happened down there. It took days to get even the most basic things, days to provide food and water. Months to bring back power. Years to clean up the mess. That was *one city*, Mom, helped by the rest of the entire nation, yet look how long it took.

"Reverse that now. We've got no national government left to speak of, no state or local people who are going to be able to help. They're stranded just like we are.

"So let's say that maybe part of the nation wasn't hit. Let's suppose help is coming, and suppose that by some miracle it could get here in a few weeks—which I honestly, no-kidding, really doubt is going to happen, but let's say that it does. That still leaves, what, a third of the country, a hundred million people, fending for themselves for three or four weeks. Winter is coming on. It's already getting cold at night. No food. No water. No doctors or hospitals. People are, you know, kind of getting weird already after the bomb in D.C. This isn't going to help that. It will be a crazy four weeks."

Sara squared her shoulders. "No, Ammon, it can't be. I just don't believe it's going to all come crashing down."

"Mom, I love you, you know that, and I respect you more than any living person in this world. I love your optimism and faith, the way you carry us and make us press on. But this isn't something that's just going to go away. This isn't something we're going to be delivered from. We get *through* this, not around it. We get through this—and we will—but the only way to do it is if we're careful and we think."

The small group was silent, the four of them lost in

thought. "Okay, then," Luke finally said. "What's the first thing we do?"

Ammon bit his lip and turned to his twin brother. "First thing, we stay together. Second thing, we protect our stuff." He gestured down the off-ramp toward their car, a hundred yards away. "The equipment in our car is our only lifeline. It's everything we have, but it might be enough to see us through."

No one answered.

"Okay," Ammon pressed them. "Everyone cool with that so far?"

"Yeah, sounds good," Luke replied.

Mary moved toward Ammon, her voice apologetic. "I'm sorry, I'm sorry, but I simply can't stay here. I've got to get my daughter home. I've got to get her medications."

"I understand," Ammon said. "But we can't do anything until morning. The last thing we want to do is to go wandering off into the night. Let's push your car onto the shoulder— maybe *someone* will come along—then split up our blankets and our sleeping bags." He turned to Luke. "You and Mom sleep in our Honda. I'll stay here with Mrs. Dupree."

Mary hesitated. "But tomorrow, I'll be home, right? We'll go to my apartment in the city. It isn't very far. Someone is waiting for me there. She won't understand what's going on. She's only been here in the country for a few days—"

They heard the sudden crash of breaking glass coming from behind them, farther down the road, the sound harsh and jarring against the silence of the night.

They stopped talking. No one moved.

Shouting. Cries of laughter. Another crash. The sound of scattering glass.

They turned toward the crashing.

"That's our car!" Ammon breathed. "Someone's breaking in!"

Sara's hands shot to her mouth, her mind racing. All their food. All that money. Their water! Their clothes and sleeping bags. She gasped and took a step back. *What if they had a gun! What if they found the gun hidden under the front seat of the car!* "Oh no!" she mumbled in horror.

"HEY!" Ammon shouted through the darkness. "HEY THERE! THAT'S MY CAR! WHAT ARE YOU DOING!"

Heavy silence for a moment.

They waited and listened.

"HEY!" Ammon shouted again.

Another crashing sound. Another broken window. "Look at all this!" they heard a man say. "Come on. I need some help!"

Sara groaned. All of their work and preparation. Everything might be lost!

Ammon shook, his hands balled into fists. Luke started running toward their car. "Come on, Ammon," he cried.

"No." Ammon ran to catch up and pull him back.

Luke pushed his arm away. "We can't just let them take it. We need it to survive!"

"What are you thinking, Luke!" Sara hissed as she ran toward her sons, fearful the thieves might hear them talking in the dark. "What are you going to do?" She grabbed her son. "Go attack them? Get into a fight? No, we'll let them take it! You understand me, Luke? Ammon? It's not worth getting killed for."

Ammon shook his head in anger. "Yes, Mom, it *is*. Everything we need to survive is in that car. We live or die over the next few weeks depending on what we do right now." He stopped, dropping a shoulder toward the sleeping child. "And that little girl," he whispered, leaning toward his mom, "look at her, Mom. She's freezing. She's sick, we can all see that, but I don't think Mary realizes how *really* sick she is. We need our blankets, our water, some of the food. If we're going to help her, we've got to have something to take care of her with."

Luke was glaring toward their car. No more crashing glass and no more laughing. "Come on," he said. "We'll rush them together from the darkness. They'll never see it coming. We can take them, Ammon."

"No!" Sara cried softly. "What if they have a gun!"

"It's okay, Mom," Luke whispered, trying to reassure her. "They're just a couple goons whose car stopped and they started walking, just like us. They saw our stuff and decided they'd take it. We can take them, I'm sure."

"I don't know," Ammon countered. "We don't know that for certain, Luke. Like I said before, things have changed now, and we've got to be smart."

"So?" Luke asked his brother.

Ammon turned to the women. "This is what we're going to do," he said.

chapter twenty-six

Aquarter mile before the station, the Metro tracks began to slope gently upward. Soon they emerged from the tunnel to ground level.

It was dark. Very dark. Not a light could be found anywhere in the city. Sam instinctively glanced up, looking for the North Star. The sky was clear and bright with a hundred million stars. For a moment he thought he was back in the desert, miles from the nearest city, there was so little light around. Then he stopped, his mind racing as a knot of fear began to form inside his gut.

Bono stopped beside him. Sam moved his flashlight left and right. A ten-foot, razor-topped fence ran parallel to the tracks. Beyond the fence, on both sides, there was a freeway. They were in the median. The train station was ahead.

They heard voices all around them. From the station. From the road. But there were no lights, no moving cars, no streetlights, no headlights, no lights in the windows of the buildings that rose up on either side.

"Oh no . . . oh no . . ." Bono started to mutter.

Sam shot him a look of confusion. "It can't be," he answered. "There's no way it's what you're thinking!"

Bono stopped and swore. His face was crunched with frustration, his lips tight. "No, no, no!" he repeated, his voice weak. "Do you understand what this means, Sam! Do you know what this is?"

Sam thought only a moment. "EMP," he answered, his voice sick with dread.

Bono turned a slow circle, concentrating on the utter darkness all around him. He checked his cell phone. No signal. He looked down the freeway. Not a single car moved. The moon was a bright red, and his eyes were adjusting to the darkness. Through the fence he saw a stalled ambulance on the eastbound lane. The back door was open and there was movement around it, men in scrubs, and a wheeled gurney on the ground. "Welcome to 1850," he said.

Sam looked at him. "Can it really be that bad?"

"Look around you."

"I don't think—"

"You have no idea," Bono cut him off tartly. "You have absolutely no idea. None of us do."

The two men stood in silence. Bono reached into a side pocket on his pack and pulled out a narrow flashlight.

"Save it," Sam told him. "Getting batteries is about to become a huge issue. We'll need to save the light." He flipped off his own flashlight, letting his eyes get used to the dark.

"I thought the EMP would fry the circuits?"

"We were underground," Sam explained. "Our gear has been protected."

"So our cell phones will work."

"Yeah, but all of the cell towers and circuits above ground will be fried. They'll make good paperweights, but that's about all they're worth right now." He pulled his cell from his pocket and started a throwing gesture, but Bono caught his arm.

"Keep it," he told him. "For one thing, you've got a good battery and good circuits. Who knows what that's worth? More important, they most likely positioned the nuclear detonations to hit the east coast. The interior of the country, the south, out west maybe, it might not be so bad."

Sam grunted, turned off his phone to save the battery, and shoved it away.

A woman came toward them from the freeway on their right. "Who is that?" she called desperately. "Where did you get that light? What's going on here?" She pulled herself over the cement guardrail and moved toward them. "I've got my babies in the car with me—we're trying to make our way up to Philly to my mom's place." She got close enough to see their uniforms. "Russian soldiers!" she cried and stepped back, her face tight with fear.

Sam ignored her. What did she think this was, a Hollywood script? "Come on, Bono, let's go," he said.

Turning, they ran parallel to the fence, heading toward the station a little more than a thousand feet ahead.

The platforms rose on each side. It was crowded, a hundred people mulling here and there. The two soldiers emerged from the darkness, Sam's flashlight illuminating the way. They stopped at the cement barricade and climbed onto the platform. Sam stood and looked around. "What do we do?" he asked.

Bono didn't hesitate. "Your mom's house," he said. "That's why we came here, and that mission hasn't changed. We go there, see what's up, and then form a plan."

Sam didn't move, his mind racing. EMP. No electrical grid. Every car with electronic ignition, basically everything made after 1978 or so, would be inoperable. No jets. No transportation. No phones. No mail. No gas. No food. Soon no water. No medical equipment that couldn't be operated by hand. No TV, radio, newspapers, Internet. Nothing. It was as if the entire nation had been transported back in time. Then he thought of Bono's wife and little girl, the two of them waiting for him a little more than seven hundred miles to the west.

But now . . . with all this . . . how was he going to get to Memphis? Sam shook his head sadly.

Bono *wasn't* going to get there. He wasn't going home.

He swallowed hard, feeling responsible again for keeping Bono away from his family. "Bono, I'm so, so sorry, man . . ."

Bono knew what Sam was thinking. His mind was on the same thing.

"This is better anyway," Bono struggled to say. "I would have been out there on my own. Who knows where, who knows under what circumstances? The last place I'd like to be after an EMP is out on the road. It's better that I'm here."

Sam shook his head. He didn't buy it. Every mile, any mile, toward his wife would have been preferable to this. "There's got to be a way," he stammered. "There's got to be a way to get you down to Memphis, Bono. We're going to get you there. I swear to you, baby, we're going to get you home."

Bono shook his head. "It isn't going to happen."

"Yes it is, man. There's got to be a way."

"I could walk there. That would only take a month."

"No, Bono, we're going to get you home."

"Come on," Bono said. "We'll think about that later. Right now, let's get to your parents' place."

He glanced around the platform, the hair rising on his neck. Something about it, something evil, made him shiver as he stood in the middle of the anxious crowd. Living under constant threat to his life had developed his sense of danger, and his senses were screaming now. There was no reason or explanation, but he had learned to trust the quiet voice inside his head. He had felt it and listened to it many times over the previous years, and he knew he was alive now because of it. "It's a dangerous time right now," he said, his survival instincts kicking into gear. "None of these people have any idea what is going on, but they'll expect the worst case and they'll act accordingly. Everyone goes bonkers when the lights go out, you know what I'm saying, especially after what happened in D.C. It's every man for himself right now. We'd better get off the streets."

Sam turned and started walking. "This way," he said.

Forty feet down the platform, a group of men started moving toward them. The four men approached together, their shoulders touching, their eyes staring straight ahead, dull and lifeless. Two wore shaved heads. Lots of homemade tattoos were scattered over their flesh. One of them had to be a meth-head: his lips were dry and cracked, his front teeth rotting, his face thin and taut, his eye sockets sunk deeply into his skull. His skin, wrinkled as an old man's, made him look like walking death.

Sam stepped aside to avoid them but the four men adjusted their path, moving to confront the two soldiers. They bumped into Sam with great force, almost knocking him over. He stumbled and caught himself. "Watch it!" Meth-man said.

Sam ignored him and turned to let them pass. Bono quickly moved to stand beside him.

"I said freaking watch it!" Meth-man cried again. His eyes were wild now, burning bright and crazy. Whatever demons were inside him were screaming in his head.

"Take it easy," Sam replied, his voice soft. "I don't want any trouble here, okay? It's cool, man, it's all good. You guys have a great night."

One of the skinheads reached into his pocket. "Who the bloody 'ey are you talking to!" he cried.

"Great," Sam muttered sarcastically but loudly enough to be heard. "We stinking lose our electricity and all the freaks spill out into the streets."

"Come on," Bono answered carefully. Pulling on Sam's shoulders, he took a wary step back. Sam felt the pressure of Bono's grip and almost grimaced at the pain. Bono was scared; Sam could feel it in the force of his steely grip.

Meth-man reached under his jacket, apparently for a weapon, but Bono didn't give him a chance. Half a second later, the soldier's pearl-handled pistol was in his hand. He took a lightning step forward and shoved it into Meth-man's face, nudging the cold steel into the fleshy skin between his eyes. One of the skinheads moved and Sam lurched forward, grabbed his arm, twisted, and bent it while jerking his knee up into the attacker's elbow. The bone snapped with a sickening *crunch* and the man fell back, screaming in pain. The other men backed up ten steps, removing themselves from the fight. Meth-man screamed while dropping to his knees. "Don't hurt us, don't hurt us," he cried in pretended pain. "U.S. soldiers like to kill us. *Please* don't hurt us. We are sorry. Please, do you have to be so *mean!*"

Sam listened, completely disgusted, as Bono shoved the gun again, forcing the tiny barrel into the man's skin.

"Stand up. Turn around. Walk away!" Bono commanded in a powerful voice. Something about the way he said it caught Sam's attention—it was as if another man were speaking—and he shot a glance toward his friend. Bono's eyes were clear and burning, his face bathed in burnished moonlight. "If you turn back around, I will kill you. Do you understand!" he said.

Meth-man nodded, his eyes dull and empty as death.

Bono slowly lowered his weapon and looked right into the

eyes of the attacker with a piercing, unwavering steadiness. "I command you now to leave us!" he said in the same powerful voice.

"Bono, what are you doing?" Sam whispered as Bono dropped the handgun to his side. "Keep that weapon on him or he'll jump you . . ."

"I command you to leave us!" Bono said again. "Go back now to your hellhole. Go back and grovel with your own."

The man stood, hesitated, sneered at Bono, then turned and started walking, followed by his friends.

Frightened now, Sam reached for Bono's left hand, took the handgun, and kept it pointed at the back of the attackers' heads. "Come on," he whispered urgently. "Let's get out of here."

Bono didn't move. Sam held the handgun at the ready position, waving it slowly back and forth, aiming at the four men, then turned toward his friend. Bono's face was ashen. He looked exhausted. Completely drained. Sam glanced down and saw that Bono's hands were shaking like winter leaves in the wind; he couldn't have hit anything with those quivering hands anyway.

Something had happened here. Something Sam didn't understand. "Are you okay, man?" he whispered slowly.

Bono shook his head, his eyes wide with terror. "That was him," he whispered back in a fear-choked voice. "I saw it in his eyes. I saw *him* in his face. That wasn't just a man there. That was something . . . someone else . . ."

A terrible shiver ran down the center of Sam's back. A deep cold seeped inside him—empty, lonely, and terribly sad. The blackness was dark and utterly complete. He swallowed hard, his throat dry, his chest clenched.

He felt it. He knew it. And for the first time in his life he was truly afraid.

Bono took his gun back from Sam and shoved it under his jacket again. "Drugs did that to them," he whispered. "They have so surrendered their bodies over to the power of the evil one that they don't control themselves any longer."

The four men had reached the end of the platform where it met the tracks, their images illuminated by the moon and stars. At the edge of the cement barricade three of them dropped and kept on walking, but the fourth one stopped and turned around.

"*My name is Balaam!*" he cried. "*I remember you, my brothers, and I will see you again.*"

The coldness deepened, sinking into Bono's soul. He started to speak, but the human form dropped onto the train tracks and walked into the dark.

The two men stood in silence, unable to speak. The crowd continued to mull around them as if they hadn't seen anything.

"Come on," Bono said. "Let's get to your home."

The two men started running.

And they did not look back.

Behind them, the dark angel stood and watched them from the edge of the tracks. After the two soldiers had merged into the darkness, he turned around and laughed.

chapter twenty-seven

Mary Shaye Dupree and Sara Brighton approached Sara's automobile slowly, calling from the darkness as they walked. "Hey there, that's my car, what are you doing?" Sara cried.

Walking side by side, the two women emerged from the dark. The moon had risen enough to illuminate the outline of their frames, but the darkness and open country made them seem so very small.

Two men were talking near the back of their car, rummaging through the trunk. Sleeping bags and clothes had been scattered up and down the road. Both of the back passenger windows had been broken, and shattered pieces of glass reflected in the yellow-reddish light. The air was cool now and Sara felt a damp breeze against her neck. She shivered as she placed her hands defiantly on her hips. "What have you done to my car!" she demanded.

The two men froze a moment, then slowly turned, taking the two women in. Sara returned their cold stares, her eyes flashing in the dim light. Cold and hard, she stood her ground, her shoulders firm. Mary glanced in her direction, then turned and squared her small shoulders too.

Inside her stomach, Sara was as tense as piano wire. She forced herself to breathe without screaming, swallowed the enormous knot inside her throat, and fought to keep the panic down. She knew it was ridiculous. She didn't care how tall she stood, how much she scowled, or how loudly she raised her voice—she and Mary were two small, middle-aged women standing in the dark. No way were they going to intimidate these men.

The strangers glared. They were young, somewhere in their twenties, and dressed in work clothes and boots. One of them laughed, a lusty, ugly sound. "I'm sorry," he mocked, "is this stuff yours?"

"Yes, of course it's mine. Now perhaps you could explain what you're doing rummaging through my clothes!"

The man hesitated, then glanced past her shoulder. "You alone?" he demanded.

"No," Sara answered far too quickly. "Both of our husbands are back there, just a little way down the road."

The man smiled, his shoulders relaxing at the obvious fabrication. He glanced toward his buddy, snorted, and turned back. "You got an awful lot of stuff here." He kicked a loose pile of clothes that had been thrown at his feet. "Looks like you're pretty much prepared for anything."

Sara didn't answer, her eyes still glaring in the night.

"We figure if you got all this stuff, you're on a long trip. Maybe you're never going back to where you came from. Which means you got some money—and we want it."

Sara swallowed. "We've got a little. Maybe fifty or sixty dollars."

The man scoffed and stepped toward her. "I'll bet you got a whole lot more than that . . ."

Mary started reaching for her purse. "I've got a little here," she cut in.

Sara watched, her anger boiling. She simply couldn't hold back. "*Money!*" she shouted at their ignorance. "Are you that stupid? Do you think money has *any* value now!"

The man stopped, shot another look toward his friend, unsure of what she was saying, then turned and took a long step toward her. "Money! Yeah, stupid wench, I want your money."

Mary saw his eyes, cold and hungry and slippery in the dark, and shuddered. "It's okay, I've got some money," she offered again in desperation. "It isn't much, but you can have it. Whatever I have, it's yours."

"No!" Sara shouted. "You put that money back." She turned toward the young men. "Do you two guys understand? Do you have *any* idea what has happened here! Haven't you *even looked around* . . ."

The man took another step and stared menacingly into her eyes. "I don't like you," he hissed, his breath stale with alcohol and smoke.

Sara met his stare. Mary shot an elbow to her ribs.

Sara stared a moment longer, then dropped her eyes. "All right," she whispered. "You can have our money. But that is the only thing that you may take."

The young man pulled back and slapped her hard across the face, sending her tumbling to her knees. She cried out, then held her voice, raising her hands toward her cheek. Reaching down, he grabbed her by the hair and pulled her to her feet.

Luke and Ammon jumped the two men at exactly the same time, emerging from the darkness like two wild animals, screaming and pounding their fists and legs. Ammon hit his mother's attacker at a flat-out run. Lowering his head, he buried his skull into the small of the man's back. He heard a sudden *huuufff* as he knocked every ounce of breath out of the attacker, then kept driving, his legs pounding, pushing the man to the ground, his shoulders crushing against his ribs. He and Luke were holding baseball-sized rocks in their hands and he brought his fist down against the attacker's head, feeling the man go limp. Beside him, he heard a high-pitched cry as his brother knocked the second man to his knees. Sara jumped into the fight, kicking and scratching at her attacker's legs, the only piece of him she could reach. Ammon held him tight, his arm around his neck, and kept on squeezing until the attacker's head fell against his chest.

WASHINGTON, D.C.

Sam and Bono stood outside the Brighton home. It had been more than a year since Sam had been there, but it all looked the same and for a moment he time-warped, feeling as if he'd never been gone at all. The old southern oaks and sycamores in the front yard whispered to him, their huge branches moving gently with the night wind. The grass was long, longer than Sam had ever seen it, with at least two weeks' worth of growth. The late summer leaves were beginning to drop, leaving patchy shadows across the walk. The house was dark, the windows staring at them, blank and expressionless in the moonlight. Although it looked the same, there were a few hints that Sam's family hadn't been there for at least several days: the swirl of twigs and dry leaves that cluttered the corner of the porch, a single newspaper on the sidewalk, the utter darkness inside. Sam moved to the front door, tested it, and found it locked. He turned to his right and felt along the wooden railing on the front porch. Under the third rail was a small crack in the wood where his family always hid an extra house key for an emergency.

Searching, Sam suddenly stopped, his mind going back to his first day in the old Brighton home in southern Virginia: Sara showing him his bedroom, his own closet, the shelf where they kept the clean towels, the Ping-Pong table in the game room. The final stop on the tour had been the front porch. She had given him his own key, urged him not to lose it, then showed him where they hid the spare in case he ever got locked out.

"We don't want you stranded out here," she had kidded him as she handed him the key.

His own key. A house he could stay in for as long as he wanted. That was what they had told him. He would soon find out if it was true. Could be that it might turn out like all the others. Foster homes, he had learned, were as chancy as a game of dice. Still, there was something about this family, something about this home, something different, he could sense it. His new mother had stood beside him, and he remembered staring up, skinny arms, shaggy hair, a healing bruise on his left cheek, his eyes wide in disbelief. She had looked down on him and smiled, and he had decided at that moment that she was the most beautiful woman in the world.

From that day on, all he had ever wanted was to stay in their home. He had tested them. He had rebelled, sometimes fought them, even pushed them away. But they hadn't given up, they had loved him, and now this was his home.

His mind turned to his father, General Brighton, and he almost shuddered with grief, thinking of the night he had found out about his father's death.

He remembered it all so clearly. It wasn't what he wanted, but sometimes he couldn't stop the memory from playing like a movie in his head.

Late at night. He and Bono flying across the Iraqi desert in the helicopter, the pilots getting an urgent message and setting the powerful chopper down on the sand. Both of the pilots were crying. Bono moved forward to talk to them. Sam watching, a sickness rising in him. Bono's face showed confusion and fear. He listened, then hunched over as if someone had punched him in the chest.

He looked up to ask another question, but the pilot shook his head.

"What is it?" Sam demanded after Bono had slid back across the helicopter floor to his side.

"Oh, geez," was all he'd answered.

"Tell me!" Sam demanded, his voice angry now.

"There was a nuclear detonation. They said that D.C. is gone. They think a quarter of a million people are dead. The president, all his cabinet, the Congress, the Supreme Court . . . everyone . . . all the city . . . everything is gone."

At first, Sam hadn't believed it. No way it could be true! Then he thought of his father in the White House, his mother and brothers west of there. "No," he muttered weakly. "Bono, you have to be wrong."

"Everything . . ." Bono stammered, his eyes staring blankly at the night. "Everything . . . everybody . . . our government gone . . ." He turned back to Sam. "I'm so sorry, Sam . . . your family . . ."

Sam angrily shook his head. "It can't be!" he almost shouted. Bono just stared at him.

Sam remembered the raw anguish in his friend's expression, and how he finally understood. He had taken a slow breath and held it, then unbuckled his lap belt and fallen onto the desert sand.

Even now, he could feel it, the sand against his face, his salty teardrops, the bitter grinding of his teeth. The sand had been cool, but as he clenched his fingers, digging deeper, he felt the sand grow warmer underneath. The night was calm, and the ground vibrated gently from the helicopter near his legs. Inside his head, a thought kept screaming, "He *might* still be alive."

But as he lay atop the Babylonian desert, he knew his father was dead.

*　　*　　*

Sam stood motionless on the porch, lost in thought, looking up at the great old house. Where was his mother? Where were his brothers? This family that had saved him, were any of them still alive? Would he ever see them again?

Bono cleared his throat, bringing him back to the present. Sam shook his head, mumbled something, then bent and moved his fingers carefully along the rough wood where the heavy paint was smooth and thick. He searched quickly along the crooked plank, then stood, staring at the front door.

"No key?" Bono asked him.

"Not where it usually is," he replied.

Bono moved around the corner of the house to the side-entry garage and tested both doors. Locked. Sam followed him, then went to the back of the house. A six-foot fence surrounded the backyard, and he worked the latch through a gap in the top planks, pushed the gate back, stepped to the patio door, and found it locked. Leaning against the glass, he cupped his face with his hands and looked in, but it was far too dark to see anything but a few shadows from the table and kitchen chairs. Bono moved to his side, pulled out his flashlight, and shone the light through the glass. The narrow beam illuminated the kitchen and breakfast nook in weak light, making the inside look even more lonely and more eerie than before.

"Should we break the glass?" Bono asked.

Sam thought a moment. "Hate to do that. We won't be

able to repair it, which means the house will be unsecured when we leave; critters, raccoons, robbers, anything could go crawling in. I'd hate to leave the house open like that when it might be weeks, maybe months, before we come back here again."

Bono nodded, understanding. He also knew it was very likely it would be much longer than a few months before anyone lived here again. Years. Maybe never. Still, he didn't argue.

Sam thought some more, then turned and trotted around the side of the house to the front porch again. Bending to his knees, he felt along the wooden planks, holding his narrow flashlight in his teeth. He slowly felt along the same crack in the wood on the underside of the railing. This time his finger touched something, and he bent to inspect the crack, holding the light near his face. The tip of a folded piece of paper caught his eye. Picking with his fingernail, he pulled the paper from the crack in the wood. It was folded four times, and he opened it carefully.

Sam:

Remember where we used to hide our firecrackers when we were in 8th grade? Take a look there. You'll find what you're looking for.

We really, really miss you!

Ammon and Luke

Sam shoved the paper into his front pocket, thought a moment, almost laughed, then moved. Bono followed him into the backyard. Sam shone his light against the tallest oak tree in the far corner of the backyard, finding the remnants of an old ladder and a tree house. He tested the wooden ladder and started climbing. Six feet up, just above the second branch, a large plywood board was still fastened against the tree. A crack formed between the tree and the plywood, and

Sam shoved his fingers between the wood, extracting a key. "Way to go, guys," he whispered as he dropped to the ground.

"Got it," he said to Bono, holding the house key up against the moonlight.

Bono didn't answer, not seeming to hear. He stared across the yard to the fence and the house across the way. "Who lives there?" he asked, nodding to the old brick Victorian.

"I don't know, an older couple, I think. The Hendricks used to live there, but they moved away about the time I joined the army. Don't remember who lives there now."

Bono answered slowly. "They're watching us," he said. "Top window, on the right side."

Sam didn't turn but instead began to pace around the grass, moving toward the tree to position himself on Bono's other side. Bono turned toward him, allowing Sam to look over his shoulder at the house next door. Sam quickly surveyed the old home, his eyes stopping on the second-floor window. Someone *was* standing there. She stared down, not moving as she watched them in the moonlight.

Sam shrugged, then turned toward the house. "Come on," he said.

The key opened the front door. The two soldiers grabbed their packs and stepped into the house. It was as cold inside as it was out. "No one's been here for a while," Sam said as he sniffed the air.

Bono nodded, noting the staleness. "Your mom got any candles?" he asked.

"Hundreds," Sam said as he moved to the kitchen cupboard. "She was a preparedness freak. The entire Russian army could survive here for years on the food and supplies in the basement storage."

He reached to a second shelf in one of the kitchen cabinets, shifted his flashlight, found a box of eight-inch candles, and pulled it down. Sam fingered the nearly empty box, pulled out his Bic (every soldier kept at least a single lighter in his pocket), and lit one of the two remaining candles. Its soft light filled the room.

The house was empty and dark and lonely. And it seemed so big. Way too big for just the two of them. Way too big in the dark. The soldiers walked from room to room. Everything seemed in perfect condition, nothing out of place. Sam called out occasionally, "Mom? Ammon? Luke?" It was obvious that no one was there, but he wanted to hear the sound of their names. They walked through every room except the basement, finding nothing that would give them any indication of the whereabouts of Sam's family, then found themselves in the kitchen again.

"So?" Sam asked as he looked around. "What do you think?"

"I think we've got some long, long days ahead of us and we need to get some sleep," Bono answered. "There's nothing we can do now. We need to save the candle. We ought to go to bed."

Sam suddenly felt exhausted. "Come on," he said.

He led the way upstairs. His parents' bedroom was on the left. Ahead of him, at the top of the stairs, was the bedroom he and his brothers had shared since they were teenagers. There was another room to the right, an unused guest room, and he pointed toward it. "There's a good bed in that bedroom down the hallway. I'll sleep in here."

Bono didn't answer. Instead, he pushed back the door to the boys' room and saw two beds. "You going to sleep in here?" he asked.

Sam nodded. "That's my old bed over there."

Bono walked into the room and dropped his pack on the other bed. "I'll sleep here," he said.

Sam hesitated, then followed, throwing his own pack at the foot of his bed. He glanced at his watch, the luminescent numbers barely glowing in the dark, but it had quit. "I'd guess it's almost midnight," he said.

"We'll sleep until sunlight. Not much we can do in the dark. Then we'll take a look around, see what we can find. Your family must have left you something, a message, a letter, something to let you know what happened and what their plan is. We'll find it in the morning, then decide what to do from there."

Sam slumped onto his mattress. "Yeah, they surely left me something . . ."

They lay atop their beds, staring at the dark, the gentle wind blowing through the sycamore trees outside the window. "I wanted to ask you something," Sam said as he listened to the wind.

"What's that?"

"We've been talking, you know, about all the things that used to happen back in the old days. The early days of the Church, but back in the Bible times too. It seems there were a lot more—you know—miracles, I guess. Strange things used to happen. People were healed. Amazing revelations. Angels. All sorts of things. You don't see things like that happen so much any longer. Is there a reason why?"

Bono thought for a long time. When he answered, his voice was tired and he spoke slowly. "I don't know for certain, Sam. I think there are miracles like in the old days, I know that I have seen some, but people might not talk about them. The Church itself is a miracle, one we might not appreciate. It also might be that we don't need the miracles quite as much as they used to. Back in the old days, there was more danger. God required much more of a physical sacrifice of his people, so maybe he helped them a little more in that way. Then life got easier, medicine and science grew. We have great doctors and hospitals now. Maybe the Lord expects us to use the tools he has given us, whereas back then they didn't have anything but faith."

Sam thought, then rolled over on his bed. "You want to know what I think?" he asked.

Bono barely grunted.

"I think that times have changed now. I think that pretty soon, the only thing we're going to have is faith. The power of darkness is increasing, but I think God's power is getting greater too."

"I think you're right," Bono answered slowly.

Seconds later, he was asleep.

INTERSTATE 65
FOURTEEN MILES SOUTHEAST OF CHICAGO

Luke and Ammon worked together. They were quick and efficient but also panting with exertion, for they were as tense as they'd ever been, the adrenaline pumping through them like a narcotic in their veins.

They dragged the two men to their feet, holding them around their necks. The first one, the man who had slapped their mother, was tall and lanky, but weak and fine-boned. The second man was smaller, with a roll of baby fat still tucked around his middle. They smelled like beer and peppermint and tacos, and their eyes were blurry from the beating they had taken.

Ammon's man cursed and halfheartedly tried to fight him, swinging slowly through the air, but Ammon squeezed his throat and shook him and he folded instantly, gasping as he clutched his chest. The broken ribs would heal, but not for a long time, and every breath he took for the next three months would remind him of this night.

"What are you doing!" Ammon shouted, rage and adrenaline pushing him to the very edge of control. "What are you doing, man!"

The man swallowed against the tightening grip against his throat. "We were . . . just . . . you know . . . looking around . . ."

"You picked the wrong guys to fool with! You picked the wrong woman to assault! I'd just as soon kill you now as look at you, you stupid, retching fool."

"It's . . ." the beaten man took a tiny breath and grimaced. "It's cool, man, we were just . . ."

"Shut up!" Ammon screamed into his ear.

"Listen, Sergeant Black," Luke hissed to his brother from the darkness. "We've been back from Afghanistan a *real* long time. I haven't killed a man in weeks now. "

"Shut up!" Ammon shouted. "Shut up, Sergeant Smith. Shut up and let me think!"

The battered man began to tremble against his arm.

Ammon shot a glance to the inside of their car, thinking of the gold coins and cash hidden there. They hadn't found it. Not yet. But they surely would have, if Ammon and Luke hadn't come when they did.

Shoving the attacker, Ammon pushed him toward the shattered window of their car, pointing to the rumpled bedding and scattered clothes. Everything had been dumped out: their suitcases, the food and water, everything searched and thrown about. The two men obviously weren't thinking of survival—it hadn't even entered their stupored minds. Beer and money were the only things they had been considering, that was pretty clear.

Ammon glanced to Luke, barely able to see him in the dark. Luke held the smaller man from behind, his arm around his throat, one hand viciously grabbing his head by a handful of hair. Ammon turned toward his mother. "Are you okay, Mom?" he asked, his voice a growl.

His mother touched her lip. "I'm okay, Ammon," she answered quietly, seemingly defeated and in shock.

Unlike her two sons, she wasn't pretending. The attacker's angry words and slap across the face had sucked the life out of her, leaving her weak and helpless as she stared at her sons. Sara had lived a peaceful life, a quiet life, and the possibility of being attacked in anger had never really crossed her mind. She had never been hit, not so much as a single time in her life, and she felt violated and helpless at what had happened to her.

"Let's just kill them," Luke sneered again, shaking the stranger he was holding by the hair. "Let's just kill them and leave them out here. No one's going to come looking for them. There'll be no police, no investigation. And we could always claim that we had to kill them in self-defense."

Ammon felt the man struggle against him and he tightened his grip, squeezing against his neck. The stranger bent his legs, dropping his weight against Ammon's arms, fighting to get away, but Ammon dropped with him, both of them landing on their knees. He pulled his arm into a death grip and felt the man grow weak. He seemed to think for a moment, then nodded to his mother.

"All right. Get the gun, Mom," he said in a deadly voice.

Sara hesitated. He sounded so serious, she was starting to believe him. "No, Ammon, you can't kill them . . ."

"GET IT, MOM!" Ammon screamed.

Sara didn't move.

Mary stepped toward Ammon, trying to remember the things he had told her to say. "I know this type," she said, her voice cold and unfeeling. "I think you ought to kill them. If you don't do it, they'll be back. We'll have to deal with them later. They'll follow us and give us trouble—or if not us, then someone else. They'll give the world nothing but trouble now. It'd be better off without them."

"You got that right," Ammon hissed. "Go on, Mom, get the gun."

The man cried again, his ribs on fire, every breath, every movement sending jolts of anguish all through his chest. Ammon squeezed against his back and he went limp. His lips were growing blue now, his broken ribs struggling to give his lungs room to breathe. "No, no, no," he begged, as if believing for the first time that he was just a few seconds from death. "Please, you don't have to do this." He started crying, his voice drunk and thick. He took a painful breath and sobbed. "We didn't mean nothing, okay. We'll go. We'll get out of here. I promise you, you'll never see us again."

"The only way I'm going to see you again is if I dig you up," Ammon snarled. He squeezed against the attacker's neck again and pulled him to his feet. "I could shoot you now or save the bullet and just strangle you."

Luke almost started laughing. That line was just too much. Like something from a Clint Eastwood movie. Ammon was *so* into this role.

These two men were no threat to them any longer, he could see that. Drunk, defeated, and scared, they were two young bulls who'd just been branded with a very hot iron.

The man stammered in fear, "I swear to you, we're sorry. I swear it to you, man, you'll never see us again."

Ammon pulled again. "I hope I do," he whispered in his ear. "If I see you, I can kill you. I *will* kill you. Is there any doubt in your mind?"

"No, man. You're crazy. You're some crazy, wagged-out soldier. I got no doubt at all."

Ammon started laughing, shrill and unhinged, then shook the man's head in rage. "Do you believe that I will kill you!"

"Yes, sir, I know you will."

"Go, then!" Ammon cried, throwing the man across the ground. "Get out of here before I kill you and bury you underneath these bloody skies!"

Luke also released his grip on the man that he was holding, then kicked him with his knee.

Both men stumbled, glanced toward the boys, their eyes wild with fear, then turned and ran.

*　　*　　*

Sara hurried over to Ammon. "Are you okay?" she asked, her voice worried, almost pleading.

Ammon stared at the spot where the strangers had disappeared. He didn't move, but kept on staring. Luke moved slowly to his side. "That was like, you know, way convincing," he said.

Ammon shook his head. "I was so scared," he answered slowly.

"You didn't sound scared, you sounded crazy. Really crazy, man. I didn't know whether I should laugh or run. You almost had me convinced."

"I was scared," Ammon repeated. He seemed to be talking to himself.

Luke chuckled just a little. "You sounded like you were going to rip that poor guy's heart out and cook it up for dinner. A regular Hannibal thing going there."

Ammon moved away. "I didn't think I could sound like that," he said. He was clearly shaken up.

Luke reached out and put a hand on his shoulder. "It's okay, dude," he tried to comfort.

Ammon didn't answer. "I'm not like that," he muttered as if trying to convince himself.

"It wasn't real, Ammon. Remember, it was part of the

plan. We knew it wasn't going to be enough to just stop them. We had to scare them." He stopped and looked at Mary, her bright eyes shining in the moonlight. "She was right," he nodded to her. "It was a smart thing to do. They would have stuck around. They'd have come back. We had to really scare them so we didn't have to worry about them again."

"All I did was scare myself," Ammon said.

"Yeah, but that's okay." Luke watched him a moment, then turned to his mother, walked toward her, and put his arms around her shoulders, pulling her close and not letting go. "Are you okay?" he asked, his voice choking.

"I'm fine, son." She rested her head on Luke's shoulder.

He pushed her back, inspecting her face. A trickle of blood illuminated in the moonlight, dark and thin. "Are you okay!" he repeated.

"Really. I'm okay. A little bruise. Nothing major."

Ammon turned from the darkness and walked toward his mom. Standing in front of her, he looked into her eyes. "That will never happen to you again," he promised, his voice filled with emotion. "I swear to you, Mom, I'll never let anything like that ever happen again." He put his arms around her, the three of them holding onto each other in the night.

*　　*　　*

Mary cleared her throat. "I'm sorry," she said, her voice soft, afraid of intruding. "I'm a little worried about my baby girl." She nodded toward her car.

"Right, right," Luke said breaking away from the others. Bending, he started picking up their scattered belongings. "Let's get this mess picked up. Don't worry about organizing it, we'll take care of all that in the morning."

Ammon seemed to think, then ran to the car, yanked open

the front door, and knelt beside the seat. Reaching under, he felt it. The gun was still there.

Sad, Sara thought as she watched him. It wasn't the money or food that he was worried about, it was the gun.

Had it come to that already?

No, she shook her head. It wouldn't come to that. Not for them. She and her family would never live that way.

Ammon stood and walked toward them.

"Okay, listen," Luke said, "we'll get this picked up, but that's really all we can do tonight. We wait until morning, then see what's going on. Ammon, you and Mom stay here. Sleep in the car. You keep the sleeping bags. Mrs. Dupree and I will sleep in her car. We'll take some blankets for us and Shelly Beth—"

"Kelly Beth," Sara corrected.

"Sorry, Kelly Beth. I'll stay with her and Mrs. Dupree tonight."

The group was silent for a moment.

"Okay," Ammon said.

* * *

Morning came. Low rain clouds had gathered again, hanging in the western sky, and a cold wind blew down from the north, sweeping across Canada and Lake Michigan, picking up a dank, fishy smell.

Ammon awoke. The night before, he had unzipped one of the sleeping bags and pulled it around him, then slept in the front seat. Sara had slept in the backseat but was already up. When Ammon didn't see her, he climbed out of the car. Even the gray, misty morning was welcome after such a dark night. He glanced behind him, up toward the freeway, then down the off-ramp toward Mary Dupree's car, which was closer than it had seemed the night before. Funny, he thought, how distances seemed so much greater in the dark. Sara and Mary were standing close together outside the black woman's car. To his left was a thick cluster of trees; to his right, the four-lane freeway was crammed with stalled cars. He could see a couple of dozen people huddled around several cars and, half a mile east of the off-ramp, he could make out the parking lot and buildings of the service stations they had been aiming for last night. Beyond the trees were fields, brown and ready for fall digging. He was surprised at how rural the scenery around him was, being so close to Chicago.

He considered, then stretched. Walking around the Honda, he checked the two broken windows, grabbed a bottled water from the backseat and walked toward his mom.

"Good morning, all," he said.

Sara turned toward him. Ammon looked at her face, seeing the bruise and narrow cut across her lip. His anger started boiling and he had to look away. "You sleep okay, Mom?" he asked.

"Pretty well, Ammon. It was colder than I thought it would be."

Ammon nodded at the sky. "The temperature has dropped quite a lot." He turned to Mary. "How are you, Mrs. Dupree?"

"I'm fine, honey, fine."

He glanced to her car. His brother wasn't there. "Where's Lukester?"

Sara nodded toward a cluster of trees to her right, a hundred feet or so beyond the road. "There was a man back there, in the trees. He was on an old four-wheeler. Luke thought he was a local. He went to talk to him."

Ammon moved his eyes to where she was pointing. Luke was just emerging from behind the trees. They waited, watching him walk toward them.

"Anything?" Ammon asked.

Luke shook his head. "There was a guy back there on a four-wheeler. He rode away before I could talk to him."

"A four-wheeler. It was running? Are you sure?" Ammon asked skeptically.

"Yeah. It was old and pretty beat-up, but it was working. Now, why is that?"

Ammon thought. "Anything built before electronic ignition and all the gee-whiz computers that control everything now, I think will work. You might have to replace some spark plugs or ignition wiring, but that's pretty easy to do."

Sara moved back and leaned against the vehicle. "We tried Mary's car again," she said, as if offering something important. "It isn't working still."

Ammon nodded, not surprised.

Mary walked over and stared through the back window at her little girl, then turned toward them. "Sir," she said to Ammon. "Please, I've got to get my little girl home. She needs her medicines—if nothing else, her pain medications."

Ammon walked toward her and leaned down, looking through the back window of the car. The little girl was still asleep. Small and thin, she looked to be eight or nine years old, but it was hard to tell, she was so slender. Her face was thin and dainty . . . no, that wasn't right . . . her face was thin and *fragile*. He watched her sleep and thought what a beautiful little girl she was.

"Did she wake up last night?" he asked Mary.

"A couple times. She sleeps all the time now, but never for more than three or four hours at a time."

"Did you—you know—tell her anything?"

Mary shook her head. "I told her we were having car trouble."

Luke came forward and stood next to them, stealing a glance toward Kelly Beth.

"It worried her," Mary concluded. "She worries way too much for a little girl. She's got a new sister back in Chicago that she's worried about now. She is terribly concerned about leaving her alone."

A gust of wind blew and the trees off in the distance began to sway, creating a muted whisper, a smooth and lonely sound.

"This other daughter, why is it that she is a newcomer to Chicago?" Sara wondered.

Mary hesitated. How much should she explain? How would these people feel about it? She just didn't know. "She's not really my daughter," she started.

They waited patiently.

"She's an orphan from a refugee camp in southern Iraq. She's Iranian, not Iraqi, though. She had no family, no one, really. She'd been bought . . ." Mary hesitated. "There are people who buy and sell young women, I'm sure you know what I mean. There's an organization in London that works to intercept and save them. My daughter, her name is Azadeh, had been bought and paid for and taken out of the refugee camp. I don't know if she knows or understands this, but she was on her way to a very bad situation, a very bad place. I don't know the entire story, but someone, apparently a couple of U.S. soldiers, stepped in and saved her."

"No kidding," Luke answered. "Some U.S. soldiers found her and saved her?"

Mary shrugged. "I don't know the whole story, but yes, apparently."

"What studs," Luke smiled. "Good ol' U.S. soldiers. Gotta love 'em, man."

Sara watched, then interjected. "We have a son in the

army," she explained. "My husband is in . . . used to be in the air force."

Mary listened, pulling her shirt collar up around her neck. "I like the army," she said. "Lots of my people, most of my neighbors, think it's a terrible thing to do. I never felt that way. I know what it's about. Good people. Unselfish people. If you've got a son in the army, you should be proud."

"Thank you," Sara said.

"Anyway," Mary continued, "the London organization worked to place Azadeh somewhere in the West. I agreed to take her. It took months and lots of money to get her here to the States. She got here just a few days ago.

"But that's not the main reason I need to get home. The biggest reason is Kelly Beth. All of her medicines, her painkillers, her vitamins, everything is back there."

The other three were quiet. "How far is it to your house?" Luke asked.

Mary nodded to the north. "It's surprisingly close. Straight up Interstate 65. That takes you almost to the lake. A couple miles before that, you come to Gary and take 90 west. It's only about four miles from there."

"So, how far, do you think?" Ammon asked.

"I don't know—when you're driving you don't pay that much attention, you know what I mean. I could drive it in half an hour, twenty minutes if I don't hit traffic."

Luke reached down, picked a piece of grass from beside the road, and stuck it in his mouth. "Maybe twenty miles?" he asked.

"That sounds about right," Mary answered.

"How far is that?" Sara asked. "I mean, could we walk it? How long would it take us? A few hours? A week? A couple of days?"

Ammon smiled at his mom. When it came to such things,

she was totally clueless. "I don't know, Mom, maybe a couple of days," he said.

"It's really not that far," Mary interjected hopefully.

"So what do we do, then?" Luke asked.

Ammon stared at his mother, then turned to the others. "We walk," he said to Luke.

"That's a long way, don't you think?"

"I guess we could stay here and spend the winter."

Luke looked away, embarrassed. "I didn't mean that, not the way it sounded."

Mary put a hand on Luke's arm. "What about my baby?" she asked, a terrified strain on her face. "We can't leave her . . ."

"We'll carry her," Luke answered.

"You'll carry her?"

"Yeah, we'll carry her, of course."

"You will do that? You would do that?"

"Of course," Luke answered, smiling at Mary. "What did you think we'd do?"

Mary hesitated. "Truthfully?" she said. "I thought you'd leave me."

Sara shook her head. "Did you hear what I said last night?"

Mary kept her head down.

"We meant it, Mary. You've got to start trusting us. We're simply not going to leave you out here by yourself."

"Isn't there a wheelchair in the back of the car?" Ammon said.

"Yes," Mary nodded.

"No problem, then," he said.

Luke glanced toward their car. "I don't know how we're going to carry everything," he wondered. "All the food and water, our clothes, the sleeping bags and camping gear?" He shot a secretive look toward Sara, thinking of the gold and other valuables hidden throughout the car.

Ammon turned and rubbed his hands through his hair. "I was wondering the same thing," he said with worry.

"I'm strong," Mary shot back. "Much stronger than I look. I can carry a lot. You can pack me down like a mule. I'll carry anything you tell me to. I'll make three or four trips if I have to. I'll steal a wagon and drag it, if you'll please just take my little girl."

Ammon smiled sadly, realizing the mother's desperation over her child. "Don't worry," he assured her. "We're going to figure something out."

Luke hunched his shoulders. "Can I talk to you?" he said, pulling Ammon aside. "We're going to figure this out," he assured Mary as he guided his brother away.

Twenty feet from the car, he lowered his voice. "There's no way we can carry all our gear. One of us to push the wheelchair. Three of us to carry. The water alone would take fully one of us. And think about the money and all that other stuff we've got hidden in the car. Are we really going to try to take that with us? That can't be too smart, walking around with a bunch of cash and gold right now."

"What's the option?" Ammon whispered back. "Leave it here? If we do that, we abandon it; I guarantee you none of it will be here by the time we come back."

They stared at each other for a moment. Ammon reached down and grabbed his own blade of grass. "What do you think about that little girl?"

Luke shook his head sadly. "I don't know. I'm sure no doctor, but I'm telling you, she looks terrible to me. Thin as a rail. Sleeping all the time. I mean, can you imagine! Can you even begin to fathom what that poor woman and little girl have been going through? What they're going to go through still? I'm as unfeeling and stupid as the next guy, but man, it tears my heart out just to look at her."

They were silent another moment. "I think she's dying," Ammon said.

Luke bit his lip and didn't say anything.

"I think poor ol' Mrs. Dupree was taking her daughter home to die. I think she knows. I think she's given up any hope. Did you hear what she said about the clinic? She went down for some kind of special treatment but the doctors wouldn't do it. They said there was no reason. That can't be any good."

"So what do we do?" Luke asked, his voice beginning to choke.

Ammon stared at his brother, the broad-shouldered high school fullback, the guy who could pound through any hole in the offensive line no matter the cost to his body. The harder the hit, the more it hurt, the more a man it meant he was and the more he loved the game. Under the sweatshirts and the sandals and the hang-by-the-edge-of-the-cliff-without-any-rope, hard-guy exterior, Luke was at least as soft as any guy he knew. "I don't know," he finally answered. "All I know is we can't leave them here."

"Of course not. I know that." Luke considered the darkening sky. "I was thinking maybe we should bury some of the gear, some of the more . . . you know . . . precious but dangerous stuff—the gold, maybe some of the cash and canned food. Let's cram everything we can into our packs. We could jury-rig some pouches around our stomachs, improvise a little in order to take as much as we can, then," he nodded toward the tree line, "bury the rest. We'll be careful, wipe out our tracks and conceal the hiding place. We'll wrap the little girl—what's her name, Kelly Beth—in a couple blankets and push her home."

"Okay," Ammon answered. "But one thing we haven't thought of. Once we get to her place in Chicago, what are we going to do then? What's our long-term plan?"

Luke shook his head. "I've got absolutely no idea."

"What about Mom? Have you talked to her?"

"We talked a little bit this morning. She has no idea either. Still, it's kind of funny, she seems in a pretty good mood."

Ammon glanced back toward his mother. "Okay," he said, "let's do it. Let's gather and organize our gear. Take everything we can, conceal or bury the rest. We'll make Kelly Beth as comfortable as possible and start out walking. The freeway, if you haven't noticed, is full of people. We won't be the only ones walking toward the city."

Luke considered. "Twenty, maybe twenty-five miles. We can do that in a day."

"I don't think so," Ammon countered. "Two days, maybe, with our gear. If we keep going and don't have any problems, we can be there by tomorrow night."

Luke looked at him and shuddered. "Listen, dude, I don't mean to sound pessimistic or overly morbid, but I don't know if that little girl is going to make it that long."

"I've wondered that," Ammon said sadly. "But if she doesn't, then let's do this. Let's make certain she is being held by someone who cares about her when she passes from this world. Let's make certain she can say good-bye to her mother. Let's keep her safe and warm. That might be all we can do, but let's make sure we at least do that."

Luke closed his shiny eyes, a small tear forming on the corner of his eyelid. He lowered his head a long moment. "I wish Dad was here," he said.

"I know," Ammon answered. "If not him, I wish we could talk to Sam. I'd give anything to know where he was. Is he okay? Is he back here in the States?"

Luke turned and looked east. "Do you think he'll try to find us?"

"I don't know, dude. I mean, he's in the middle of a war, after all." Ammon glanced toward the freeway. "I wish he was here," he repeated. "I wish Dad was here. I feel so uncertain."

Luke slapped him on the back. "Come on," he said.

The two brothers turned and walked back toward their mother.

Sara was staring down the road toward the freeway, firm as stone. She lifted her hand to her eyes to shield them against the gusting wind and squinted.

"Mom," Ammon started, but she quickly held out her hand to cut him off.

"Look at that," she whispered. Ammon turned, looking into the distance. Crowds of people crammed the freeway, most of them heading north toward Chicago. Some were dragging suitcases, some holding boxes and bags, briefcases and sacks, a great migration of lost and lonely souls.

"That's an awful lot of people," Ammon said.

"Shhh," Sara interrupted again.

Ammon fell silent.

"I thought I heard gunshots," Sara whispered.

Ammon waited, holding his breath.

Then he heard it, a distant *crack!*

"Oh no," was all he said.

chapter twenty-eight

Morning came. Sam awoke the moment the sun began to lighten the room. He got up, checked the lights, walked into the bathroom, checked the water, pulled on some pants but no shirt, and walked downstairs.

Bono followed. Sam grabbed a large bowl, went into the basement, and drained some water from the water heater tank. The two men cleaned up and finished dressing. To most people it would have been an inconvenience to wash up from a bowl of barely warm water, but after months in the desert it seemed a luxury to them. They opened a couple of cans of fruit, found some nuts and beef jerky in the basement, and ate until they were full.

After they had eaten, Sam asked tentatively, "What would you think about saying morning prayer together?"

Bono didn't hesitate to fall to his knees. Sam prayed, his eyes clenched tight. After he said amen, Bono continued kneeling, staring at his friend. "That was kind of cool," he said.

Sam's face was expressionless. "What's that?"

"What you said. In your prayer. The thing you asked for."

Sam thought. He really didn't know what Bono was talking about.

"That angels would guide and help us."

Sam blushed. "It wasn't an original thought. I'm not capable of that. I got it from a scripture my dad showed me one day. I was just a kid, but you know how some things kind of stick in your mind. Believe me, with my background with my real old man and lady—you know what I'm talking about—fights and beer and drugs were lots more common in my home than any scriptures, I can promise you that. So it took a while after I came to the Brightons' before I paid much attention to this whole scripture thing. There were lots of times when the scriptures went way over my head. But there was this one time when Dad said something that I remembered: "*I will go before your face. I will be on your right hand and on your left, and my Spirit shall be in your hearts, and mine angels round about you, to bear you up.*" I've always believed that. Don't know why, it doesn't make any sense, but sometimes it's almost like I felt their presence, angels, old friends, standing at my side. So I just figured, you know, if we're going to find my family, if we're going to get you home to your wife, we could use a little help."

Bono stared at him, amazed. "I love your faith," he said.

Sam shrugged. "Is that what that is?"

Standing, Sam started searching the house. Five minutes later, he found the letter on his father's desk in the study. Sara had placed it underneath a set of scriptures with the corner of the paper poking out, his name on it. The note was dated just a few days before.

> *Dear Sam,*
> *Time is short. We feel a sense of urgency to get moving now that we have decided what to do, so this letter will not be long. More, the things I really want to tell you,*

I want to say face-to-face when I can hold you and tell you how much I love you, how proud I am of you, and how much you mean to me, to our entire family. Because of this, and for other reasons I can't go into right now, this letter will be fairly brief and to the point.

First, I want you to know that we have tried to call you, left you email, messages at the army, everything we could think of to get in touch with you. Having not been able to talk to you since the explosion in the city, I leave you this letter with a prayer that you will find it, that you are okay and healthy, and that we all will very soon see you again.

By now you must know that your father is dead. We know that he was on duty at the White House when the nuclear detonation took place. Although we don't know for certain, it appears that he didn't even make it into the underground command post. Most of those who made it didn't survive anyway—the floors and ceilings collapsed, trapping many inside. There was a fire, it wasn't pretty, although a few people did escape. Two days after the explosion we got a short letter from our good friend General May. (He had to send it by private messenger.) He said Neil was last seen at his desk, calling the Pentagon to warn them of the impending attack. That was just seconds before the detonation. It appears he waited too late to seek out shelter.

Your father died trying to save the lives of others. Tell me, does that surprise you? Frankly, I would have been surprised if it hadn't ended that way.

He loved you, Sam, I hope you know that. From the first time he saw you, he felt that you were one of his sons. He would often talk about the strange path God took in order to bring you to our family. He also understood that the bonds of family must have started before this life, and he always felt that you and he must have been like brothers in the premortal world. You have been as much a part of our family as any of our other sons. Ammon and Luke look to you as their older brother, and in many ways, you are the patriarch now, the leader of our family. I know that's kind of a bummer, putting all that on you right now, but it's just how it is.

The rest of us are okay. A couple of days before the attack on D.C. we were warned to leave the city. We took what we could and left, and were well clear of danger by the time of the attack. It was a miracle, Sam, it really was, how the Spirit warned us to leave. The afternoon of the explosion, I had scheduled a lunch appointment with a friend at Union Station . . . Luke and Ammon would have been downtown on the campus . . . we all would have been in the center of the explosion . . . I just don't know what might have been.

We were saved by the Spirit, and we continue to feel his gentle guidance in our lives and the decisions we must make.

It's been a week since the explosion. We've done all we can do here and have spent the last few days just wondering what to do. Last night I got the answer. We are heading west, to Salt Lake City. But the funny thing is—and I haven't said this to anyone, not even to Ammon or Luke—I don't think we're going to get there. Something's going to happen on the way. What it is or what we will do, I don't know for certain. We'll take it one step at a time and see what happens, always relying on the Lord.

I do know this, however: He didn't bring us to this point to fail. He didn't protect us for no purpose. There are great days still ahead.

So . . . Lieutenant Brighton! (Yes, General May sent us word in the same message that he told us about your dad), don't lose faith or give up hope. This is not the end, but the beginning. There is so much left to do yet, so many happy days still ahead. I know it won't be easy. I simply can't imagine ever being happy without Neil, but that is my challenge now, and I'll do the best I can. I'll say the words, even when I don't see how they could be true. I'll keep my faith and keep on going, believing there is a purpose and some happiness yet to live.

We will be on the road for six or seven days, depending on how it goes. We have our cell phones. You can call us. If not, try to reach us in SLC. I'm leaving a home phone and address where we'll be staying at the bottom of this page. Try to reach us there.

In closing, let me tell you what I told Luke and Ammon just a few hours ago. It isn't fair that your father died. Believe me, no one understands that more than I. But sometimes life isn't fair. God never promised that only the evil ones would die in these days. Even the good, sometimes especially the good, will be asked to sacrifice. I think there is more to come, maybe much more, a few heartaches, I suppose, but some incredibly good things are coming too. There will be more opportunities to help and teach other people than we've ever had before.

Sam, you are the fulfillment of scripture. I know that might not mean a lot to you, and you may not understand what that means right now, but you were sent into this day for a reason and a purpose. You are a light unto the world. You were sent here to be a savior of men.

It won't be easy. It never is. But the things you're going to do, the good you're going to do, the good you have already done, it staggers me, leaving me weak but so, so proud.

Find us, Sam. Whether in Utah or en route, find us. We will need you. Do for us what you can.

Until that time, know how much I love you. Keep the faith. Say your prayers. NO ONE loves you more than God does, but I love you pretty close.

Mom

Sam sat on the edge of the leather couch and read the letter over again. Bono stood near the doorway, giving him time. After reading it the third time, he passed it to Bono.

While Bono read, Sam found another piece of paper on the neatly tidied desk, a note that Luke had hidden under Sara's letter, which read:

Sammy, dude, you Cherokees or Sioux, or whatever your top-secret, He-man Special Forces unit is called these days, are REALLY hard to get a hold of. Like Mom said, we've tried everything to get in contact with you, but nothing yet. (By the way, I read her letter. Three pages long. Good thing she said she'd keep it brief, huh.)

Anyway, it's been a hard couple days, Sam, and I get the feeling we might not be on the back end of the storm. Things have gotten kind of weird here. Like REALLY kind of weird. As you can see from mom's letter, we're heading west. Try to contact us when you can. I'd really like to talk to you.

By the way, the main reason I am writing is to tell you that I made it over the ledge on that rock down on the Potomac River. You know, the one you couldn't get over when you tried, the one with the six-foot ledge that juts almost straight out. Yeah, I did it. And I did it

*without a rope. Let's see you do that, dude. I'll tell you the
story sometime. It was an . . . interesting experience.*

   *Ammon says to tell you he's up to 248 in the bench
press. I've never seen him do it, but that's what he says.*

   *We miss you and love you. Dad was proud of you.
We're proud of you too.*

                        *Hugs and kisses,
                        Your studley bros*

Sam read the letter, smiled, then read it again. Then he
started to chuckle, the laughter building into great, heaving
sobs. Tears of relief, joy, and pain combined together and
streamed down his face.

"What is it?" Bono asked him, reaching for the note.

Sam passed it to him. "Just my stupid little brothers," he
stuttered with relief.

                    *   *   *

"You said your family has a lot of storage?" Bono asked
when Sam had finally quit laughing.

"Pretty much," Sam answered.

"They kept it in the basement?"

"Yeah. It's kind of a dungeon down there. You know these
old homes—walk-out, sunlit basements weren't the norm."

Bono looked satisfied. "That's good. It actually gives me
some hope." He stomped his foot on the floor. "Thick walls.
Thick foundations. These houses were built to last five hundred years. It might be enough . . ."

Sam watched him carefully, not sure of what he meant.

"Do you think your parents had an emergency radio in
their storage?"

"I'm sure they did. But with the EMP, it won't matter
anyway."

"Maybe so. But let's give it a try."

The two soldiers rooted around the basement. The cement and rock foundation was old and dry and at least two feet thick. The house, built more than a hundred years before, had been designed for a former plantation owner and army officer as his summer home. The labor and materials were meticulous in quality even if growing old. The men found the two-year supply: jugs of water, cans of grain, all the normal stuff. A windup radio was sitting on a shelf at the back of the room. Bono wound it, turned it on, heard the static, and smiled. "Give me a few minutes with this," he told Sam. "Take a final look around the house to make sure we haven't missed anything, then we'll make our plan."

Sam went through the house, looking for another message from his family, checking for any valuables that might have been left behind, making sure all the windows and doors were locked. Then he sat down on the sofa. Bono had brought the radio upstairs and tinkered with it some more. Now he switched it off and turned to Sam.

"You realize what's happened, don't you, Sam?" he started.

"You mean with what . . . my family . . . ?"

"No. I'm talking bigger picture now. Last night, the loss of power."

"An EMP, I thought we decided."

"Yeah, that's right. A world-class blast of destructive electromagnetic power. Anything unprotected that's electronic, it takes it out. Fries the circuits through and through. It's a miracle, if you ask me, that this radio is still working, but these thick walls must have been enough to blunt the pulse.

"So far, I've only been able to pick up one station, a government emergency broadcast. Right now it's repeating the same message again and again, nothing live, just the same recording. Yes, it was an EMP. Four nuclear detonations, evenly spaced across the entire United States. They won't say yet, but I know what that means. A single detonation, at the right altitude, and with enough power, would have been enough to take out most of the country. With four, they would have reached from central Canada to central Mexico, which means that what we see here is pretty much what we're going to find across the nation."

Sam didn't answer. A long silence filled the room.

"They say they're evaluating the situation and expect to make progress very soon in restoring normal services," Bono concluded.

Sam watched him carefully. "You surely don't believe that?"

Bono looked away and thought again. "Electromagnetic pulse isn't something I know a lot about, other than the basic stuff they teach us. I remember one thing, though: It becomes a vicious cycle of destruction. What few basic capabilities or electro-infrastructure does survive is quickly overwhelmed. It becomes swamped and soon fails. Yes, I think we'll rebuild, it's not impossible, but it will take months, likely years, and meanwhile everyone has to rely and live on what they can provide for themselves—which, if you understand America, isn't a lot."

Sam nodded slowly. "So what do we do?"

Bono stood. "First, we've got to get in contact with our unit. As you know, a majority of critical military C4 command, control, communications, and computers are hardened against an EMP. The military is the one thing that isn't going to crumble, at least not right away."

"So what then?"

"How far is it to Fort Belvoir?"

"I don't know, maybe eighteen miles."

"Is that the closest army installation?"

"Yeah, probably."

Bono reached for his pack. "All right, Cherokee, that's where we're heading. We gear up, take what we'll need from your house, then head out. Eighteen miles. We can be there by late afternoon if we run."

Sam stood and looked around the empty house. "I guess we don't see our families, then." He said it as a statement, but he meant it as a question, though he pretty much knew what Bono was going to say.

"I don't know," Bono surprised him. "Everything is suddenly pretty crazy. I don't really know what to expect now. But I do know this. I've been away from my family for more than a year. I've been home a total of three weeks in twenty-two months. So I'd better have a chance to go home and check on them or I'm going to be one unhappy soldier. Low morale isn't even going to begin to describe what I'll be feeling then."

"Roger that, dude. Same for me. My family is out there somewhere. I've got to find out how they are."

Bono walked into the kitchen. "Let's pack up anything we can carry that's not going to spoil." He opened the fridge. It was already growing warm. No electricity, no refrigeration, one of the nastiest results of the EMP. He shook his head, knowing that lots of people around the United States were going to be hungry before the day was even through. And what was true in every home was true in every business, from local restaurants to small markets and huge grocery stores. A billion pounds of food was going to spoil in the next few days.

"You got any extra canteens?" he asked Sam as he closed the refrigerator door.

"Downstairs in the storage."

"Get 'em. Fill 'em from the hot-water tank. No one's going to have any water and it's going to be very dear. Any iodine pills?"

"No, but we have portable water filters."

"Even better. Short of our guns, they're the things that are likeliest to save our lives. Grab them, anything else you can think of, and let's head out. We'll report in at Fort Belvoir, get our orders, then beg them to give us a little time. After all, it's not like they need two such highly trained combat killers. Snipers, Counter-intelligence Ops, Counter-insurgency Ops, those are the things we're good at, and I don't think they need that particular field of expertise inside the U.S. right now. Riot control, traffic control, medics, nurses, civil engineers, JAGs, civilian affair officers, those are the specialties that will save us, not combat troops."

"Kind of nice to let someone else carry the water for a while, isn't it, Bono?" Sam smiled. "They might need us in a few weeks, but probably not right now."

Bono hoisted his pack. "Let's get going. Eighteen miles to Fort Belvoir, nothing but a gentleman's hike. No desert. No one shooting at us, at least we hope not. No IEDs or roadside explosions. Like a day in the park. We'll go report in, find out what they want us to do, beg for some time to see our families, then see what happens after that."

chapter twenty-nine

It started raining, first a drizzle, then a solid pour.

Before the clouds broke open, Ammon and Luke had cut through a barbwire fence and pushed their car and Mary's the short distance to the cluster of trees that separated the freeway off-ramp from the farmland to the east. Using a hatchet they had packed in the trunk, they cut branches and piled them atop the vehicles to conceal them from the road. Mary and Sara worked together to organize and pack the things they would take with them. While Mary was distracted, Ammon pulled the cash and gold coins from the car, moved farther back into the trees, and dropped the valuables in a hole Luke had dug. The boys buried the money, then covered their tracks and moved back toward the road.

The packing was almost finished. "Can we go now?" Mary pleaded. "I want to get my little girl home. And I can't leave Azadeh any longer. She has no idea what's going on."

Ammon nodded toward the freeway, looking north toward where they had heard the gunshots, thinking of the two goons they had had the trouble with the night before. "Before we leave, I want to go up there and check it out," he said.

224

Mary flinched. "It won't take long, will it?" she wondered.

"Not too long. But after hearing the gunshots, I want to know what's up there before we head out."

He looked at the dark sky. The rain had settled in for the day. Sara pulled out a dry poncho and handed it to him. "You be careful, then," she said, kissing him on the forehead. She and Ammon had obviously discussed his leaving them to check out what lay ahead—and it was clear that she didn't like it.

"I won't be gone long," he assured her. "A half hour. Maybe an hour. Be back as quickly as I can."

Ammon hugged his mom, nodded to Luke, and set off through the trees.

An hour passed. Another hour. Luke started pacing. Sara's face grew more and more tense, her eyes more wide. They had cleared off the brush so that Kelly Beth could rest in the back-seat of Mary's car, and Mary climbed in and sat with her. Luke paced among the trees, feeling worthless, growing more frustrated with each passing minute.

Sometime midmorning, Kelly Beth woke and asked for some water, then complained of the growing pain inside her bones and back and side. She closed her eyes as Mary held her, clutching her tightly to her chest.

"Mama, is it time to take my medicine?" the small girl asked hopefully.

"Yes, baby, it is. But we don't have any right now."

"Can you get some for me, Mama? My body hurts."

Mary shook her head. "I'm trying, baby."

Luke and Sara listened, realizing that the child wasn't even really aware of where she was. Sara turned to Luke and whispered, "She's in a lot of pain."

Luke grimaced. "I can see that."

Sara dropped her voice even lower. "Luke, how are we going to get her to Chicago? She'll never make it. She can't even sit up in her wheelchair. She'll get soaked, sitting in the rain."

Luke stared through the back window, watching Mary. "I will carry her," he said.

"It's a long way, Luke."

"I know, Mom, but I'll carry her. What else are we going to do? I mean, this isn't what we would have asked for, taking responsibility for this little girl, but at least it *gives* us something, something to work for, something . . . I don't know, something worthy. Otherwise, what would we be doing? Sitting here and worrying where to go and what to do. This way, we have a purpose, a goal to work for, a place to go, which might turn out for all our good anyway."

Sara nodded, understanding. The rain started falling harder, splattering on their raincoats and running down their cheeks. "I'll carry her all the way to Chicago if I have to," Luke assured her.

"I just hope . . ." she hesitated. "I just hope she makes it home."

Luke wiped a raindrop clinging to his nose. "I hate it, the thought of her dying out here, in this mess."

"She needs a blessing," Sara offered slowly.

Luke shook the rain from his poncho, avoiding his mother's eyes. "I don't have the Melchizedek Priesthood, Mom."

Sara just looked at him, apparently lost in thought.

Luke pressed his foot against the muddy ground. "We should pray for her," he offered.

"It's not enough."

"I know, Mom, but what else do we have to offer?"

Sara was silent for a few moments longer. Finally she took a deep breath and said, "We keep on praying, then."

*　　*　　*

Forty minutes later, Ammon made his way back through the trees, crouching as he went. The rain had let up, leaving a heavy mist in the air.

Sara and Luke moved toward him, running through the wet leaves and trees to meet him. His face was tight and he was out of breath.

"Are you okay?" Sara asked, rushing toward her son.

"I'm fine, Mom," he answered quickly.

Luke handed his brother a small towel, and he wiped his face and wet hair. "What's going on out there?" Luke asked.

Ammon glanced back, his eyes tense. "We can't go that way, not along the freeway. It's not safe anymore."

"What is it?" Sara asked, moving closer to her son.

Ammon wiped his face again and shook his hair. "We'll have to stay here awhile," he said. "At least a night, maybe more."

"What is it!" Sara repeated.

"A couple miles up, there's a group, I don't know who they are, they seem like locals. They've set up a barricade across a bridge and aren't letting anyone pass. Only those who are willing to pay are getting by. Some are heading off across the fields. The men at the barricade are chasing after them, but some are getting through. Some are heading for a small river that's up there and getting across. The river isn't very wide, but it won't be easy, and we sure couldn't carry any of our things if we decided to try to cross it. I'm not a strong enough swimmer to cross a river, even a small one, with a pack on my back. None of us is. And as far as Kelly Beth . . ." he paused, the problem obvious.

"That's crazy!" Sara answered. "I mean, they can't do that. What right do they have to stop people from traveling on the road?"

"They've got no right, Mom, but they don't care right now. There's a lot of people heading north, toward the city. Everyone who was leaving the city is heading back, and everyone, like us, who was heading toward the city is still trying to get there. With all these stranded travelers, these guys seem to think—and so far they're right—that no one is going to stop them from doing pretty much whatever they want. The police don't know about them yet. How are they going to find out? No one can call them. And when they do learn what's going on, they may try to send someone out, but how are they going to get there? It might take a couple days."

Luke pressed in anger, "Who are they, Ammon? A handful of goons? Some vigilantes?"

"I guess that's a pretty good description. A group of a dozen, maybe fifteen men. They all seemed to know each other. They're demanding money, watches, cell phones, whatever people are willing to give them in order to pass."

"Okay," Luke said, "we'll do what everyone else is doing. We'll go and pay them to let us pass."

"That might be a problem," Ammon answered.

"And why is that?"

Ammon shot a wary glance toward his brother. "Those two guys from last night are up there."

Luke turned away, gritting his teeth.

Sara drew a quick breath and held it. "Do you think they'll recognize us?" she pleaded desperately.

"Oh, they'll recognize us," Ammon answered. "I've already tested them. Believe me, they recognized me."

Luke turned and looked away, holding his hands to his head. "No, no, no," he repeated, then glanced toward Mary's car.

"I know," Ammon said, as if reading his mind. "I understand the situation with Kelly Beth. But we can't go up that way, not right now, anyway. We need to wait here until morning, give it a day. Maybe the Highway Patrol or National Guard or someone will show up. Until they do, there's nothing we can do. We simply can't make it up that road."

INTERSTATE 495
WEST OF WASHINGTON, D.C.

Sometimes they ran, sometimes they walked, sometimes they stopped to rest while adjusting their packs. They stayed on the roads, knowing better than to try to cut through the backyards and fences and highways and barriers that made a cross-country hike through the city virtually impossible.

As they ran, they were shocked at the state of the city. To their left, thin trails of smoke still rose from the downtown area. They knew what it was like down there, the rescue efforts under way, the death and destruction. Both of them shuddered, thinking of the devastation just fifteen miles to the east. The nuclear warhead was small and had been detonated too low to generate an enormous cloud of radiation, and most of the radiated material had already washed away in the wind, but being so close to the detonation still required them to move cautiously.

Once or twice the soldiers stopped while Sam pulled out a portable radiation detector. As he worked, Bono looked up, covering his eyes to protect them from the sun.

"You notice anything?" he asked.

Sam didn't look up from his work as he answered, "Like the fact there are no airplanes in the sky?"

"Yeah. Like that. Dulles is just west of here. Reagan International and BWI to our east. On a normal day, you'd be able to count dozens of aircraft landing or taking off."

Sam kept on working, hooking a small wire from a

portable battery into his detector kit. "Guess that makes this, what . . . an un-normal day."

Bono grunted. "Yeah. Pretty much un-normal. I mean, how weird is this? Civilian air travel within the United States is a thing of the past. The military birds will keep on flying—I'm guessing most of them were hard-wired to protect against EMP—but civilian airliners, they're all but gone now."

"I'm just glad I wasn't in one when the blast hit," Sam said.

Bono lowered his gaze, looking east. He knew that most of the residents of D.C. were surprised, even shocked, to discover that, having survived the initial blast, their lives wouldn't immediately come to an end. It was a common fallacy, the thought that nuclear fallout would kill everything within an enormous radius of the explosion. Bono knew that wasn't true. Yes, many would die. The total death toll wouldn't ever be known, since it would extend for many years into the future as a result of the radiation exposure that had taken place. But he also knew that most Americans expected downtown D.C. to be uninhabitable for a thousand years, which wasn't the case. The half-life of the initial contamination was relatively short, as little as seven hours for the worst of the radiation. The city was located near the eastern coast, where the prevailing winds blew from west to east, which meant that most of the nuclear fallout—the dust, debris, and water vapor that had been sucked up, superheated, and radiated from the nuclear bomb—had already blown out to sea. The area upwind of the explosion received little radiation. Cities on the west side of the city—Fairfax, Falls Church, Arlington—had not received any fallout at all, and wouldn't, if the west winds kept blowing for another week or so. Areas downwind would surely suffer, but even those would be relatively safe to travel through within six weeks or so.

Looking skyward, Bono imagined the cigar-shaped area of nuclear contamination that had spread east. Washington, D.C., was at the tip of the cigar, and the band of fallout, twenty to thirty miles wide, spread eastward for a couple of hundred miles.

He dug into his pocket for the copy of the report that had been given to the U.S. soldiers on the flight back to the United States.

In a nuclear detonation, large amounts of soil or water will be pulled into the radioactive cloud by the fireball. This material becomes radioactive when it joins with radiated contaminants in a process similar to water vapor condensing around dust particles to form rain. This is what is referred to as nuclear contamination, or fallout, when it falls back to earth.

The large particles (larger than 50 millimeters) are too heavy to rise into the stratosphere and will fall back to earth within 18–30 hours. The smaller contaminants (less than 100 millimeters) will remain aloft and be dispersed by stratospheric currents.

The ground track of fallout from an explosion is a long and irregular ellipse that will extend downwind from the location of the explosion. Individuals within this contaminated area are at greatest risk.

Perhaps more than any other variable, meteorological conditions will influence local fallout. A nuclear detonation with a significant body of water nearby (i.e. the explosion that was experienced over Washington, D.C., with the waters of the Chesapeake Bay within range of the fireball) will produce water vapor particles that are lighter and smaller than an explosion over land. This generally creates less contamination in the immediate area but more downwind, covering a greater area.

Effects of fallout vary. Rapid death will follow high doses of radiation. Low exposure to contaminants may not preclude an otherwise normal life, although the development of delayed radiation effects may produce late-term effects.

At the writing of this report, tests indicate significant fallout, with its anticipated effects, over all the eastern portions of the District (Suitland, Clinton, New Carrolton, etc.). This band of fallout extends from roughly Annapolis in the north to the southern Maryland coast along the Potomac River, the western shore of the Chesapeake Bay, the eastern shore of Maryland, and the Atlantic Ocean.

Except for the immediate area around Washington, D.C., much of the contaminated area is sparsely populated. Still, some casualties are expected beyond those already killed in the blast.

Bono shrugged. Funny, he thought, as he folded the paper and put it back into his pocket, who would have thought the destruction of the nation's capital would be the least of their worries now?

The radiation meter was clicking at his side. Sam studied the readout, then carefully put the dosimeter back inside its protective cover and tucked it in his backpack.

"Still good?" Bono asked him.

"Kind of amazing," Sam answered. "I'm not getting anything."

"Yeah. But remember, we're upwind. And a long way from the detonation site."

Sam looked around, his eyes always moving.

They stood on the median of the 495 Beltway, the

twelve-lane freeway that surrounded D.C. An enormous series of cement overpasses was before them where Route 66 merged with 495. They were halfway to Fort Belvoir Military Reservation. It had been a long day, the traveling much harder and slower than they had hoped it would be.

The freeway was a mass of stalled cars. Virtually nothing moved. Some of the people still waited in their vehicles, convinced the government was going to send someone out to save them—to pick them up and drive them home. Most of the drivers and passengers, however, along with other travelers like Bono and Sam, had finally started walking, and the freeway was crowded with weary people moving along the unending line of cars. Most of them avoided the sides of the road, walking between the stalled cars, realizing that traffic wasn't going to start anytime soon. As Bono watched, he knew that few of them, if any, had any idea what was going on. The radios inside their automobiles would have been fried along with the electronic ignition, fuel injection, and computer circuits, and without their cell phones they had no way of knowing about the EMP.

He smelled smoke and turned around. They'd been watching the growing flames for the past hour or so. Just outside the Beltway, somewhere south of 66, a fire had broken out inside a complex of tightly packed townhouses. What had started as a small fire (Bono suspected from something like some idiot trying to fry a hot dog on a hibachi inside his kitchen) had spread to the entire building, then to the building next to it. With no water pressure and no fire trucks to respond, there was little anyone could do but watch the buildings burn. That was a serious ongoing danger. Since there was no practical way to fight the fire, who knew how far it might spread? The smoke was growing thick and mean, billowing upward in mushrooming clouds that rose several hundred feet before being carried in a long line to the east.

Bono nudged Sam, pointing toward the fire. "How far do you think it might go?" he asked.

Sam shrugged. "A long way, I guess."

"Think it could burn all the way to 66?"

"Maybe. I mean, how are they going to stop it? No pressure in the city water lines. What are they going to do, beat it back with shovels? If things get bad enough, I guess they could bring in bulldozers, tear down a line of buildings to create a firebreak . . ." He paused, realizing that wasn't going to happen either, and then asked, "Do you think the electrical circuits in heavy demolition equipment would be fried as well?"

"The new stuff? Probably. But there's lots of older equipment, bulldozers and land-movers built before the 1980s, that probably doesn't have electronic ignition and all the modern circuitry the new machinery has. I'm sure they could round up some old stuff. But let me ask you this." Bono nodded toward the freeway. "How're they going to get it to the fire? The roads are all impassable. Nothing's going to move. It could be weeks, maybe months, before these roads are clear. Think about that, Sammy. You start with a single fire. You've got no way to fight it. You can't even get equipment to it, the small amount of equipment that wasn't destroyed by the EMP in the first place . . ." His voice trailed off. "You could lose an entire city. It could all burn away and there wouldn't be anything we could do."

Sam watched the billowing smoke, then looked south again. "Come on," he said. "We've got another eight miles. It's getting late. I want to make the army post before nightfall." He hoisted his pack and started jogging.

Bono fell in behind him. They stayed on the embankment of the highway, away from the people as much as possible.

Angry, frightened eyes stared at them as they passed. Most everyone called to them, recognizing the uniforms.

"Hey, you! Soldier! What's happening here?"

"Stop there! Can you help us?"

"Hey, I've got a carload of kids with me! I need some help. Why are you running? I *demand* to know what's going on!"

The shouting was insistent and angry; the soldiers just ignored it. It would take a month to get to Fort Belvoir if they had to stop and explain what had happened to everyone they passed.

Ten minutes later, Sam saw them. Three men. Two young women. Lots of leather, lots of chains, and a bunch of ugly, moody eyes. They stood around their car, cursing and shoving all the strangers that walked by. He watched them carefully as he and Bono approached, still at a gentle run. One of the men saw the soldiers coming and reached toward his hip. *He's armed,* Sam thought, instinctively moving his hand toward the weapon underneath his camouflage uniform. He was in the lead and he turned to the left, moving farther off the road to give the men a wider berth.

A screaming woman ran toward him, her eyes wild, her arms flailing in the air. "He shot someone!" she cried. "There's a dead body up there! Between those two cars!" She motioned frantically toward the men on the road.

Sam slowed. Bono came up behind him. "Are you certain?" he whispered toward the woman.

She didn't answer, her hands darting to her mouth.

Sam watched the three men and two women. The girls had backed off. The men turned to face the soldiers, maybe forty feet away. "You got no business here, grunt boys," the nearest man shouted to him. "You ain't the freak'n police. You ain't nothing. Go on, keep on jogging. You got no business here."

Sam shot a look to Bono. "What do you think?" he asked.

Bono looked at the mass of empty cars and walking people all around him. "I don't know. We don't have time for this. And we don't really have any authority . . ."

"But if they're armed . . . if they've already popped someone . . ."

Bono nodded slowly. "We ought to do something, I guess."

"I know the world's gone crazy, but man, Bono, it's only been a day. Wouldn't you think these people could hold off the barbarism for at least a week or two? And murder is probably still illegal. Inadvisable, at least." Sammy had a habit of slipping into sarcasm when he was working up to combat mode.

Bono studied the men, who had grouped together now.

"If they've hurt someone, I don't think we can just leave them here, not with a weapon," Sam said.

"Okay," Bono finally answered. "Check it out. See if it's true. But we're not the judge and jury. We don't want to hurt anyone, you understand. All we want to do is make it impossible for them to intimidate or hurt any of these travelers, okay?"

Sam nodded. "You got me?" he whispered softly.

Neither of the men had pulled their weapons, but Bono nodded slowly. "Left hip for one, right hip for two," he said.

Sam started walking toward the group of hoods.

"Go on, soldier boy," the first one sneered, waving him back. "You got *no* business here!"

Twenty feet between them. Two lanes of cars. Sam looked down. Between a set of tires he saw the body. Brown leather shoes. Expensive suit pants. A pool of drying blood beneath the ankles. He quickly moved his eyes, not letting on that he had seen. A young woman hunched in the backseat of a nearby Lexus: dark hair, lots of makeup, her head slumped against the window, her face stained and bruised and purple beneath her dark eyes. Half a second was all it took him to understand what had happened here.

"No worries, buddy," he shouted back. "I just wanted to ask you something."

"Stay back!" the man screamed in fury. Pulling out a weapon from under his loose shirt, he aimed at Sam. "Go on, keep on running, you got no business here, soldier boy." His voice was thick and hopeless. Nothing left to lose. Nothing left to gain. The world was over anyway, why not have some fun, stake your claim while there was something left to stake a claim to.

Sam moved his eyes again, evaluating the threat. Three men. The first one armed. The second one? . . . almost certainly, from the way he held his hand beside his hip, just a few inches from the small of his back. The last man stayed away, his eyes darting between the soldiers and his friends. He was no threat.

Sam swallowed, moved two steps to his right to allow Bono a clear line of fire, and lifted his hands, palms toward the screaming man to show that he was not holding a weapon.

"Go back or I *will* kill you!" the man screamed again. He moved his finger to the trigger and squinted down the short barrel of his gun.

Sam slowly dropped his right hand toward his hip.

The bullets passed by his ear. *Buzz, buzz.* Hot and angry. There was no other sound like a passing 9mm bullet.

The first man screamed in pain and dropped his gun, the blood already spouting between his fingers as he held his shattered hand. The second man fell back, his shoulder bloody, his right arm hanging worthlessly at his side. The window behind him burst as the flattened bullet passed through his shoulder and into the car. The two men screamed and cursed together, crying in pain and fear. Their buddy, the oldest of the three,

swore, his eyes wide, then turned and ran, sprinting like a rab-
bit down the line of empty cars. One of the young women
screamed, fell to her knees, and threw up, her long hair falling
into the watery flow. The other girl, no more than a teenager,
ran toward her boyfriend, bent over him, saw the blood, then
stood and ran, following the other man.

Sam drew his weapon and held it with both hands, his face
deadly and intent. He moved toward the hoods with careful
steps. "Get down," he told them, his voice low and calm.
Behind him, Bono kept his weapon trained on the attackers.
Sam made certain he maintained a line of fire for his friend.

He moved toward the Lexus and pulled open the back
door. The woman stared up, her eyes wide with dread and fear.
She seemed to be as afraid of him as she was of the other men.
"You okay?" he whispered as he pulled her from the car. She
felt heavy, fragile, too weak to help herself. "Come on," he
urged, his voice harder now. "Get up. You've got to get out of
here."

She stood, brushing her hands across her face. Sam saw the
tear in her dress, the bruises and scratches across her cheeks.
She had fought them. He was proud. She was going to be
okay.

Across the highway, among the passing strangers, two
older men were hiding behind a nearby car. "Over here!" Sam
shouted to them.

The two men hesitated, then came toward him. "Take care
of her!" Sam said, gently prodding the battered woman toward
the men.

"What?" the first man answered in surprise.

Sam nodded impatiently to the scene of carnage: the dead
husband, the bleeding attackers, the injured woman. "Take
care of her!" He cocked an eyebrow.

The two men understood. "All right, sir. You got it." The

first man reached out for her hand. She cried, then fell into the stranger's arms.

Sam turned toward the two young men who were crying on the ground. He moved toward the first one, who sat holding his bleeding hand against his chest. "You've been a bad boy," he muttered, kneeling down by his side.

"He shot me! He shot me in the hand!" The young man cursed and swore at Bono, calling him every foul name that Sam had ever heard.

"He could have shot you through the mouth if you'd prefer that," Sam said in disgust. "And if you don't shut up, I still might let him."

"He shot me, man!" the man screamed. "I'll get you, you stinking soldier. I'll kill you!" He swore again.

Sam bent over and looked the young thug in the eyes. "Tell me, what is there in this situation that would lead me to believe that?" he asked.

The man sniffled, then closed his mouth. Sam reached out and took his hand. Examining it carefully, he pulled a thick gauze pad from his first aid kit and compressed it into the man's palm. "You'd better count your blessings," he said. "My buddy there is good enough he was able to miss the major tendons and nerves. Believe me, tough guy, that was no accident—he could have destroyed your entire hand. He did you a huge favor: Your hand will heal okay. You'll be able to stand trial for this murder with no problems, you slimy scum."

The man shook his head, then turned away.

While Sam was working, Bono had moved toward the other man, kicked away his handgun, and examined his shoulder. It took them a few minutes to administer first aid.

Standing, Sam gathered up their weapons. Bono wiped his hands on the attacker's pants, then moved and stood at the side of his friend. Sam nodded toward the injured shoulder.

"Just a flesh wound," Bono told him. "It'll be okay."

Sam tucked their two handguns inside his backpack, then turned toward the men. "You made things a whole lot harder than they needed to be," he said. "Think about it, guys. Things are going to be tough for everyone right now, but they're going to be a lot harder for you. How are you going to get to a hospital? What kind of care do you think you're going to get? I wouldn't want to be either one of you. But you made your own bed."

Bono reached into his backpack and pulled out some plastic bands they used as handcuffs to handle captured insurgents when working in Iraq. He dragged the two men together, cuffed them to each other, then ran another cuff around the dead man's wrist. "A murder was committed here," he said as he cuffed the men. "It would be a whole lot better if you didn't leave the scene of the crime."

Sam wrote a brief note, explaining what had happened, wrote down his name, rank, and contact number, and left it on the windshield of the dead man's car.

"Come on," he said to Bono, "we've still got a long way to go."

*"And now, O all ye that have imagined up unto yourselves
a god who can do no miracles, I would ask of you, have
all these things passed, of which I have spoken?
Has the end come yet? Behold I say unto you, Nay;
and God has not ceased to be a God of miracles."*

—Mormon 9:15

chapter thirty

L ook, I don't know what to tell you," the army colonel said. "I mean it, guys, I've got my hands full right up to my elbows, and the last thing I need is a couple lieutenants asking favors and hanging around my neck."

"We understand that, sir," Bono answered respectfully. "But please remember, our Cherokee unit was brought back from overseas just a few days ago. Everyone has already scattered, heading off to see their families. Our unit has been gone for twenty-three of the past twenty-four months and we were all anxious to get home. The problem is . . ."

"The problem is, now that you're all split up, there's no way Special Forces Command is going to reconstitute your unit. Not right now. Not under the circumstances we find ourselves in."

"Exactly, sir."

"What does your boss want you to do, then?" the commander of the helicopter aviation unit at Fort Belvoir demanded.

Bono slid to the edge of his chair. His face was tight and

sweaty. And he looked tired. Really tired. Not so much physically—although the hike across D.C. had worn him out—but there was a much deeper weariness and worry on his face. "He wants us to stay available," he started to answer, "but frankly, sir, he knows it's unlikely our particular unit is going to be called on anytime soon. So he's giving us two weeks to go home and see our families. Two weeks. Not a lot of time when we've been gone for two years, but hey, we're not complaining; we're very happy to have any time at all. The problem is, of course, we've got no way to get there. We don't own any horses, which might be the only way to get around right now. So we need a ride, sir. One of your helicopters out there. If we could get out to Andrews Air Force Base or down to Langley, we might be able to catch a hop from there. I've got to get to Memphis and Lieutenant Brighton here needs to get to Salt Lake City, or . . ." Bono hesitated . . . "somewhere in between."

The gray-haired colonel raised an eyebrow and turned to Sam. "You don't know where you're trying to get to?" he asked, his voice tired and sarcastic.

Sam shook his head.

"What, your family lives in a Winnebago or something? Your dad packed up his three wives and headed out when things began to hit the fan?"

Sam blushed with anger and looked away. Bono huffed as he leaned back against his chair. "Where did that come from, sir?" he demanded, his voice hard. "Are you so ignorant as to assume that (A) anyone from Salt Lake has to be a Mormon, and (B) members of the LDS faith are running around with half a dozen wives?"

This time the colonel blushed. "Sorry," he said, lifting his hand in apology. "Really. I wasn't thinking. You know, guys, I've been working for weeks on about two hours of sleep a night. It was a bad joke, a weak attempt at humor, but I meant nothing, okay?"

Sam shrugged. "A joke. Oh, I get it. Funny, sir."

Bono slumped. He was too tired to really care. "No sweat, sir. And as a matter of interest, it turns out that you probably knew Lieutenant Brighton's father . . ." The colonel's face began to soften . . . "General Brighton at the White House."

"Of course, of course, I knew your father well." He turned to Sam. "I hope . . . you know, I hope he's okay. Did he, you know . . ."

"No, sir, he didn't. He was killed in the explosion." Sam stared at the colonel, his face blank.

The older officer cleared his throat. "I'm sorry to hear that. I really am. I had the honor to fly your father many, many times. Even got him the front seat in one of those UH-60 helicopters out there. He did a pretty good job for an air force guy. Couldn't ever learn to hover, but he was a right good ol' pilot. More, he was a really decent fellow. Everyone who knew him liked him. Everyone knew how hard he worked."

"Thank you, sir," Sam answered.

Bono watched Sam for a moment, then glanced around the boxy office. Typical army: brown, faux-wood desk, a dozen pictures on the walls, an American flag in one corner, the regiment flag opposite it, a small window where the colonel could stand and count the choppers—mostly Sikorsky UH-60s and Bell UH-1s—out on the flightline.

They were sitting on the east side of Fort Belvoir, a section of the military installation known as Davidson Army Airfield. A component of the U.S. Army Military District of Washington, Davidson's most important mission was to provide air transportation for army bigwigs, foreign dignitaries, and senior members of the Department of Defense.

"So, sir, what do you say?" Bono pressed. "Please, it would

only take a few minutes to fly us to one of the air force bases around D.C. It would take us a week, maybe longer, to walk, the way things are right now. It's turning crazy quickly, you surely know that, and this may be our only chance. We've been gone an awfully long time, sir."

The colonel walked to the window and stared out on the flightline as he thought. "Do you have any idea how dear these helicopters are right now? They are literally the only transportation left inside the District. I've got my pilots flying twenty hours a day and we're not even close to keeping up. Now you want me to what, gin up a sortie so a couple Special Forces soldiers can go home and see their families?"

Bono shook his head at Sam and raised an eyebrow. *It doesn't look good,* his frown said.

The colonel stood in silence. Sam fidgeted nervously. Bono watched the colonel's back.

"I've been flying some critically important missions," the colonel continued. He thought another moment and then added, "But some of it is bogus. Yesterday I had to fly some congressional staff out to one of the bunkers in West Virginia. Bunch of snot-nosed college kids. They couldn't have explained the difference between national security and a security blanket, but they are *so* critical to the survival of our nation that we *had* to get them out there. I've got senators' wives demanding to be taken home to mama, some pukes down at the DNC—the Democratic National Committee, for pity's sake—demanding we get them out of town."

Bono started smiling.

"And you want me to take a couple grunt lieutenants down to Langley just so they can try to hitch a ride. A couple guys whose only excuse is that they've been living in the desert for the past twenty-four months, eating snakes and burying themselves in the sand to get away from the heat. Senators' wives or you two pukes? Now, who do you think I should put as my priority?" The colonel turned around.

Bono looked him in the eye. "Us, sir?" he said.

"Dang straight there, lieutenant. It'd be an honor to help."

Bono grinned. "Really, sir?" he asked.

"Yeah," the colonel answered indignantly. "After what you guys have been through, it's the least I can do. Believe me, guys, I would rather fly this mission than almost anything else I've done in the past week."

"Thank you, sir," Sam said.

The colonel turned toward them. "You do realize, I hope, that it's extremely unlikely it's going to do you any good anyway. No flights are going in or out of Andrews; the radiation levels are still too high. Now, we can get you two down to Langley, but what are the chances the air force is going to be able to help you? It's not like they're scheduling regular service down to Memphis." He turned to Sam. "And you don't even know where you want to go."

Neither of the younger officers said anything.

"I could make a pretty strong argument that the best thing you could do is stay here. We can take care of you. You could help us," the colonel said.

The soldiers immediately shook their heads. "No, sir," Bono said. "Thanks for the offer, and it might turn out that you're right, but we've got just two weeks, and this might be our only opportunity. Who knows how long it will be until our unit cuts us loose again? Months? More likely years. We've got to try to get there while we have the chance."

The colonel nodded. "Oh, to be so young," he muttered wistfully.

Sam cocked his head toward Bono. "If you saw his wife, sir," he said with a sly grin, "believe me, you'd understand."

"Got it," the colonel laughed.

"No, sir, you really have to see her. Go on, Bono, show him some of your pictures." He smiled teasingly at the colonel. "I'm telling you, sir, he's got the cutest little kid in the world. Go on and show 'im, Bono."

"I'm not going to show him . . ."

"Come on, don't be humble."

"There's no reason," the colonel broke in. "You don't have to convince me, okay."

"Thank you, sir," Bono said, shooting a deadly look toward Sam. Sam smiled again and shrugged.

The colonel walked back to his desk, calling to his aide. "Specialist Anderson, get in here."

The office door pulled back.

"What's the schedule on our Hueys?" the colonel asked.

"We've got two birds flying medical and rescue teams back and forth to the mobile hospitals. A four-ship has been requested to ferry some surviving congressional staff out to Mount Weather. Our last scheduled sortie before nightfall is a bird heading up to CIA headquarters. Scheduled takeoff is 20:00."

"Okay. Tell the pilots I want them to take off early and run these guys down to Langley before they head up to the CIA."

The army specialist hesitated. "Langley, sir? As in Langley Air Force Base, not CIA headquarters, Langley?"

"Yes, that is right."

"Sir, that's a forty-minute flight."

"I know that, Specialist Anderson."

"With all the birds we already have committed, not to mention our fuel situation, sir, do you really think that's wise?"

"I don't know, Specialist Anderson, I'm not that wise of a guy. But wise or not, I do think you ought to leave command decisions such as this up to the boss."

The specialist nodded and left the room. The two young soldiers stood up and thanked the colonel with a shake of their hands.

"Bono?" the colonel questioned as the lieutenants moved toward the door. "Like what . . . the Korean running shoes?"

Bono stopped and turned around. "That's it, sir. Twenty bucks. They'll last forever."

"Sure, sure, I had a pair myself. Picked 'em up at Osan. Not much of a nickname, though. Like being called Nike or Reebok or white-tennis-shoe guy or something."

"I've heard many worse," Sam broke in.

"How's that?" the colonel asked.

"Well, sir, for example, roughly translated the Persian word *parvân* means *pretty butterfly*. As a call sign, I think that would be a whole lot worse than Bono."

Colonel Parvan snorted, then laughed, walking them to the door. "Good luck, guys," he said.

The soldiers walked down the hall.

The colonel watched them and then added quietly, "Get on home and see your families. It might be the last time that you see them in a very long time."

* * *

Two hours later, Sam and Bono found themselves tucked inside the back of an old Huey UH-1 helicopter. The noise and vibration made it impossible to talk as the chopper lifted off from Davidson Army Airfield and headed south. Behind them, through the sunset haze and smoke, Sam could see a huge, irregular circle that changed in hue from brown to gray to black as it got closer to the center of the nuclear blast. A mile square, the scene went from broken buildings to torn-up buildings to steel frameworks jutting out of the ground to nothing but a blackened circle of dust and ash. He stared, then turned away and closed his eyes, knowing he was looking at his father's grave.

Forty minutes later, the chopper set up for its final approach into Langley. As they descended from 500 feet, Bono pushed the cabin doors back.

Langley Air Force Base, Headquarters, Air Combat Command, was situated on a jut of land that extended into the mouth of the Chesapeake Bay. The enormous runway ran east and west, with most of the aircraft parking on the south. Two taxiways led north, one to the alert fighter facilities, one extending farther through the trees toward a NASA test facility. Trees, bushes, and half a dozen small rivers and inlets from the Chesapeake Bay surrounded the base. As the chopper slowed, Sam noticed that the main road had been blocked with portable cement barricades. HUMVEEs and guard posts lined both sides of the access road. It looked more like Iraq than America, and he found it hard to draw his eyes away from the soldiers manning the gates, knowing that foreign fighters weren't the primary security concern anymore. He thought of the scene in D.C., the chaos they'd experienced back on I-495, then turned in his seat to look down at the center of the base. The aircraft parking ramp was crammed with dozens and dozens of aircraft: air refueling tankers, C-130 tactical freighters, C-141, C-5, and C-17 airlifts, F-15 fighters, contract airline carriers, and white C-21 VIP transports.

Sam nodded toward the crowded parking ramp. "You ever seen so many aircraft?" he shouted above the noise.

Bono shook his head. "Looks like half of our air force."

"No. Not even close. But that is a *bunch* of aircraft, lots more than I've ever seen here before."

The chopper turned east and set down on the VIP helicopter pad outside of Base Operations. A red sidewalk had been painted on the tarmac from the center of the helipad to the front door of Base Ops. The two soldiers stepped out of the old chopper, grabbed their gear, and walked quickly, heads lowered, toward the building where a large sign was positioned over the door:

Welcome to Langley Air Force Base
Home of the 1st Fighter Wing

They walked in, dropped their gear against the wall, and looked around. Offices left and right. A flight planning room down the hall, which would contain all the charts, maps, regulations, Notice to Airmen, and other pilot information required to plan a local or international flight. The weather shop was around the corner; off to the right, farther on, were a crew lounge and small cafeteria. The building was packed. Twenty or thirty pilots moved here and there, intent on their work. Sam noticed the different unit patches on their shoulders: C-141 crews from Washington and Germany; C-17 crews from South Carolina; tanker crews from Oklahoma, Japan, and Maine; aircraft and aircrews from all around the world. The place smelled like sweat and Chinese food and had a certain sense of urgency that came only with war. The two army soldiers moved toward the crew lounge and stopped.

"Okay," Sam said, "what now?"

"I don't know," Bono answered. "Haven't figured it out yet."

"My plan is a good one. And it's really all we have."

Bono hesitated. He was clearly not convinced.

"What else you going to do?" Sam pressed. "None of these aircrews or airplanes are going to take you down to Memphis. There's not even an air force base down there. And remember, with my plan, we don't have to ask them to land anywhere—which ain't going to happen, friend. But get them to divert a little, you know, just turn a couple degrees and fly for thirty minutes, that's a doable thing. Get us close, just fly over, and we can take it from there."

Bono turned to him, frustrated. "You don't even know where you're going. Your family couldn't have made it to Salt Lake before the EMP went off. You've got the entire country lying there before you. How you going to find them? *What is your plan!*"

Sam shook his head. He didn't know. Bono watched him, then turned away. "I'm sorry," he said. "I don't mean to sound pessimistic, but it's a real problem, Sam."

"I know that."

"What are you going to do, then?"

"I don't know."

"Are you going to—"

"Look, Bono, I don't know, okay? I mean, everything has happened pretty quickly. It's only been a day."

Bono sucked his teeth, then turned away. "I'm going to talk to the guys at the Operations Center and see what sorties they've got heading southwest." He turned and walked toward the center of the building, where an elevated platform had been built.

Sam waited, then went into the mission planning room with its lines of charts and maps, bulletins posted on the walls, notices of airport and airspace closures from all around the world, and a bunch of other things he didn't understand. He paid it all no attention as he walked to the back of the room where a huge map of the United States had been mounted on the wall. He stood before it, staring. Langley Air Force Base was on the tip of Virginia—hard to go farther east without getting wet. The entire nation lay to the west, thousands and thousands of miles. Eight states between Salt Lake City and Langley. A dozen major cities. A thousand smaller towns. Two mountain ranges. The great, barren plains. Half a dozen major rivers.

How would he ever find them? How could he possibly know where they were!

He located I-70, the main highway heading west from D.C., and traced it with his finger, following its course through Maryland, West Virginia, Ohio, Indiana . . . still only a fourth of the way to Utah. Such a long, long way to go.

And just two weeks to find them.

He stared and then shivered.

Who was he kidding? His family could be anywhere along a highway that extended for more than two thousand miles. They could have taken I-80 farther north or any one of a dozen highways to the south.

He took a breath and sighed, his shoulders slumping as he thought. Bono was right. He wouldn't find them. There wasn't any hope.

*   *   *

The man entered the room quietly. Sam didn't notice him until he was standing at his side; then Sam turned, looking at the man's profile as the stranger also considered the large map on the wall. Sam started to turn away but couldn't, for there was something about the stranger that seemed out of place. For one thing, he wasn't wearing a uniform, just a white shirt and tan slacks, making him one of the very few civilians in the building. His hair was short and blond and he was tall and strongly built, with bare arms and a thick chest. Some kind of security badge hung around his neck and Sam glanced toward it, trying to figure out who he was.

The man turned toward him and smiled so warmly that Sam couldn't help but smile back. "How you doing?" the stranger asked.

"Pretty good," Sam replied.

The man nodded, then leaned against a large table in the middle of the room.

Sam watched him a moment before turning back to the wall. They stood in silence as Sam studied the map.

"Are you the fellow who's looking for his family?" the stranger asked.

Sam looked around, then nodded. "You must have talked to Bono?"

"Bono? I'm not sure what you mean."

"Lieutenant Calton. The other army officer I came in with."

The man didn't answer.

Sam shrugged, his eyebrows creasing. The stranger looked at him and smiled again. Dark eyes, determined, almost piercing, gracious and comfortable. Sam felt an instant liking, almost a drawing to the stranger. "Sir, how did you know about my family?" he asked respectfully. Something about the stranger seemed to demand his deference.

The man thrust his hands into his pockets. "Go to Chicago, Sam." He stepped forward and pointed with his finger, tapping the map. "Stay on the south side of the city. You will know what to do."

Sam's eyes were drawn to the map. "Sir, what are you talking about?"

"Listen to me, Samuel Brighton."

Sam hesitated, almost afraid to answer. "Chicago? Why Chicago! That doesn't make any sense."

"Trust me, Sam. Chicago. Both of them will be waiting. You have to save their lives."

"I can't go to Chicago. I have to find my family. I don't even know what you're talking—"

He didn't have time to finish his sentence. Bono burst into

the room, running toward him. "Come on," he almost shouted. "I got us a ride!"

The stranger looked at Sam intently, reached out and patted him on the shoulder, then turned and walked out of the room. Bono paid the man no attention as he ran toward his friend. "Come on, man, we don't have much time." He was flushed and excited, his pack already on his back.

"What is it? What you got?"

"There's a C-141 heading down to Little Rock. They don't have much room, but I talked to the loadmaster and he'll get us on . . ."

"Little Rock, are you kidding? Man, that's perfect! You'd only be, what, I don't know, but not too far from Memphis!"

"Yeah, but it's leaving right now. I mean *right* now! The aircraft is out on the ramp, the engines running. They've got a hard takeoff time and they can't let it slip or they'll be here for six hours waiting for another slot. We've got to go. *I've* got to go! I've got to take this, Sam."

Sam hesitated, shooting another glance toward the map. "I understand. This is great. Go on! Go and get it."

Bono didn't move. "What about you?"

"I don't know . . ." Sam stepped aside, looking toward the doorway, but the stranger was gone.

"Come with me, Sam. Come with me now. Come down, spend some time with my family. My wife would love to have you. And I could use your help."

Sam slowly shook his head. "I can't do that, Bono. Dude, I've got my own family, my mom and my two brothers."

"Stick with me, Sam. You're never going to find them. Not like this! Not the way things are right now. Luke and Ammon, they're no dummies. They'll take care of your mom."

Sam thought, then turned away. He paced, his lips tight

with worry, the words almost screaming in his head. *"Go to Chicago. They are waiting. You have to save their lives!"*

Bono watched him, confused, then spread his arms toward the map. "Look, Sam, I understand what you're thinking, but you've got to be realistic, okay? You've got to consider the very real possibility that you might not be able to find your family right now. I don't need to remind you what is happening out there. I don't need to tell you just how difficult . . . no, Sam, how impossible this is going to be. You can't travel. You've got no transportation. You don't even know where you're going!" Bono was almost shouting now, his voice rising with frustration. "Come with me. Come to Memphis. This might be our only chance."

Sam took a step toward him. "I just can't do that, Bono."

Bono took a breath and held it, then slowly let it out. "All right, then." He glanced down at his watch. "I've got to go, Sam. He gave me five minutes, not a second more."

Sam paced again and then stopped, his face crunched and tight.

"What's your plan, Sam? I need to know."

Sam glanced behind him at the map on the wall. "I'm going to Chicago," he answered softly.

Bono took a step toward him. "Chicago! Are you crazy! Why are you going there? Why, Sam, would you go up to Chicago . . ." Bono stopped, his voice trailing off. He stood frozen for a moment, the color draining from his face. Ten seconds passed in silence. "Yes," he mumbled softly. "Yes, that's what you should do."

Sam nodded to him. "Go now," he said.

Bono hesitated. "The aircraft won't wait a second for me."

"Go, buddy, go!"

Bono raced to Sam, threw his arms around him, and drew him to his chest. "I don't know . . . I don't know what's going on. I don't know why you have to go to Chicago, but yes, I am certain that's the right thing to do."

Sam pushed him away. "Don't you miss that aircraft."

Bono turned and started running, almost getting to the door. Then he stopped and turned around. "Take care of yourself, Lieutenant Brighton."

"Roger that. Now go, go, go."

Bono gave a quick salute, then started running down the hall.

Sam stood a moment, silence and peace settling all around him, then walked to the doorway. Bono was already gone, the door that led toward the flightline swinging shut. Looking out, he could see that it had grown dark outside, the lights from the building casting yellow squares across the tarmac.

He stood, feeling alone, then walked toward the Operations Desk. "You got any flights heading west?" he asked the duty officer.

The sergeant shook his head. "We're not opening up any spots right now, sir," he answered curtly.

Sam hesitated, still not used to being called "sir" or "lieutenant," then leaned toward the sergeant. "Come on," he pleaded. "There's got to be something. Can't we work something out?"

The sergeant stopped his work and looked up. "Are you kidding me, lieutenant? I mean, you've *got* to be kidding me. Look out on the ramp there, look out on the *stinking* world, then turn back and tell me that you should be my priority right now. The nation has just been kicked in the throat, and you think my most important job is to try to get an aerial taxi for some army puke."

Sam was taken aback. "Dude, you know I was . . ."

The sergeant slid a notepad across the counter. "Give me your name and information and I'll put you on the list."

Sam glanced toward the notepad, thumbing through it. Five pages long. More than a hundred names already on the list.

He sighed, his shoulders slumping, and reached across the counter for a pen.

* * *

Sam spent the next eight hours stalking up and down the halls of the Base Operations building, talking to every pilot, copilot, or cargo master he could find. He made himself obnoxious, hounding everyone. With each passing minute he grew more anxious to get a flight.

He felt it, deep inside, a growing twist of worry that pulled his stomach into knots.

He didn't understand it. He'd never felt anything quite like it before. But like in a dream, he sensed there was a monster coming at him and he couldn't turn to run.

"Come on," he repeated as he paced up and down the hall. "Come on, come on, I've got to find a flight!"

* * *

Flight operations continued on a twenty-four-hour cycle, and every hour that went by, the place became more frantic and intense. Sam kept himself awake for as long as he could, terrified of missing his chance, but sometime after four in the morning he finally fell asleep, crashing in the crew lounge across a leather couch with a couple of pilots just in from Germany. As the sun rose, he forced himself awake, washed up in the bathroom (wondering how the military base maintained its water pressure), and started stalking again.

Eight hours later, after hounding and begging and threatening all sorts of things that no one really believed, Sam got the best offer he was going to get. A KC-135 air refueling tanker was heading out to Portland. Yeah, they had some room, and yeah, they'd allow him to take up one of the small seats in the back, but it was a five-hour flight across the States with no stops in between. Sam begged again, but lost the battle. No way were they going to make a stop for him.

"It's cool, it's cool, you don't need to," he pulled back. "Just get me close. That's all I need. I'll take care of the rest."

The pilot, a pretty major with short brown hair, camouflage flight suit, and puffy eyes from spending too much time in the air, stared at him, suspicious. "Don't you go fooling around with my sortie, you hear me, Lieutenant Brighton?"

"No, ma'am. Nothing stupid. But if you'll just fly a *little* farther north than you were planning on, it would really help me out."

"I already told you, we're not stopping."

"You won't have to, major. All you've got to do is get me close."

"But if ye are prepared ye shall not fear."

—DOCTRINE AND COVENANTS 38:30

chapter thirty-one

The afternoon passed, rainy and wet, and dark came quickly because of the low clouds.

An hour before nightfall, Ammon and Luke set off, hiking north. This time Luke reluctantly carried the gun tucked between his waistband and the small of his back. He also wore a poncho, which concealed his hands, allowing him to reach for the weapon without being detected if he needed to.

He desperately prayed it wouldn't happen. He had shot a gun before—their father had insisted on his sons knowing how to handle a weapon—but he was hardly an expert. More, he was completely unprepared to shoot an actual person. Would he do it? He didn't think so. When it came right down to pulling the trigger, he simply didn't think he could. To save his brother's life? Maybe. But he probably couldn't shoot to save his own.

The two young men moved quietly and quickly through the growing darkness, staying near the tree line, which paralleled the road. A mile passed and their boots became heavy with rain and mud. The rain let up and, to the west, the clouds began to thin. On their left, sometimes a hundred yards, sometimes more or less than that, the freeway had grown less crowded. There were a few people here and there, but most had given up traveling for the night and were hunkering down, setting up camp inside other people's cars.

Approaching the edge of the trees, Ammon crouched and pointed. "There," he said.

Luke knelt down at his side. The men were still there, guarding the bridge. They stood together in the rain, baseball hats and wet hair and clinging clothes.

"Who are they?" Luke wondered. "Where do they come from? Why are they doing this? It makes no sense."

"It's crazy," Ammon said, then pointed farther up the freeway. "You see that?" he asked.

Luke strained to see against the growing dark. "Looks like . . . what is that . . . is that a car that's been overturned?"

"It's a Highway Patrol," Ammon explained. "It was easier to see it this morning when there was more light."

Luke sucked in a breath. "You sure?"

"Really sure."

"What's it mean?"

"Don't know. But it leaves a lot of questions. Where's the patrolman? What happened to his car? You saw what happened—the EMP didn't cause a big explosion or anything. Everything just quit working, coasting to a stop. That trooper didn't flip his car. Someone overturned it. Why would they do that?"

Luke thought as he stared. "You didn't tell Mom anything about this?"

"No. I was going to, but I changed my mind. No reason to make her worry more than she already is."

Luke lifted his hand and pointed to the crowd of men. "Is that the guy I fought last night?"

Ammon squinted. "Yeah, I think that's him. I got a little closer this morning, but it's hard to be sure in this light. I tell you this, though, the guy you took last night had a mean gash down the side of his head."

"I whacked him pretty good," Luke explained with pride. "I had a fist-sized rock in my hand when I popped him."

"Yeah, well, I don't think he's very happy. They sure weren't happy to see me this morning."

The two young men stared. Ammon's knees started cramping from bending in a squat. "There is some good news, I think, in what happened to the trooper's car," he said.

"What's that?"

"Maybe I'm wrong, but it just seems to me that sometime the authorities are going to realize they've lost a man out here. Sooner or later, apparently later in this case, they're going to notice they have a man down. When that happens, I have to believe they'd send someone out here to investigate."

Luke thought, then nodded slowly. "You might be right."

Ammon stared at the group of ill-dressed men, counting them. "There aren't as many of them as there were this morning."

"Maybe they've figured it's time to head out? Get home to their families or whatever. Take their share of the cash and run."

"That's what I was thinking, especially if they believe the authorities are going to show up."

Luke moved his eyes up the road, toward the turned-over car. "You never saw the trooper? You have no idea where he is?"

"None at all. But he's got to be around here somewhere. Unless he took off and started walking."

Luke shook his head. "He's not alive," he said.

Ammon shivered. "I was wondering about that."

They crouched another five minutes, watching the men guard the road. While they watched, a dozen people walked up to the blockade. The negotiations seemed to take a long time and were evidently complicated. Of the dozen who approached them, the outlaws let a few more than half go through.

Ammon shivered again. It was getting cold, but that wasn't what was driving a chill up and down his spine. "What do you think?" he finally asked.

Luke reached up and pulled his poncho close, feeling the same chill. "I don't look forward to confronting those guys we met last night."

Ammon grunted in agreement. "I think we should wait until morning. We'll leave really early, before the sun comes up. Might be these goobers will have dispersed by then. If so, good enough, we head up the road. If not, we'll reevaluate then and decide what's best to do."

Luke bit his lip, thinking of the little girl huddled in the old car a mile or two behind them. "I heard Mom talking to Mary just before we left," he said. "Sometime last week, Mary started giving Kelly morphine to control the pain. She doesn't have any more pain medication with her. Mom thinks Kelly might be going into shock from morphine withdrawal."

Ammon nodded slowly. "That and the pain."

Luke stared across the empty fields toward the freeway. "If we don't get Kelly Beth home pretty soon, I don't think it's going to matter."

"Understood," Ammon said. He got up. "Come on, let's go."

Capri 44
Thirty-Two Thousand Feet over Southern Ohio

The inside of the old KC-135 air refueling tanker was cold and noisy and full of light mist from tiny leaks in the pressure and heating systems. The cabin walls were gray-stitch insulated material with the metal ribs of the fuselage showing through, and the floor was scarred and worn from an untold number of cargo pallets being rolled on and off. The main purpose of the aircraft was to carry and offload fuel for other aircraft, refueling them while in flight, and its belly was a series of enormous, interconnected fuel cells. Tonight, because the old tanker was not scheduled to air refuel, it didn't carry as much fuel, and so the loadmaster had loaded up the cargo compartment with military supplies needed in the west. Three dozen tightly packed wooden pallets, double-wrapped in thick plastic, took up the entire cargo compartment.

A row of uncomfortable web and aluminum benches ran down each side of the plane. Sam sat alone, his head resting on his chest, his mind racing behind closed eyes.

The tension had never left him. It was growing worse instead. A deep sense of . . . he didn't know . . . a sense of *lateness* crept upon him, making him irritable and intense.

Time was slipping by. He was falling behind.

But he didn't know for what.

Yet he was growing more tense by the minute, his mouth dry, his muscles tight.

He felt a gentle push on his shoulder and looked up. The loadmaster was standing there. "Boss wants to see you in the cockpit," the master sergeant said.

Sam nodded, stretched to pull the tired muscles in his back, then stood and followed the sergeant to the cockpit. He stepped around the forward bulkhead, between a narrow entry, and through the cockpit door.

The aircraft commander was sitting in the left seat, one foot propped up against the lower portion of the cockpit display panel. Sam moved forward and stood between the two pilot seats. Looking through the cockpit windows he stared, completely stunned. It was like flying through the emptiness of space. A few stars above them. Endless blackness down below—not a single ground light anywhere. Utter darkness straight ahead.

He stared until the pilot interrupted his thoughts. "Kind of strange, isn't it?"

Sam shuddered at the darkness.

"So you really want to do this?" the pilot asked.

"Absolutely," Sam replied without hesitation. He thought of the growing tension deep inside him. "I've *got* to do it," he said.

"You don't know what you're jumping into, do you, Brighton? You don't have any idea what's going on down there."

"Doesn't matter, really, does it, ma'am? It's going to be the same everywhere. Here. Portland. Everything in between. Everyone's going through the same thing right now."

The pilot thought again. "We've never done this before, you know. We just don't do such things from a tanker. C-141, C-17, yeah, any day, but we're a different kind of aircraft, a different system. We don't have a ramp that can drop down. And we're supposed to be trained and qualified before we go tossing people out."

The radio sounded in her headset and she paused and listened as the other pilot responded to the radio call.

Turning in her seat, she looked at Sam. "You understand how many rules and regulations we'll be breaking?" she asked. "Tons. Way too many."

"I understand," Sam replied. "But I'm telling you, ma'am, it's no big thing. Descend as low as you can to equalize the pressure and get a little warmer, slow down as much as you can, and give me a thumbs-up when we're there. That's all you've got to do."

The pilot dropped her foot and sipped from a bottle of

water. "I don't suppose too many people are going to be so concerned about peacetime regulations right now," she concluded, then shrugged and glanced toward the other pilot, who gave her a "whatever" kind of look. "Okay," she said. "If you're willing to take the chance, who am I to tell you no?"

"Thank you," Sam said, his face illuminated by the subdued white and green fluorescent lighting in the cockpit.

The pilot checked her NAV readout. "Twenty-one minutes, then," she said. "Go get your gear on. We won't delay if you're not ready."

Sam nodded, then turned and left the cockpit without saying any more.

INTERSTATE 65
FOURTEEN MILES SOUTHEAST OF CHICAGO

It was very dark. Luke and Ammon moved silently back toward their cars. Sara was waiting for them, standing near the edge of the trees. Hearing movements through the brush, she quietly called their names. Minutes later, they emerged from the darkness.

"What do you think?" she asked them as they approached.

They stopped and explained the situation. While they talked, Mary moved toward them, listening intently.

"We really ought to wait until morning," Ammon concluded.

Mary's face sank. "Another day!"

"Another night, Mary. We'll try to leave for the city in the morning."

"We've *got* to leave in the morning. I can't stay here another day. My baby needs her medicines!"

Ammon glanced toward Luke, looking for support. Luke shook his head in sympathy. "I understand," he said, turning back to Mary. "But Mrs. Dupree, we need to think this through and be careful. It's dangerous right now. It will get better—I don't think it's going to be like this forever—but right now, with those guys out there, we need to wait."

"But my little girl, my little girl . . ."

Ammon started to answer her, then fell silent. Mary's little girl was going to die. He was certain of that now. Kelly hadn't wakened since midmorning. She didn't shiver anymore. It seemed she hardly moved. Sometimes she mumbled, but her eyes, when they were open, had taken on an opaque, filmy texture. She hadn't eaten anything, as far as he knew, and had swallowed only a sip or two of water all day. No, there was nothing they could do now. She was going to pass away. Here. On the road to Chicago. Back at her apartment, maybe, if things went just right, but it was going to happen—that was the dreadful truth.

He sighed, a heavy sadness creeping over him, then turned and walked to Mary, extending his arms. She stepped quickly back. He took another step toward her and paused. Twenty-four hours ago, she had been a stranger. Now he felt a kinship for her that expanded beyond any emotion he had ever felt before. He wanted to help her. He cared for her. He even loved her.

But there was nothing he could do.

He couldn't help her.

He couldn't help her daughter.

He couldn't make it go away.

And he ached, a dull and painful throbbing in his heart.

He lifted his arms again and stepped toward her. Mary held back for a moment, then fell into his chest. He put his arms around her, almost completely supporting her weight. "I'm so sorry, Mrs. Dupree, I'm so sorry. If there was something we could do . . . if there was anything we could do . . ."

The small black woman started crying, tiny shudders of

emotion in his arms. She knew now. They all knew. And as he supported her weight, his arms around her, Ammon thought he actually felt her heart break.

CAPRI 44
EIGHTEEN THOUSAND FEET OVER SOUTH CHICAGO

The aircraft slowed, the engines pulling back to a quiet hum as it descended, gradually slipping out of the dark sky. The loadmaster had already moved to the rear door on the left side of the aircraft reserved exclusively for emergency evacuation situations. He had never actually opened the door even while on the ground, let alone while in flight. He had strapped an oxygen mask with a built-in microphone and headset receiver over his face and was ready to depressurize.

"Fifteen thousand," he heard the pilot announce.

"What's the airspeed?" the loadmaster queried.

"Slowing through two hundred knots."

The loadmaster turned to Sam, who was finishing a final check of his equipment. "You want one-sixty?" he called above the noise of the aircraft.

"Slow as you can get her." Sam pulled his leg straps tight.

The loadmaster turned back to the door and spoke into his mask. "He's looking for one hundred sixty knots. I don't know, we're kind of heavy to be going that slow, don't you think?" The aircraft kept on slowing and descending as they talked.

"Okay," the pilot said after two more minutes had passed. "One-seventy now, and ten thousand. We're on oxygen up here. How about you in the back?"

The loadmaster checked himself and the boom operator, getting a thumbs-up from the young airman who was going to help him with the door. "Two good masks in the rear," he said.

"Ready to depressurize."

There was a sudden *thump* and rush of air as the cabin pressure was released, forming an instant cloud of mist inside the cabin. Bitter cold. Lots of noise. Building pressure in Sam's ears and gut.

"How's everything in the back?" the aircraft commander asked after the aircraft had depressurized.

"Good back here. Clear to open the aft emergency hatch?"

"Sergeant, you are cleared."

The loadmaster gave Sam a quick thumbs-up. Sam moved forward and stood before the door, hands on his chest straps, bracing himself against the bone-chilling cold and blast of wind that would suck the oxygen right out of his lungs. He bent his knees and waited, just two feet from the door, his muscles tense, ready to pull his legs up tight against his body so they didn't flail around him when he stepped into the night.

He knew that, twenty feet behind him, the enormous tail of the aircraft angled outward from the rear of the fuselage. It was possible the wind would blow him back into the tail before he cleared it, in which case he would be cut in half. Would it happen? It wasn't supposed to. But he'd never heard of anyone bailing out of a flying KC-135 before, so he really didn't know.

Seconds passed. The parachute straps cut into his legs. The loadmaster released the latch holding the access door release lever, then turned to Sam. "You ready?" he shouted. Sam nodded and stepped six inches forward. "Keep balled up. It's going to blow you." Sam nodded again, wishing he had some goggles.

"Twenty seconds," the pilot said through the loadmaster's headset.

He moved toward Sam, slapped his shoulder, and yelled

against his ear, "I hope you find your family." Sam nodded and shouted, "Thank you." The loadmaster slapped again.

"Doors coming open," he said into his mask, then pulled the door back six inches and slid it to the side.

Piercing cold. Bone-crushing wind. An unbelievable howling from the four jet engines and the blast of air. The sound filled the entire aircraft and vibrated against the fuselage walls with the force of a tornado.

The sergeant lifted a hand and showed the count with his fingers. Five. Four. Three. Two. He slapped Sam on the shoulder.

Sam tucked his head and stepped into the howling night.

He tumbled head-over-head, the freezing cold around him, feeling as if he couldn't breathe. Spinning, his arms pulled into his chest, he fell through the darkness toward the even darker earth below.

INTERSTATE 65
FOURTEEN MILES SOUTHEAST OF CHICAGO

The two men stood together at the lip of the bridge. The sun had set and the other thugs had scattered, heading off to their trailers and homes, leaving the two men standing in the misty air alone. The shorter of them pointed, lifting his arm halfway up his side. "He was there again," he said. "The one you saw this morning."

The taller man hesitated, gently touching the scab that was forming at the back of his head. His ribs still burned and he walked carefully, every misstep sending bolts of pain through his chest. Worse, he'd been nauseous and weak-kneed all morning, his eyes bleary, his tongue thick. It seemed he could actually feel the bone plates in his skull grind together every time he moved his head. He'd suffered concussions a couple of times before, the worst one back in high school after a particularly bitter fight, so he knew the symptoms pretty well. And he knew that, as with the fight in high school, the only thing that would make him feel better was either passing time or revenge.

He stared toward the darkness. "You sure it was him?" he demanded of his drinking pal.

"Yeah. It was him. The one who attacked you. The other one was with him, too."

The taller man snorted. "You really think they're soldiers?" His voice was cynical. No way was he going to mess with a pair of Army Rangers. His old man had always told him he was stupid, but even he wasn't that dull.

Baby-fat man shook his head. "No, they ain't soldiers. They're just a couple punks who jumped our backs in a chicken of a fight. A couple cowards who had to use rocks and sticks to beat us 'cause they couldn't take us straight-up."

The leader moved his head and grimaced. "You don't think that was his mama?"

"I don't really care."

The other man considered. "She was a pretty good-looking woman . . ."

More silence as he thought.

"They're back there somewhere," he hissed. "Sitting in their cars, waiting for rescue. But no one's going to save them. Not tonight, anyway."

His buddy swore. "We could 'rescue' them," he sneered.

"I think we should," the tall one answered with contempt. "I think it's time for payback. Only this time, we'll be the ones who come sneaking up from the dark."

chapter thirty-two

They built a fire, more for the light than the heat, for Sara simply couldn't stand the thought of another dark, empty night. The wood around them was soaking wet and it took a while to get the fire going. When they did, they kept it low, sitting close to the flames, not wanting to broadcast their position in the trees. As they sat, the clouds began to thin and then break up overhead, the moon and starlight shining through the cracks.

"I wonder what time it is," Sara said, staring quietly at the flames.

None of their watches, all electronic, worked anymore, and no one responded for a moment. The dancing fire had cast its spell, pulling them deep into silent thought. "I'm guessing something between ten and twelve," Luke finally answered.

Mary, a dozen feet away, said, "It's just after eleven-thirty."

Sara watched the fire cast yellow shadows across Mary's face. She looked tired. They all were tired, but Mary was especially so. "How do you know that, Mary?" she asked.

Mary kept her eyes on the flame. "I don't know, I've just always had a sixth sense when it comes to time. I've never worn a watch in my life, but I can always tell you within a few minutes of what time it is."

"That may come in handy," Ammon laughed.

"Happy to be able to contribute something," Mary smiled.

"Does your internal clock work while you're sleeping?" Ammon asked.

"Pretty good," Mary answered. "Sometimes, if I'm sick or something, I seem to get off, but mostly I can count on it."

"So you could set your brain-alarm for, say, five in the morning? That'd give us time to pack our things and be ready to head out by sunrise."

Mary seemed to concentrate, rolling back her eyes. "Got it," she said.

Ammon watched her, then laughed. "Five o' clock, right?"

"Got it," she repeated.

Ammon nodded, satisfied.

"Of course, you'll never be able to prove it if I'm wrong," Mary giggled.

Ammon smiled back at her. "True that," he said.

Sara held her hand up. "What was that!" she whispered suddenly.

The others fell silent. Ammon stood slowly, moving away from the light of the fire. He listened, his ears straining. Sara also stood up. Luke remained where he was, cocking his head.

A tiny flit of movement from behind him. A brush of leaves. The stir of wet grass. Everyone heard it. Ammon tensed. Sara's eyes grew wide, the whites shining fearfully in the flame.

Ammon shot a deadly look toward their car, thinking of the gun that was hidden in the trunk. He motioned to Luke, then started walking slowly toward it. Sara watched him go, then turned back around. "So, Luke," she said nonchalantly, "do you think it's going to rain any more tonight?"

"What did you say, Mom?" Luke asked a little too obviously as he stood.

The two men emerged from the darkness, their faces yellow in the firelight, the sockets of their eyes cast in shadows from the flame. "Well, well, well," the first man drawled, "look what we have here! Our U.S. soldiers and their mamas. What a lovely, lovely sight."

He wobbled, his eyes unfocused, both hands hidden behind his back. A mean drunk on the best of nights, he'd gotten his initial momentum from the Jack Daniels, but it was the pain in his head and ribs that drove him now. The more pain he felt—and he felt a lot of pain—the more angry he became. He sneered at Ammon. "Don't move there, soldier boy!"

Ammon turned toward him. "Listen, pal, we don't want any problems, okay?" He kept his voice from choking. "We didn't come looking for trouble. We were just defending ourselves."

"Defend your . . . shelves," the drunk man slurred. "That's a good idea, tough guy."

Luke's mind raced. "Come on, boys. Come and stand with us by the fire."

The first man belched and spit. "I don't think so," he said.

Ammon slowly backed toward the car.

The drunk dropped his right arm. The steel tire iron he was holding angled sharply to the right. Ammon's eyes grew wide, darting back and forth. The adrenaline shot through him, the rage starting to build.

Luke took an angry step toward the man. "I'm not afraid of you!" he snapped. "I took you last night, no problem. Believe me, boys, we can take you down again."

"I don't think so." The drunk dropped his other hand. An old Colt .45 shone in the dim light, the short barrel glistening like liquid metal. "Not tonight, baby," he sneered at them again.

Ammon froze. Sara screamed. Mary's eyes rolled back and she went limp, slumping to the ground, her arms tucked underneath her like a rag doll. The second man stared at her and wobbled. "Look at that," he laughed, "she's as drunk as we are!" Mary twitched, then lay motionless, completely unconscious. Ammon moved toward her.

"Get back," the first man screamed.

"Look at her. She's—"

"I don't care about her!" he screamed again.

The second man giggled and pointed. "Good place for her," he laughed. "Good place for the black mama, down there in the mud."

Ammon stopped, silent and sweating, even in the cold. There was something about these men, something unstable, unpredictable—something dangerous. He could see nothing but unhinged fire in their eyes.

"Look at her," the second man continued mocking, his voice thick with bigotry and hate. "This is where all these African mamas belong!" He took two steps and kicked Mary in the ribs, lifting her tiny body off the ground. She didn't move, absorbing the entire force of the blow, her eyes still closed.

"LEAVE HER ALONE!" Sara screamed.

"Shut up!" the first man hissed.

"She's done nothing to you! It's us you've got a problem with."

"Got that right, you wench!" The man took a raging step toward her.

"Stay back!" Luke cried, racing to stand between the stranger and his mom.

The man stopped, then took a step back. He wobbled, smiled, and lifted the barrel of his gun.

Ammon lurched suddenly toward the men.

"Don't move!" the first man cried, turning the Colt .45 on him. Dropping the tire iron, he shifted the gun into his other hand. "Showtime!" he hissed.

A deadly silence settled over them, full and heavy and not of this world. Evil. Raging evil. The spirit of Satan filled the night.

They were standing right beside him. They were speaking in his ear. Murder was their greatest pleasure and they shivered now with glee.

To the man, it seemed as if time stood still. His heart crashed inside his broken rib cage, his eardrums pounding. Slowly, he lifted the heavy gun, squinted one eye, and aimed at Ammon.

"Do it!" Satan hissed.

He held the gun out, his arm extended, pointing it at Ammon's heart.

"Kill him!" Satan shouted. "Kill him! Do it now!"

The drunken man took a breath and held it. Time crawled, so warped and slow it seemed a full minute passed with each beat of his raging heart.

"Kill them both! Then kill the women!"

Ammon stepped back, moving in slow motion. His eyes were focused like a laser, never leaving the barrel of the gun. It was all he saw now, all he knew, his entire universe nothing but the barrel of the gun.

Sara screamed, but the man couldn't hear anything but the hissing voices in his head. His eyesight narrowed, then tunnel-visioned as he focused on a two-inch spot on Ammon's chest. Luke cried and ran toward him, flying through the air. The man jerked the gun around and fired, sending a geyser of mud

and dirty water into the air. Luke cried again and fell back-
ward, landing spread-eagled in the mud, his face contorted in
pain. Sara screamed and ran toward him, falling on her knees
beside her son. The man turned in fury and aimed at Ammon's
head.

*"Kill him," Balaam cried, his voice filled with ice and rage.
"You've killed one. Your fate is sealed. Might as well kill them all
now."*

The drunk moved his finger to the trigger, the flesh press-
ing against the cold metal.

*"WE COMMAND YOU TO KILL THEM!" Balaam and
Satan cried together in his ear.*

The man swallowed and stared at Ammon, time flowing
back to normal now. Looking down the barrel of the gun, he
saw Ammon staring at him in shock. Sara cried again in
anguish as she pulled Luke's body close.

"This is for last night," the drunk man whispered, press-
ing the trigger of the gun.

The tire iron came down with sickening force on the back
of his head, sending him slumping to the ground.

Mary stood over him, her eyes wild, the tire rod in her
hand. The man dropped, completely unconscious, his face
pressed into the mud, his eyes open but lifeless, his open
mouth gasping in the sludge.

Mary dropped to her knees, pulled the gun from his
clenched fingers, held it up in terror, then threw it toward
Ammon. He caught it and, with one motion, turned it, pulled
the sliding lever, and aimed it at the other man.

The fat one stood there speechless, his eyes wide in shock
and fear. Where *had* she come from! How had she risen like
that! One moment he had been the hunter—now the gun was
aimed at *him!*

She had been faking! She had tricked them! Stupid, deceiving liar!

Mary stared at him, her eyes flaming. "I'm not an African," she sneered.

The man slumped, then turned and ran into the dark.

chapter thirty-three

R*un!*" the Spirit whispered to him. "*Run, Samuel, run!*"

The young soldier stood motionless in the moonlight, unsure of what to do. He actually looked around him. Where had the voice come from?

"*RUN!*" the voice seemed to whisper once again, more urgently this time.

Only seconds earlier had he even hit the ground. The parachute was strung around him, streamer lines tangled underfoot. He pulled the parachute release buckles at his chest and wriggled out of the harness, then bent and grabbed the thin parachute material and started wadding. Rolling it into a loose ball, he tossed it aside.

"*RUN!*" the Spirit whispered.

So he started to run.

Through the brush, toward the road. Up the embankment, onto the pavement. A small country road. He stopped, jerking his head left and right.

"*RUN!*"

He looked north. The night was quiet. Half a dozen dead

cars sat around him. No one was in sight. He bent over, looking inside. The cars were empty.

He turned and ran again.

A mile later, the country road grew narrow. The blacktop ended. The road turned to loose gravel. He stumbled in the dark, rolling onto his shoulders as he fell. His backpack was heavy, loaded with all his gear. He didn't even come to a stop but kept on rolling until he came to his knees from the inertia, then pushed himself to his feet again and ran.

A line of trees. He kept on running. His lungs began to burn. His legs were loose and in rhythm, his backpack bouncing as he ran.

The road turned east, but he kept north. Through a ditch, half-filled with muddy water, his boots and pants getting wet, up the other side, across a narrow field now, always running toward Polaris, the navigation star. Was it the right direction? He didn't know, but the dread inside him kept him moving as beads of sweat started rolling down his face to burn his eyes. His breathing was deep and heavy, but still he didn't slow.

The moon broke through the scattered clouds, casting the emptiness around him in dim light. Shadows up ahead of him. A row of houses, dark and empty. He passed a winding driveway and heard a barking dog. He turned right to move around the empty homes and almost crashed into a barbwire fence. Bending, he forced his way through. The barking dog was getting closer. He pushed his pack against the wire, got caught for a second, then forced through and turned and ran.

A freeway up ahead of him. He scrambled up the embankment. Hundreds of abandoned cars. Voices to his right. Movement there. A group of people on the road, to the south. He started moving toward them, gasping for breath.

"*No*," he heard the whisper.

So he turned north again and ran.

chapter thirty-four

Sara screamed and held her son, cradling his head in her arms. The mud, slippery and wet, was cold against her legs. Luke's eyes were closed and he lay motionless, his body heavy and lifeless to her touch. His mouth opened and he gasped and closed it again.

It was nearly impossible to see in the dim light, so Sara searched carefully along his chest and abdomen with her fingers. She felt it before she saw it and lifted her hands, holding them against the firelight. Seeing the stains of blood, she sobbed in ripples, unable to control herself.

Ammon watched the fleeing man disappear into the night, then turned away, his face tight with anguish. "Watch him!" he cried to Mary, pointing to the man who had slumped unconscious at her feet. "Smash him if you have to, but DO NOT let him stand again."

Mary nodded, her trembling hands holding the tire iron in a powerful grip. Ammon rushed to his brother and dropped on his knees. "Luke . . . Luke," he repeated, whispering his name. "Hang in there, brother, hang in there. You're going to be okay."

He shot a look toward his mother, who was staring into her son's empty eyes. His face was ashen now, and lifeless. Ammon gently lifted his mother's arm, which was draped across Luke's chest. The bullet wound, a quarter-size hole, dark and red, had penetrated his abdomen right beneath the ribs. "Oh Luke, oh Luke," Ammon repeated in agony, completely unaware that he was saying anything.

Sara kept on crying, overcome with shock. She rocked her wounded son like a baby, cradling his head in her arms. His eyelids fluttered and he murmured, and she pressed her ear against his lips.

"Mom, can you hear me?" he whispered softly.

"Yes, Luke, I'm here."

He opened his eyes and looked up at her. "Don't worry about me, Mom. It doesn't hurt that much."

He forced a painful smile, then gurgled on his blood.

EAST SIDE, CHICAGO, ILLINOIS

Azadeh walked into the living room, felt her way past the small table to the counter, and stared through the kitchen window. The city had turned black now. Not a streetlight. Not a candle. Not a ray of light anywhere. Though she couldn't see them, she knew the mob was there. The streets were filled with people and had been all day.

She hadn't been outside of the apartment since the power had gone off. Throughout the day she had listened to hurried footsteps and calling voices and, more than once, angry fists beating on her door. Huddling in the corner, afraid to even move, she had waited without speaking until the people had gone away.

Afternoon melted into evening and she started pacing, sometimes glancing out the kitchen window to the busy street below. Lots of people. Thousands of people. Where had they all come from! The rain that had been pelting the apartment window finally broke. The night returned, leaving her in the dark once more.

Standing at the window, she looked outside and shivered in the cold air.

With every passing voice and footstep in the hallway, she turned, hoping desperately that Mary and Kelly would walk through the door. The hours passed. The mob grew louder. She paced the vinyl floor.

She was dreadfully thirsty now, her mouth thick and dry. But there was no water from the tap and nothing else to drink.

The night grew darker. She paced again. A deep feeling of dread began to haunt her, a feeling she'd felt too many times before: the day they had killed her father; the night she had left the village, heading off on her own; the last days at the refugee camp.

Experience and instinct were her teachers, and both were screaming now.

She looked around the dark apartment in desperation, not knowing what to do.

Suddenly, she thought of Pari al- Faruqi, the small Christian woman she had known in the Khorramshahr refugee camp. Why she thought of her at this moment, Azadeh didn't know, but the memories came back, flooding her mind with incredible detail.

Most of the six hundred refugees in Camp Khorramshahr lived in small, semipermanent plywood structures—bland, one-room huts, barely warm, ugly and inhospitable. But Pari had decorated her small home with a delicate touch: colorful murals on the walls created from pieces of broken chalk and paste, tin cans filled with wild chrysanthemums and croton plants she had gathered along the fence, scraps of abandoned material she collected to sew dresses and colorful quilts for the younger girls in the camp, one of which lay on top of her own cot. The image of Pari's small home filled Azadeh's mind and she pictured every detail: the mural, the plants, a half-finished dress . . . Pari's bed . . . the patchwork quilt . . . the silver cross on the wall at the head of her cot.

The silver cross . . . the silver cross . . .

A warm shiver ran through her as Pari's words filled her mind. "God loves you, Azadeh. He knows you are here. You can talk to him anytime that you need to. You can pray to him and he will listen. I swear to you, that is true."

Azadeh thought of her friend, tears welling in her eyes, then did the only thing she could think of to do. Unsure, but having faith, she knelt on the kitchen floor and started praying.

*　　*　　*

Satan watched her pray and trembled, rage and fury racing through his mind. This was the one great weapon for which he had no response, the greatest tool of the Enemy, which he could simply not destroy.

A humble prayer. Oh, how he loathed it! It gave them such comfort. It gave them such light.

And it was the light that brought him fury.

So he cursed and raged again.

INTERSTATE 65
FOURTEEN MILES SOUTHEAST OF CHICAGO

Sam was completely exhausted. His lungs burned, his legs were liquid, his calf and thigh muscles were cramped and tight. He slowed to a jog, his arms hanging at his side, then started walking as he gasped.

He couldn't run another step. It was as far as he could go.

The moon had risen higher and the clouds had parted, providing moonlight and starlight to illuminate the road. He continued north along the freeway, walking between the lines of stalled cars. Passing one, he glanced through the back window, then stopped and slowly turned. Hesitating, he walked back, peered closely at the window, then looked around again. "Hey!" he called out, his voice tight with thirst. "HEY! IS SOMEONE THERE?"

A head bobbed up from the backseat of the car.

Sam sensed the movement and swiftly turned. The stranger reached for the door, pushed it open, and climbed out, his eyes wide in uncertainty and fear. Sam moved toward him quickly. The man was young, maybe thirty, with a bald head and baby-smooth skin. "Is this your car?" Sam demanded.

The bald man looked around sheepishly.

"Sir, is this your vehicle?" Sam repeated.

The man eyed Sam's uniform. "Are you a U.S. soldier?" he asked.

Sam nodded quickly. "I am. Is this your car?"

"No, it's not, and I'm sorry. I didn't break in or anything. My car is stranded ten or fifteen miles south of here. I was trying to walk home when it got dark and I decided to sleep here for the night."

"You're not LDS, then?" Sam demanded.

The man cocked his head. "LDS? What do you mean? Why do you want to know?"

"It's cool, man, I'm not some anti-Mormon vigilante. Tell me," Sam said, almost hungrily, "are you a Mormon?"

The man shook his head. "No, I'm not."

Sam deflated with disappointment, his shoulders slumping. "I'm sorry, I thought maybe you . . . there's a BYU sticker in the back window of this car."

The man glanced toward it, his face expressionless. "Like I

said, sir, I'm just camping here for the night. I didn't think anyone would mind. I didn't break or steal anything."

Sam shook his head in frustration and turned away. "I didn't mean to scare you, I was just . . ." He quit talking. It didn't matter. And he didn't have time to explain. He raised his hands in apology and started walking again.

The man watched in desperation as Sam began to merge into the dark. "Hey," he called out, "what are you, a lieutenant, is that right?"

Sam slowed and turned back to him.

"Tell me what has happened here, lieutenant. Please, will you explain?"

"I can't. I've got to go." He turned away again.

The bald man took three steps to follow. "A couple of the doctors at my school are Mormon. They're good doctors, from what I hear."

Sam stopped. "What school are you talking about?"

"Northwestern. I just graduated from the medical school there."

Sam took a step toward him. "You're a doctor?" he demanded.

"Almost. I still have to finish my internship . . ."

A tremble ran up and down Sam's spine, warm and flowing and full of heat. A feeling of certainty and calm. He was on the right track. And he was getting very close.

"What's your name?" he asked.

The bald man looked around, still uncertain, then answered slowly, "Jerry Woodson."

"Come with me, Jerry!" Sam shot back, taking a step toward him.

"Come with you? Why? Where're you going?"

Sam ran forward and grabbed his arm. "Have you got a black bag? Any doctor stuff or gear?"

Jerry didn't answer. Sam pushed him toward the car. "Come on, we've got to hurry."

"Where are we going?" Jerry asked again.

"I don't know," Sam answered quickly as he dragged the man along.

*　　*　　*

Sara held onto Luke, cradling his head against her chest. Rocking back and forth, she whispered in his ear. Ammon crawled away, his eyes blank. His hands grew cold and lifeless and he dropped the stranger's gun into the mud. Looking around in desperation, he fell against a tree. For a moment, he was transported back in time. He was a little boy, small and hopeless. He needed someone's help. But there was no one to help him. He was completely on his own. No one was going to save him. He felt a crushing weight.

No transportation.

No telephone.

No police or ambulance or rescue.

Miles of walking to the nearest hospital.

Who knew if anyone could help them even if they made it there?

There was nothing he could do now. His brother was going to die. He shivered, thinking of the bleeding hole in Luke's chest. He pictured Luke's gasping face and pale lips, then dropped his head between his knees.

He wanted to scream. He wanted to cry. He wanted to shake his fist toward the heavens and demand an answer *why!*

We did everything that you commanded! We did everything you ever asked us! We did our very best, we tried to follow, and this is what we get!

He raged and cried inside, overwhelmed with grief and helplessness and pain.

Then he turned cold and clammy, beads of icy sweat forming on his brow. His heart was racing and he was panting and his face was growing pale.

He felt a soft touch against his shoulder. It took a moment before he gathered the strength to look up. Through bleary eyes he saw Mary standing there. "Do you have a first aid kit?" she asked him.

Ammon didn't seem to hear.

"Do you have any medical supplies?" she pressed again, her voice more firm.

He shook the mud from his hands but didn't answer as he spread his legs across the ground. "Yeah, sure, we've got some stuff. It's there . . . I don't know . . . it's somewhere in the back of the car."

"You need to get it," Mary told him.

"Don't know where . . ." he mumbled again.

Mary knelt down and looked him directly in the eye, the fire casting shadows across one side of her face. "Listen to me, baby, I know it's hard, but you've got to stay together, at least for a little while. You need to stand up, find your first aid kit, and help me. You've got to help your brother. I've got to help your mom. We've got to do everything we can to save him until we can get some help."

Ammon shook his head in rage. "Are you *kidding* me!" he shouted. "Do you think it's going to matter! Your little girl, my brother, both of them are going to die. Both of them are going to die here! And there is *nothing* we can do!"

Mary leaned even closer to him and took his face in both of her hands. "Can you hear me, Ammon?" she demanded. Her voice was hard but calm. "Can you hear me, son?"

He nodded but didn't look at her.

Mary squeezed his face again. "Listen to me, Ammon, this is important. You don't know what's going to happen here!

It's not up to you to decide who will live or who will die. It's not up to you to decide who's going to suffer or what God has in his plan. It's not up to you to complain about the situation or feel sorry for yourself.

"Your job is to do everything you can to help your brother! Do you understand what I am saying? I don't care, it doesn't matter, if you don't think it's going to help. Your brother needs you and so does your mom. You're going to stand up now and do everything to help them. You understand me, son."

Ammon stared into her face, his eyes coming into focus once again. "I understand you," he whispered sadly, his face clouding with embarrassment and shame.

"Good boy. I knew you would. Now, come on, we've got to find that first aid kit."

Mary stood, reached down, took Ammon by the hand, and pulled him to his feet. Turning, Ammon walked toward the cars hidden in the trees. He uncovered the back of the Honda, opened the trunk, and started searching through their supplies.

A shadow fell behind him.

Mary gasped, "Who goes there?"

Ammon turned, dropped to his knees, and reached out for the gun.

The sound of heavy breathing. Footsteps running through the trees. Shadows flashing in the darkness.

Ammon turned toward the stranger, lifted the gun, and took a breath.

Sam stepped out from the darkness.

Ammon stared at him, not believing. He was an angel. He was a vision. There was no way that he was real. Sam turned to him and smiled, and Ammon cried out in relief.

Sara looked up, her eyes wide.

Sam saw his brother lying there.

Sara tried to called his name but her mouth hung open, teardrops rolling down her cheeks.

chapter thirty-five

Sara laid her dying son gently down, then stood and ran to Sam. Grabbing him by the shoulders, she fell into his arms, repeating his name over and over again. She leaned back, looked into his face, brushed away her tears, then grabbed his hand and pulled him toward Luke, falling on her knees again. Ammon stood and ran toward him, throwing his arms around his neck. Sam slapped his shoulder, then stepped back and knelt down by Luke. He checked his eyes, looking into the pupils, then moved his flashlight down to see the blood that was soaking through his shirt and jacket. "What happened here?" he demanded.

"Please, Sam, you've got to help him," Sara pled.

Sam turned toward the dark trees and called out, "Come on, Jerry, run!"

*　　*　　*

"Look," Jerry said, "I'm not a doctor. Almost, but not really, and I don't have any experience with this kind of thing. I've done a couple stints at Cook County Emergency Room, but nothing even close to this. And there were always other doctors I could turn to when I didn't know what to do. I don't have any light or the right equipment to examine him, and the conditions here aren't really conducive to—"

"Just tell us!" Sam demanded. "Is he going to live?"

The student looked away. How much should he tell them? Did he even know himself? He glanced toward the young man, who was now lying in the backseat of the car. "He's lost a lot of blood. I can stop most of the external bleeding, but I can't stop the hemorrhaging that is going on inside. We've got to deal with shock, infection, dehydration, hypothermia . . ." His voice trailed off as he rubbed a vinyl-glove-covered hand against his face, smearing a thin swath of blood across his forehead. "I just don't know," he said again. "The thing I'm most worried about is the hemorrhaging. He really needs a transfusion—"

"I'm the same blood type," Ammon interrupted.

The almost-doctor thought. "I could jury-rig a transfusion. It would take a little time, but it would help."

"Do it," Sam commanded. "Whatever it takes to save my brother, you understand? Whatever it takes, we're going to do it."

Jerry looked at him and nodded. "I'll do everything I can. If we can get him through the night, then tomorrow, if we can get him to Chicago . . ."

"We can't wait," Sam shot back. "If I have to, I will carry him, but I'm going to get him there tonight."

"No. It wouldn't be smart, Sam, moving him right now. He needs to rest a few hours. He needs the blood transfusion."

Sam shifted his weight. "I won't wait . . . I can't wait. My brother needs surgery, even I can see that. If we stay here, he's going to die."

Jerry shook his head. "You'll cause more injury if you move him before he's stabilized a little bit. And how do you propose to transport him in the dark?"

"I'll figure it out," Sam said, his voice determined.

Jerry thought quickly. He understood what Sam was feeling. And though he had known him only a few hours, that drag along the road had been enough to show that he was a charge-the-bunker kind of guy. Jerry respected him already. This was a man he wanted for a friend. But Sam was wrong, and Jerry had to convince him before he made matters worse. "I know you want to help your brother," he answered calmly, "but you need to listen to me, Sam. If you try to move him tonight, he's going to die. You can't just reach into the car, throw him over your shoulder, and head off into the night. He couldn't take the jostling. He couldn't take the cold. He needs to rest. I need to control the hemorrhaging. I need to get him warm and stable, to treat the shock and get some blood into him. Let me do my job. *You* figure out how you're going to move him while keeping him lying down. You've got to build some kind of stretcher. I'll take care of your brother. You take care of the rest."

Sam stomped his feet in frustration, Ammon and Sara standing at his side. "I want to know the odds," he demanded, though his voice was much less certain now.

Jerry shook his head. "I'm not an oddsmaker," he answered firmly. "Medicine 101: Stay away from the fortune-telling. It brings heartache to everyone."

"Please." Sam glanced toward his mother and lowered his voice to barely a whisper. "Please, I understand why you don't want to do it, but I'm begging you."

Sara reached out and placed her hand on Sam's shoulder, then turned to Jerry. "I want to know," she said.

Jerry hesitated, staring off into the dark. "My best guess—

and it is only a guess—but I think if we move him tonight, he's going to die. Do I know that for certain? No. Sometimes we're surprised. But I believe that if you try to move him, there's maybe a ten percent chance he's going to live."

Sara swallowed, looked away, then turned back. "But if we wait, if we stay here until morning and let you do what you can to stabilize him?"

"I don't know. I just don't know. I don't know what kind of damage has been inflicted by the bullet. Did it hit his spleen? The liver? Did it perforate the large intestine? I'm sorry, I want to give you as much hope as I possibly can, but there's no way I could even guess."

"Fifty-fifty?" Sam was pleading.

Jerry thought, then shook his head. "I'm sorry. I really am, but no, I don't think his chances are that good," he said.

Sara's hands shot to her mouth and she quivered. Sam turned and held her, folding the delicate woman into his arms. Ammon stood beside them, then moved forward and put his arms around her too. Mary stood beside the young doctor, staring sadly at the ground.

Jerry watched the family, then touched Ammon's arm. "We need to start the blood transfusion as quickly as we can . . ."

Sara closed her eyes, holding onto Sam, then pushed away. "No. Not yet," she said to Jerry, wiping her eyes with the back of her hand. "There's something else we need to do first, something more important."

She turned and stared at Sam, a great weeping in her heart. He was such a good man, such a strong man. She loved him as much as any soul she'd ever known. But he had never seen the vision. He'd never grasped the *plan*. He was good enough and worthy, but he had just never been interested. Church.

Religion. Things of God, things of the Spirit, he had never understood.

She smiled at him weakly. Even though she loved him, he couldn't help her now. And the thing that she was asking was the most important thing that they could do. She was as certain of what Luke needed to survive as she was of anything.

She lowered her eyes, then turned to Ammon. "Your brother needs a blessing," she said.

Ammon turned away. "Mom, you know I can't."

"Your brother needs a blessing!"

"Mom, I don't know how. I've never done it before. I don't have the Melchizedek Priesthood. I don't have any idea what to do!"

"You've got to do it!" she repeated. "I will show you how."

Ammon shook his head and turned away, his shoulders slumping. "I don't have the proper priesthood . . ."

The night was silent.

Sam stepped forward with hesitation. "I can do it," he said.

Sara turned to him, her eyes wide. "What do you mean, Sam?"

"I have the Melchizedek Priesthood." He seemed to shrink with sudden uncertainty and he kept his head down.

"You do, Sam?" She stared at him uncomprehendingly. "You do?" she repeated.

"I was ordained in Iraq a couple months ago. A good friend named Lieutenant Calton ordained me. I was going to tell you, but I thought, you know, I wanted to tell you in person . . ."

"You're kidding," Ammon whispered, shaking his head in disbelief.

Sara gazed at him, her eyes soft and glowing. "Are you prepared?" she asked.

Sam looked at her, thinking deeply as a long moment passed, the wind blowing gently through the trees. "I'm not afraid," he said.

Sara closed her eyes and raised her face toward the heavens, her cheeks stained with tears and mud.

Sam walked to a patch of thick grass under the front bumper of the car where he'd laid his pack to keep it dry. Lifting it, he pulled out a small chrome container of consecrated oil.

He moved to the other side of the car where he could reach Luke's head and knelt down beside him. Sara and Ammon followed and stood nearby, their heads bowed. Mary remained beside Sara, desperately grasping her hand. Jerry stood back but stayed close enough so that he could hear what was said.

Sam lifted the container of sacred oil and removed the lid. At that moment, a sweet spirit fell around them, as powerful and overwhelming as a rush of hot wind. They felt it, they *all* felt it, everyone who was standing there. Poignant and powerful, it filled the dark night with peace and comfort that could not be denied. Sara closed her eyes again, and Mary gasped. Jerry squinted, his forehead creasing in peaceful thought. Sam took the oil and placed a drop on the crown of Luke's wet head. He anointed his brother, teardrops rolling down his cheeks and splashing on his wrist. He lifted his hands and replaced them for the blessing.

He waited, uncertain, his face stained with tears. Then he felt it, another pair of hands being placed upon his own. Then another. And another. He felt their heat. He felt their pressure.

He was not alone.

The Spirit deep inside him told him what God needed him to hear.

"Sam, this is my son. I love him more than you could ever comprehend. His work is not finished, so listen and I will tell you what to say."

Sam took a breath and started speaking. The words came slowly at first, but were full of faith and power. "My brother, Benjamin Luke Brighton," he started, "by the power of the Holy Melchizedek Priesthood and in the name of our Savior who loves us, I seal this blessing upon your head."

Sam paused a long moment, then spoke again, his voice confident and assured. "The Spirit whispers to me that your purpose in this life is not yet finished. There is a greater work for you to do. So in the name of Jesus Christ, I command you now to live. You will sleep in peace. You will be stable and in comfort until such time as we can get you to the doctors who will then take care of you."

Finishing the blessing, Sam kept his hands upon Luke's head and, as he lingered, he felt the weight lift as the unseen hands were pulled away. Then he heard his mother weeping. Standing, he turned to her. She stood strong, her shoulders square, her face peaceful now, and calm.

Mary was leaning on Sara's shoulders, her cheeks completely wet with tears. "There were others there," she whispered slowly. "A young man. He looked like Ammon. Another man. I don't know who."

Sam nodded slowly. "I felt them," was all he said.

"They were kneeling right beside you." Mary's voice was choked with sobs.

Sara held her close. "I saw them too."

Mary pulled back and looked at Sara. "What is this thing you call the priesthood?"

Sara thought before she answered, unsure of what to say.

"My little girl . . ." Mary murmured slowly. With pleading eyes she turned to Sam. "Can you do this thing for Kelly? Can you give her a blessing too?"

Sam looked around, uncertain of who or what she meant.

Then he heard the same Spirit whisper to him that he had heard before.

"There is another child, one of my daughters. Her work has just begun. I have sent you here to save her. Now you must listen once again."

chapter thirty-six

By morning, the rain clouds had completely blown away. The sun rose, casting a white beam of light through the small portion of the kitchen window that caught a patch of sky. The warmth fell upon Azadeh's face where she was sleeping on the kitchen rug.

She lay there, feeling the heat until the sun had passed, then rose and looked around. Stretching, she rubbed her eyes, feeling the empty loneliness return again.

She was so thirsty. And hungry now. There was a little food in the pantry, but she was afraid to eat it all. What if Mary and Kelly returned and needed something too?

Looking around, she knew she had to find something to drink. She couldn't go another day without water.

Then she heard it. Slow. Somewhere in the distance. *Droink . . . Droink . . .* The sound of dripping water.

She turned, her eyes wild with excitement. A pool of wetness had formed under the refrigerator and she ran toward it.

Opening the door, she traced the dripping water. The upper freezer was closed, and she pulled it open to find a small, swinging, plastic door. She pushed the tiny door back,

302

revealing the automatic ice-maker. Melting chunks of ice floated in the ice container. She almost cried with relief as she gently pulled the plastic container from the freezer, placed it on the kitchen counter, took a cup, and dipped out a drink. Another cup and then another. The cold water washed down her parched throat, giving instant life. Satisfied, she looked around, pulled a kitchen towel from the oven handle, dipped one corner into the water to get it wet, and wiped her face and hands.

A slice of bread and two raw eggs for breakfast kept the hunger down.

Walking to the small living room, she sat down on the cloth-covered sofa and thought.

It had been two days now since all the power had gone off, two nights since the mobs had formed out on the streets, three days since she had been outside the apartment, and a day since Mary and Kelly Beth should have been back.

Something had gone wrong. Maybe deathly wrong.

Azadeh realized they might not ever come home again.

She glanced toward the tiny kitchen. There were still some eggs and bread and a couple of cans of food in the small cupboard, but that was about all. If America was the land of plenty, it was hard to understand why Mary had so little food around. Azadeh and her father had kept more supplies in their mud and wood home back in Iran than Mary kept in her apartment in Chicago. Still, it was what it was, and the small amount of food would have to do. The bigger worry was the water, of course, and she glanced at the small plastic container she had taken from the freezer. It was enough for two, maybe three days if she was careful, but that was all.

She could survive here for three days. If Mary didn't come back before that, she would have to venture out of the apartment on her own.

She stood and walked into the kitchen and looked through the window once again, staring down.

The world outside her apartment was as strange and foreign to her as if she had landed on the moon. The streets were full of angry people. There had been fights, she could see that, and she was shocked to see what looked like a body lying on the street, the mob mulling around it as if it weren't there. She shivered as she studied the growing crowd of people. There was danger down below.

She did not want to go out there. She knew it would be dangerous. An Iranian girl wouldn't be welcome on the dirty streets of East Chicago.

But what choice did she have?

She would die inside the apartment if she stayed after the water and food were gone. Friendless, without any money or ability to travel, she didn't know where she would go, but she would have to leave eventually.

She watched a long time, studying the swelling crowd, then walked back and sat on the sofa once again. For at least the hundredth time she picked the phone up and listened, but heard nothing. She punched the buttons on the handset, but the phone was clearly dead. She tried the lights and television but nothing worked.

I'm on my own again, she thought miserably. *But that's okay, I'll work it out. I've been on my own before.*

Two more days, maybe three, before she'd have to leave.

Her stomach grew tight at the thought.

Curling on the sofa, she pulled a woolen blanket tight around her neck. The sun was bright now, but it was cool inside the apartment, the cold wind blowing in across the great lake. She shivered, then rolled on her side and stared at the far wall, listening to the sounds drifting up between the buildings from the crowded streets below.

* * *

The day passed. Azadeh walked quietly from room to room, not willing to reveal to those in the apartment below her that she was still there. There were occasional steps in the hallway, and sometimes shouting, but they were growing less frequent now. Sometime in the late afternoon, she ate two more raw eggs and a slice of bread, then drank a little water. About half of it was gone.

Night came. Dark. Colder than the night before. She drank half a cup of precious water, then went into her bedroom and curled up into a ball on the bed. The room was too lonely, too dark. She lay there for an hour or so, then walked back into the small living room and settled in on the couch instead.

Time passed. Halfway through the night, she heard some cries and shouts coming from the street. Walking to the window, she looked out, but it was far too dark to see what was going on below. Moving back to the couch, she lay down again.

Morning would come eventually, she knew that, but the night was dragging painfully on.

She drifted to sleep sometime before the sun rose. In her dreams, she heard happy voices from her village from when she was a little girl. She felt the mountain sun on her face and smelled the alpine flowers. Her father was calling her to breakfast, and she pulled a lungful of cool air, smelling the cooking lamb, wheat patties, and hot tea. The faint hint of smoke drifted from the kitchen and she pushed herself out of bed, running from her bedroom. Her father stood beside the cookstove: thick work clothes, dark skin, and warm eyes. She ran to him, the feel of his closely cut beard upon her face.

His voice was soft, but growing distant now. "Azadeh, can you hear me . . . ?"

She looked around the kitchen.

Her father was gone.

"Azadeh, baby, open the door for me."

She sat up suddenly. She was not back in her village. Her father wasn't there. Still, the voice was calling.

"Azadeh, are you in there? Azadeh, it's me. It's Mary. I don't have my keys."

Her eyes darted around in confusion, then, crying with relief, she ran toward the door. "Miss Dupree!" she shouted. "Mary! Kelly Beth! Are you there?"

"Yes, Azadeh. I need you to let us in. I don't have my keys."

Two chains and two deadbolts held the door shut. She snapped them back and threw it open.

Mary rushed into her arms. "Azadeh, baby, are you okay?"

Azadeh cried with relief. Mary held her tight, then stepped back.

Azadeh saw it immediately: It was as if a beam of sunshine had been turned on inside Mary's soul. Her eyes were alive and dancing. Her face was warm and bright. She beamed with joy and pleasure, her smile a brilliant dazzle against the gray morning light. Azadeh watched her, then broke into a smile of her own. She simply couldn't help it. Mary's pure joy was infectious. And she was so relieved to see her, it was impossible to hold it back.

The two women stared at each other, each of them holding the other's shoulders. Then Azadeh looked past Mary, momentarily confused. "Where is Kelly Beth?" she asked with worry, staring at the empty door.

Mary turned around, her face still beaming, as Kelly Beth walked into the room. Her tiny frame was weak and fragile, but she was walking still. No wheelchair. No IV drips or medications. Her eyes were lively and dancing and she was smiling too.

"Kelly Beth . . . Kelly Beth . . . !" Azadeh quivered with emotion as she stared down at the child. "Kelly, what has happened!" Breaking into tears, she dropped to her knees in front of the little girl.

Kelly looked at her, then motioned to the hallway at her right. Raising a hand, she beckoned to him, and Sam walked into the room.

Azadeh froze, her eyes wide, her face full of wonder, her mouth opened in an unheard cry.

The American soldier looked down at her. "Do you remember me?" he asked.

Azadeh didn't move. She *couldn't* move. She couldn't think. She couldn't talk. It took every ounce of energy just to breathe.

Yes, she remembered him. She remembered him from the mountain on the day her father died. She remembered him from the night on the river when he had come to save her life.

She remembered him. She knew his spirit.

She remembered him from long before—before this life, before this darkness. Then she sensed it, something further, something longer, something more eternal, long ago.

She knew this was her brother.

And she closed her eyes and cried.

chapter thirty-seven

The old man stood near the forty-foot windows that looked out to the east on the blank desert sky. The sun was a few minutes yet from rising, and the moon had set behind them, leaving the desert in the gray and lifeless twilight of predawn.

The king remained behind him, unwilling to interrupt his thoughts.

"You have proven to be reliable," the old man said without turning around.

Abdullah looked past his shoulders to the rising sun. The sky was turning red, creating a glorious desert dawn. "Every warhead was successful," he boasted. "The destruction has been carried across the entire country. It was much more powerful than we had even hoped for." He paused, a shiver of excitement running through him. "I don't think they're going to make it," he concluded. "I actually think we have destroyed them."

The old man turned. "You are wrong," he said.

The king waited.

"They will rebuild," the old man told him. "We hurt

them, it is true, but there is still enough light, enough good-ness, enough courage and strength inside their people. Yes, millions are going to die, but they will strive to rise again."

The king stared into his filmy eyes. "You have people, though, friends inside the country, who will see to it that—"

The man cut him off. "Yes, many of our friends inside the United States have already done their work. For years now they have torn at their foundations, destroying the people's faith in their nation, their god, even in themselves. These friends have been fruitful and creative, but in the end it may not prove to be enough."

The old man sniffed, then frowned, his bony nose so thin a dozen blood veins showed like spider webs through the skin.

Abdullah watched him for a moment. Then he looked away, too pleased with himself to be brought down by the old man's constant gloom. "Think about it," he bragged again. "They're just now beginning to understand how dangerous their situation is. They're just beginning to get thirsty, just beginning to wrestle with their first hunger pains. They're just starting to feel the panic. I really think we have destroyed them. Now the world lies in our hands."

The old man turned and looked blankly to the east, his reaction as vacant as the empty sky. If there was satisfaction in the victory, he certainly didn't show it. "You know your brother has a son who is still living," he said.

The king nodded, the princeling the least of his concerns.

The old man surmised his thoughts and shook his head. He knew better. He had seen it too many times before. He thought back on the great Jaredite people, remembering two thousand years of family strife and fratricide over kingship and power. "He is young now," he said, taking a step toward the king. "But think, King Abdullah, he will grow into a man. Everyone around him will remind him of who he really is, who his father was, what he has lost. They will tell, even goad him, that one day he must be king. They will remind him of everything that has been stolen from him. No, you cannot let him live, or one day, when he is older, he will come and claim your kingdom for his own."

Abdullah shook his head. "Don't worry about him," he sneered. "I have taken steps to find him. It won't be long until he's dead."

The old man stared, then compressed his lips and turned back to the rising sun. The two men were silent a long moment.

"Do you remember the first time that I met you?" the old man finally asked.

The king thought back to that morning on the distant beach in France, so far away—another life, another universe, another measure of time ago.

"What did I promise you?" the old man demanded as Abdullah thought.

"You promised me many things. You promised me freedom. Power. You promised anything that I could think of. You promised me it all."

"Have I delivered on my promise?"

"Yes, sir, you have."

Silence another moment. The sun was just beginning to peek across the distant, flat horizon, sending its first shafts to light up the world.

"There was another thing I promised you."

Abdullah thought, but didn't answer.

The old man waited, then turned. "I promised, King Abdullah, that I would show you the truth."

The king thought. Yes, he remembered now, those had been the old man's words.

The old man pulled out a thin cigarette, lit it quickly, and shoved it in his mouth. "Do you want the truth now?" he asked.

"Of course," Abdullah said.

The man walked until he was standing right before the king, then smiled bitterly. The brilliant sunlight shone behind him, casting his outline in a shadow that spread across the room. "The truth, my King Abdullah." His voice was wicked and sarcastic now. "The truth is, my King Abdullah, that I was lying to you then. I promised you everything, but *none* of it is real. None of it will last forever. It will all come crashing down. We can fight and scratch and murder, we can lie and cheat and kill. We can plot and plan and muster, but *we are never going to win*. The sun will still rise in the morning. Light will always chase the dark. We cannot win. We never could.

"And that, my friend, is the only truth that really matters. You have sold your soul for nothing." He stopped and put his arms around the king. "You have sold your soul for nothing," he repeated more softly. "Now, welcome to my world."

epilogue

MOUNT AATTE
NORTH OF PESHAWAR, PAKISTAN

The storms came, deep and cold, the clouds covering the mountain peaks in crowns of gray and white. The steady rain fell in fat drops before the temperature plunged to almost freezing, turning the cold rain to thick snow, breaking limbs away from the fruit trees and beating down the wheat under a heavy blanket of snow.

Then the storm clouds passed just as quickly as they had come, blowing north toward the mountains that towered 20,000 feet above the fertile valley floor.

The shepherd waited out the storm from a shallow cave in the granite mountain. As the dark clouds bore down, his hot breath turned to mist and he pulled his leather jacket close.

Glancing to the back of the shallow cave, he watched the young boy sleeping. The child was lying on his side, rolled up in a rough, goat-hair blanket, his eyes fluttering lightly as he dreamed. He was a good lad, gracious and accommodating, deferential and bright. But he was also strong, the shepherd could see that. There was a sturdy will inside him that was even greater than his own.

Was he going to be a child-warrior? The Pashtun didn't know.

Eight hundred years before, his people had fought the terrible Genghis Khan when the Mongol and his army had come sweeping from the north, killing, eating, or destroying everything in their path. Legend said the Pashtun boy-warrior was only fourteen when he was called to lead their army against the coming hordes. For years the boy had commanded a guerrilla campaign, hitting the Mongol armies in the mountain passes, then disappearing with his soldiers like a ghost into the night.

Some thought the story of the child-leader was just a legend, but the Pashtun shepherd knew that it was real. God could send his warriors. Sometimes he chose the old ones. Sometimes he chose the young.

The tribal leader pulled his worn jacket around his shoulders again, then turned and walked toward the sleeping child. Reaching under the rough blanket, he touched the slender chain on the young boy's neck. The diamond was pure and perfect, and even in the dim light it reflected a dozen shafts of brilliance. He fingered the diamond slowly, knowing full well its worth.

Kneeling, he lifted the young prince and held him close. The boy squirmed but didn't waken as the shepherd held him safe against his chest.

about the author

Chris Stewart is a bestselling author and world-record-setting Air Force pilot. His previous military techno-thrillers for the national market have been selected by the Book of the Month Club and published in twelve different countries. He has also been a guest editorialist for the *Detroit News,* commenting on matters of military readiness and national security. Chris is president and CEO of The Shipley Group, a nationally recognized consulting and training company. In addition to the highly acclaimed series *The Great and Terrible,* he is the coauthor of the bestselling book, *Seven Miracles That Saved America.* Chris and his wife, Evie, are the parents of six children and live in Utah.